FOOTPRINTS IN THE SAND

PAM LECKY

Storm

Previously published in 2020 as *Footprints in the Sand* by Pam Lecky.

Ebook ISBN: 978-1-80508-695-6
Paperback ISBN: 978-1-80508-696-3

Cover design: Ghost
Cover images: Arcangel, Adobe Stock, Shutterstock

Published by Storm Publishing.
For further information, visit:
www.stormpublishing.co

ALSO BY PAM LECKY

The Lucy Lawrence Mysteries

No Stone Unturned

The Art of Deception

A Pocketful of Diamonds

Dedicated to my father, Gerry Lecky,
Whose Love of History
Has been my Inspiration.

PART 1

DREAMS & SCHEMES

ONE

The Mediterranean Sea, Late September 1887

The *Regina del Mar* steamed south towards Alexandria. Lucy Lawrence stood on the starboard deck of the ship, sheltered from the breeze and watched the sun's dying flourish of pink, yellow and orange. It was another spectacular end to a day at sea. For the first time in weeks, Lucy felt at peace with the world.

Her original plan had been to explore the Continent for the summer months, as she was now an independent and wealthy woman, having claimed the two rewards for the recovery of the Maharajah's stolen sapphires. However, her meandering journey had come to an abrupt halt in Nice. Inclement weather and the aftermath of the earthquake in February meant she had been denied the pleasure of exploring the quaint cobbled streets of Nice's old town. But far worse, she soon realised she was the subject of much gossip. Between her dead husband Charlie's shenanigans and her brother's trial for fraud, the family had well and truly fallen off its pedestal in the eyes of society. What's more, the London based newspapers were widely available in Nice and most of the hotel guests were British. Despite other more worthy world events, the woes of the Somerville family had therefore reached the eager ears of the tabby cats who frequented the hotel's salons. Side-eyed glances and muttered asides soon had Lucy silently seething and contemplating an early departure.

She could have borne it all if her friends had stayed true. But apart from letters from Lady Sarah and Judith and a few heart-rending missives from her brother Richard from prison, there had been silence from London. Not that she'd expected Phineas Stone to keep up a regular correspondence, but it was confusing that she'd heard nothing at all. Was it a case of out of sight and out of mind? Lucy had always found him a very private person, but that parting in London had given her hope of something between them. His gift of the painting of Abu Simbel had been such a personal one. Had she misread him?

And then, just as she had decided to leave the French Riviera, everything changed. She met the handsome Egyptologist Monsieur Armand Moreau.

It had happened one evening, about two weeks earlier. Driven almost mad by boredom, Lucy had ventured outdoors despite a steady drizzle. As she had strolled along, mulling over a side venture into Italy, she had come across an excited crowd waiting outside a nearby hall. The poster on the wall outside proclaimed that this evening there was to be a lecture, in English. Emblazoned, in large letters the poster read: *The Wonders of Ancient Egypt*; *a Lecture by the Esteemed Archaeologist, Armand Moreau.*

Even as a child, Lucy had been fascinated by Egypt, an interest born of hours poring over books on the subject, including *Description de l'Égypte,* in the library at Somerville Hall. It was too tempting. She ducked inside, not intending to stay long.

Two hours later she was deep in conversation with the

archaeologist, a very charming Frenchman. The following afternoon, much to the horror of the gossiping tabbies—which afforded Lucy some delight—Moreau joined her for afternoon tea at her hotel. As he spoke of his work, Lucy had become enthralled. And although she knew she was being drawn in far too easily, when Moreau had tempted her with tales of Cairo, and his difficulties in sourcing funds for his next important dig, Lucy found herself offering to be his patron for the upcoming season in Sakkâra, Egypt. From there it seemed the most logical step to agree to accompany him to Egypt. If anyone had told her she would embark on such an adventure when she had left England, she would have laughed and shook her head. But, here she was. She was Egypt-bound and could barely contain her excitement.

Who was she trying to deceive? There was, of course, another reason for her impetuosity. Phineas. She might not have heard from him directly but that didn't mean she hadn't heard about him from another source. Lucy sighed and glanced down into the water, a sudden tightness in her throat. It was all because of the letter from Lady Sarah, a letter that was burning a hole in her pocket even still. It had arrived, forwarded from Nice, the day they had left the port at Brindisi.

With a quick glance across the deck to ensure she was alone, Lucy pulled it out. It was an innocuous note except for a couple of paragraphs that had sent her brain into a spin. Like a scab that itched, she couldn't resist scratching the wound. Lucy scanned the letter once more. She skipped through the home news until she found the section she wanted.

I have some other odd news to impart. Perhaps you've already heard about it from Phineas, but it's only just come to my notice in a letter from Geoffrey's sister, Agnes, in London. About two weeks' ago, there was a frightful scene at the Royal Academy

*involving none other than Alice Vaughan, her husband and
Phineas—*

Lucy breathed hard for a few moments. She wasn't a huge
fan of the woman in question and hadn't thought about Alice
Vaughan for months. The lady had been engaged to Phineas
and then jilted him. Lucy had met her once and had been
surprised at the woman's hostility towards her. If she didn't
know better, the woman regretted marrying another man. Lucy
continued to read:

*I don't believe the Summer Exhibition has ever been so talked of
as a result. My understanding is that Alice, at the top of her voice
(and most insistently, according to Agnes who witnessed it all)
invited Phineas to dinner at their home. Citing a previous
engagement, Phineas declined (like a sensible man!). This,
however, did not go down well with Mrs Vaughan. She threw a
tantrum so violent in nature that the staff had to request the
Vaughans leave the premises. Quite shocking behaviour, I think
you will agree. Naturally, London was buzzing with it.*

*Of course, this all would have died down eventually but for what
happened next. Alice Vaughan disappeared the very next day.
The family tried to keep it quiet, but one of the servants went
tattling to the newspapers. The official line from the family is
that she has gone somewhere quiet to 'rest her nerves'. My first
thought was that she'd been shipped off to an asylum, and you
could hardly blame the family if that were the case. However,
there is a further twist to my tale. Phineas has also disappeared.
He hasn't been seen since the debacle at the Royal Academy.
Now, my dear, I must ask if you know where he is. Is he abroad
on a case? Has he sought you out on your travels? London is agog
to know where he could be. The gossips are having a field day, as
you can imagine. I for one do not believe Phineas capable of*

*absconding with someone else's wife, but the pair do have some
unfortunate history...*

Lucy exhaled slowly, folded the letter, and put it back in her
pocket. Phineas must have been called away on a case; it was
the only possible explanation for his sudden disappearance.
And yet, why would he not let someone know where he was
going? It was odd behaviour on his part. Of course, Lucy had
often wondered if Alice Vaughan regretted breaking her
engagement with Phineas. He had explained to Lucy that it was
Alice who had backed out and that he, as well as her mother,
were concerned for the lady's sanity. Perhaps he was more than
concerned? Perhaps seeing Alice distressed, his feelings had
returned, and he had decided to rescue her from her marriage.
But that didn't make sense, surely? Lucy had seen how Alice's
behaviour had repulsed him. Then an awful thought struck her.
Maybe they'd been meeting in secret all along. Lucy groaned as
she recalled posting that one letter to him last month. Desperate
for some communication she had used the excuse of asking him
to recommend places to visit. Phineas had never answered, and
now she knew why.

From Phin's silence, Lucy could only draw one conclusion;
whatever might have been between them was now dead. He
had forgotten about her and was forging on with his own life.
She must do the same, no matter how hard it would be. Her
vision inexplicably blurred, and she hurriedly wiped her eyes.
This was silly; she needed to buck up! Staring out to sea, she
slowly calmed down.

Tomorrow they would reach Alexandria. For now, though,
with no land references in sight, they could be on any ocean,
destination unknown. With that notion came a sense of
freedom Lucy could almost taste on the salty air. She gripped
the handrail, her heart pounding. Real, meaningful change was
within her grasp. Lucy glanced south across the vast emptiness

of the Mediterranean, wondering what might lie ahead. A winter living with strangers was appealing. She might be anyone she wished, do anything she desired, and who would know back in England? Cairo society, from what Armand Moreau had told her, was a lot freer than England. As if the universe were in league, in two days' time her widowhood would be at an end and life might begin afresh. Lucy had the money now to indulge her interests, and she had certainly earned the right to enjoy life to the full. Would her stay in Egypt help her make the decisions that would mould the rest of her life? Behind her lay the life most familiar. But of late, it had not brought her much joy.

Then as she watched the sky change colour, a traitorous thought sneaked into Lucy's mind. Was Phineas enjoying such a sunset? Where and with whom? Lucy thumped the handrail. Every time she thought she was free of him, he cropped up in her thoughts. If only she knew, one way or the other, if the rumours about Alice Vaughan were true. Then she could find peace. What's more, here she was with all the ingredients for a new start: a beautiful sunset, the romance of foreign lands ahead and a charming and attentive Frenchman. How could a woman resist the allure of entanglement? And there was no mistaking Moreau's wishes in the matter. Their friendship had deepened over the last few days, as they talked about plans for the dig and what they would do once they reached Cairo. The more time she spent with Moreau, the more fascinating he became. Where Phineas chided, Moreau coaxed and flattered. Moreau delighted in the ridiculous while Phineas scoffed at it. Both men were intelligent, but sometimes Phineas could be a little patronising... she would have to stop comparing them; it did nothing for her equilibrium.

Other passengers were taking their evening stroll before dinner. Mostly couples, of course. But Lucy liked the solitude: it was the reason she'd come up on deck so early. It gave her time to reflect before Moreau joined her. The crossing had been uneventful, other than a few sticky moments with her maid Mary who was convinced the trip was a mistake.

Lucy heard a step behind her. *'Bonsoir, madame.'*

She turned away from the rail on hearing Moreau's greeting. She had to admit he was a striking man with his dark complexion, emerald green eyes and unruly brown hair streaked with silver. Lucy guessed him to be in his late forties. His clothes, although of excellent quality, showed tell-tale signs of wear, in particular the cuffs of his coat and the glimpse of a shirt no longer sparkling white. From their conversations during the voyage, she had learned that archaeology was not a lucrative business.

'Ah, M. Moreau, isn't it a beautiful evening? I wish it wasn't our last on board.'

Moreau's smile was warm as his gaze lingered on her face. 'I, however, will be much happier on dry land. But we have been lucky. Sometimes the crossing is horrible. Of course, having your company this year, madame, has made it so agreeable that I have barely thought of my fears. Come, let's take a turn about the deck before dinner.'

Lucy took his arm as they set off. 'What is it you fear? That you will be ill?'

'No, not that,' he said. 'Drowning, of course.' Lucy felt the shiver run through him as they walked along. She was surprised. He was usually so unflappable. But then she had an unreasonable fear of spiders. She only hoped she wouldn't become acquainted with any on her travels, particularly as a hot country was bound to have large, nasty ones. Hurriedly, she dismissed the notion.

'But drowning must be a quick death. There are far worse ways to meet your maker,' Lucy said.

Moreau glanced down at her, one brow raised. 'Is this something you've given a lot of thought to?' There was an uncomfortable edge to his voice.

'Well, as I mentioned when we first met, my husband met a brutal end. My visit to the mortuary on the day he was killed is difficult to forget.'

Moreau grunted. 'That can't have been pleasant for you. I, on the other hand, encounter death all the time in my line of work, but of course, it is the ancient dead of which I speak.'

'Does it not feel—forgive me—but surely it is almost sacrilegious to disturb their resting places and handle their mummies?' Lucy asked. 'They took so much trouble to hide their tombs.'

'It is not a profession for the squeamish, but we owe it to science to find out everything we can about them. To try to understand how their astonishing civilisation emerged at a time when the rest of the world was so backward in comparison. The ancient mud houses of the ordinary people have long ago crumbled to dust or have been claimed by the Nile or the desert. Only the tombs and temples of stone can reveal the past. You must understand, madame: archaeology is an obsession, not a job. Egyptology is the most addictive form. The geography of death.' His voice rang with a fervour that made Lucy's heart race. She listened in awe as he went on to recount his experiences on entering his first tomb at Dashûr.

Lucy could visualise herself standing beside him at the dig, overcome with emotion. Would she be lucky enough to experience something similar during her time in Egypt? 'It sounds wonderful, M. Moreau, and so exciting for a young man starting out on his career.'

'Oh yes, it was exciting but frightening also, for it is a precarious profession. Even now, with an established career and something of a reputation, I'm not a rich man. My parents still despair. They wish I'd studied law or medicine and settled back in Nice, but it was history that fascinated me, and I can't imagine doing anything else. After my first expedition to Egypt, there was never any doubt about what my life would be, and my mentor wouldn't have had it any other way.'

'I suspect that sense of awe for your subject hasn't diminished,' she said with a grin.

Moreau chuckled softly. 'Ah! You come to know me so well, Madame Lawrence.' He bent his head and whispered. 'Don't tell anyone, but I'll admit my love of Egypt has increased with each passing year. She's much like the most fascinating of women, for she reveals her beauty in layers, each more fascinating than the last. As time passes, you begin to realise you can't live without her.'

His words echoed with sadness, and Lucy wondered if he was hinting at a lost love. Why else would he describe Egypt in such terms?

They halted at the bow and stood in silence. As Lucy had often observed while travelling in his company, Moreau was wont to drift off, deep in thought, particularly if the conversation turned on Egypt and its treasures. It hinted at a deeper, more serious side to his nature, and one she found far more attractive than the flirtatious behaviour he often indulged in when in the presence of ladies. Lucy realised he was a complex man. Was he too good to be true, though? There was a dangerous edge to him but, after all she'd been through, a soupçon of danger and risk were to be welcomed. Surely, she was wise enough not to get sucked into anything too perilous to her heart. Time, however, was on her side. Lucy would have months to get to know him better. She needed to analyse what it was about him that drew her in. Was it his flamboyance which attracted her? It was in such contrast to... No. It was a mistake to compare. And unfair. An open nature such as Moreau's was far more appealing than the tightly controlled temperament of an Englishman.

As Moreau turned to her, his gaze deepened. A sudden gust of wind tugged at Lucy's hair. Moreau reached out and tucked a wayward strand behind her ear, his fingers caressing her skin. It was such an intimate gesture she caught her breath. Slowly, he leant towards her, his eyes locked to hers.

Lucy couldn't move, barely aware of the other passengers walking past. But one of the passing ladies greeted Moreau loudly, and suddenly the moment was shattered and the warmth left Moreau's expression. Confused by her own disappointment as he pulled away, Lucy struggled to find words.

'I must admit I envy you, M. Moreau. You have been lucky enough to find a profession you love.'

Moreau gave her a somewhat sad smile. Turning away, he looked out to sea. 'Yes. Egypt is, and always will be, my life.'

Later That Evening

Lucy sat at the small dressing table in her cabin as Mary brushed out her hair. She closed her eyes briefly and tried to envisage what Cairo would be like. Would it be as exotic as she imagined? Her heart began to race, and she smiled slowly. A childhood dream was about to become a reality.

'I'm glad to see you so happy, ma'am,' Mary remarked, dragging Lucy back to the present. 'But I'm thinking we might regret this... adventure of yours.'

'Oh, come now, Mary. The crossing from Brindisi has been very pleasant. I'm sure it's a good omen.'

Mary sniffed and placed the brush down with a snap of her wrist. 'Hmm,' was her ominous response. 'I suppose it was better than the English Channel. I thought we were goners then!'

Lucy vividly recalled the voyage to France earlier in the summer and Mary's distress. There had been numerous decades of the rosary recited and frightened tears. Lucy had never been so glad to see dry land.

'This foreign travel can be very dangerous, I'm thinking,

ma'am. Maybe we should have stayed in Italy? 'Twas lovely there, and one of the other maids was telling me about some wonderful sites to visit nearby.'

Lucy sighed. They'd had this conversation already. She needed to find out what her maid specifically feared, or the next few months would be tiresome. She couldn't risk Mary abandoning her either.

'And I intend to do them justice when we return from Africa, Mary. Consider how agreeable it will be to spend the winter in Cairo with its climate. There are lots of famous sites to explore there too and, most exciting of all, M. Moreau will be taking us to Sakkâra. How many people are lucky enough to experience such a wonderful adventure? I'm sure we would soon exhaust the glories of Brindisi and would become impatient for home, whereas Egypt's amazing sites could take a lifetime to explore.' Mary's eyes popped with worry. 'Not that I'm suggesting we stay any longer than the forthcoming winter,' Lucy quickly added.

'But ma'am... I'm not sure as I should be going to such a place. Me mother in her last letter said Fr O'Brien wouldn't like it. He told her that the country is full of heathens. My soul could be at risk.' Mary's eyes welled up.

Lucy smothered a sigh. At last, the real reason. 'Mary, the Islamic religion offers no threat to you or anyone else. I assure you, your soul will remain intact. Your mother's fears are groundless. Besides, I wouldn't bring you somewhere unsafe. And before you say it, Yorkshire, last spring, was an exception.'

Mary's mouth quirked. 'If you say so, ma'am.'

'I do! Now, best finish the packing. We reach Alexandria tomorrow,' Lucy said glancing towards the pile of folded clothes on the bed. But Mary remained standing behind her, shifting her weight from one foot to the other. 'Is something else bothering you?'

'It's just that Mr Hopkins, M. Moreau's American assistant.

Me and Hopkins were alone on the quay while the luggage was being taken on board. He started asking me a lot of questions. I didn't like it, to be honest. Now that man's what my Ned would call a shifty cove.'

'What did he ask you about?' Lucy asked, mildly curious. She had only met Hopkins once they had arrived in Brindisi, and he had seemed polite enough, if a little abrupt.

'About you, ma'am. A bit cheeky, I thought.'

Lucy frowned. 'Anything in particular or just general questions?'

'He wanted information about your family and was especially interested in your late husband. Had the nerve to ask where your money came from. But you needn't worry; I told him nothin'.'

'I don't doubt you were discreet but inform me if he's impertinent enough to question you again.' Mary nodded. 'But perhaps bear in mind that Americans tend to be forthright, Mary, and expect everyone else to be the same. It is most likely curiosity. As I'm partly funding their dig, Mr Hopkins wants to be sure I'm solvent. Once we get to Cairo, he will be heading out to the desert to set up the excavation. We are unlikely to see much of him after that.'

'That would suit me just fine,' Mary said, with a toss of her head. 'I'll have enough to do fending off those heathens!'

TWO

The Excelsior Hotel, Cairo

The exotic tones of the *Fajr* drifted into Lucy's subconscious, chasing away dreams of the desert and a blistering sun. Blinking into wakefulness, she lay listening as the call to prayer echoed around the rooftops of Cairo. It was still and dark in the hotel room. But she knew the dawn wasn't far off on this first anniversary of Charlie's death. There was something fitting about waking up here today. A new beginning in every sense.

As the *Fajr* ended, Lucy pulled back the mosquito netting and headed to the window. She pushed open the shutters. Before her stretched the city, pink-toned in the light of the dawn. Lucy stepped out on to her first-floor balcony and stood perfectly still, breathing in deeply while around her the city awoke. Her eye was drawn to a beautiful minaret some distance away. It rose above the haphazard jumble of rooftops, a blaze of white against the early morning sky.

Then movement drew her attention to a terraced rooftop nearer the hotel. A woman robed in black walked along its length, a flock of pigeons flitting about as she scattered grain.

Lucy watched her for several minutes, presuming it was the lady's morning ritual. Her task completed, the woman disappeared from view. The scene struck Lucy as almost dreamlike, for there was nothing in all of England or her recent experiences in France or Italy to compare.

Within touching distance was a giant date palm swaying gently in the breeze, its maroon and amber fruit hanging plump and enticing. Lucy plucked one. As she bit into the date, enjoying its sweetness, a black crow swooped between the trees, its call melancholy, momentarily reminding her of Somerville Hall, her childhood home in Yorkshire. It sent a chill through her. Lucy cast it off with a determined shake of her head.

Her party had arrived in Cairo late afternoon the previous day, having taken the express train from Alexandria. For most of the four-and-a-half-hour journey Moreau's assistant, Mr Hopkins, had dozed. Hopkins was a lanky young man with light brown receding hair and a manner Lucy did not care for. After Mary's revelations about his probing, Lucy intended to be on her guard. He barely spoke to her, and it had often struck her he was not best pleased she'd joined them. On more than one occasion, Lucy had caught him staring at her in a not too friendly way. As Moreau's second-in-command, she understood he would be located at the dig for most of the time, supervising the workers and logging the finds. But, she supposed, he must be good at his job, for Moreau indicated he had been lucky to secure him.

Lucy was too thrilled by the passing scenery to rest as the others did. There was so much to take in. Would it be possible to grow weary of the magnificent views as Hopkins evidently had? The vast landscape of endless blue sky and parched earth made Lucy wonder what secrets lay beneath the constantly shifting sands. How would you know where to start digging?

'Instinct and luck, Madame Lawrence,' Moreau answered when Lucy put the question to him. 'Often a shard of pottery or an item of jewellery is revealed by the sandstorms. Sometimes, if you're lucky, you will discover more, and hope ignites.'

'But not always, I assume?' Lucy remarked.

'The desert is, at best, fickle. Most of us concentrate on the sites that have already revealed some of their glories. One might waste years digging somewhere on a mere hunch. Fortunately, the ancients were creatures of habit and tended to use the same site over many centuries.'

As they travelled east, Moreau had been only too happy to point out the places of interest, and Lucy's hastily-bought copy of *Baedeker's Guide* was left unopened on the seat beside her. Soon after leaving Alexandria, Moreau had pointed out the bay of Abukir, the site of the Battle of the Nile. But of more importance, in his opinion, it was also where ancient cities lay submerged beneath the Mediterranean, frustratingly out of reach.

As they travelled further away from Alexandria, the landscape gradually changed. Trees and rich cultivated land became more prevalent. And then, as if by magic, the pyramids of Giza appeared in the distance. Lucy blinked several times, unsure if it was wishful thinking on her part. But their outline against the brilliant blue sky gradually became clearer. Lucy pointed them out to Mary. The young maid exclaimed how like the pictures in M. Moreau's book they were, which made Moreau chuckle. Mr Hopkins, now awake, treated Mary to a look of disbelief and took up a book. How unpleasant he was and such a snob, Lucy thought, but she was too interested in what lay ahead, and turned her attention back to the passing landscape. Mesmerised, she kept her gaze fixed on the pyramids as they approached the outskirts of Cairo.

It was strange how nervous Lucy felt as she stood in the doorway of the hotel dining room where breakfast was being served. It was a beautiful, richly ornamented room with floor to ceiling windows looking out onto the exotic gardens. Everything was pristine, from the décor to the table settings. The buzz of conversation in the room was welcoming. Lucy desperately wanted to fit in with these guests, whereas she'd been more than happy to dine alone in France rather than face the impertinence of the tabbies. A waiter approached, but just then a dark-haired young woman, seated at a large table nearby, caught her eye and beckoned her over.

As Lucy moved towards the table, the welcoming lady rose up. '*Buongiorno*! You're very welcome to join us. I'm Isabella DeLuca.' They shook hands.

'Lucy Lawrence,' Lucy replied with a nod to the other company seated at the table, as the waiter drew out a chair for her beside Miss DeLuca.

'It is your first time at the Excelsior?' the Italian lady asked as soon as Lucy was settled.

'Yes, and Egypt.' This was met by exclamations of pleasure around the table.

'You never forget the first time, isn't that right, dear?' an American lady said, gazing fondly at the man beside her.

'No, indeed. I'm almost envious, ma'am. To experience it all again for the first time would be wonderful,' he informed Lucy. 'I'm Robert Hamilton, by the way, and this is my wife, Sophia. We are very happy to make your acquaintance.' He jerked his thumb at an elderly gentleman at the other end of the table who treated Lucy to a grave look. 'That's old Metaxas, a Greek gentleman, but he doesn't have any English. Rich as they come. Nice chap; great listener.' This comment made the others roar with laughter. Lucy began to relax.

'I'm very pleased to meet you all,' Lucy replied. 'You're all regulars here?'

'Oh, yes,' Miss DeLuca said. 'I work here during the season. I'm a photographer.'

'How marvellous!' Lucy exclaimed.

'And we just love it so much, we come back every winter,' said Mrs Hamilton. 'It is such a fabulous country and the climate suits Robert's constitution so.'

Miss DeLuca quirked a fine brow at Lucy. 'So, tell us, Lucy Lawrence, what brings *you* to Egypt?'

Later, Lucy awaited Moreau's arrival out on the garden terrace where lunch was served. After a distracted greeting, Moreau sat down. But as lunch progressed, although his manner was polite, Moreau's inattention spoke of a busy or worried mind. During the time they'd spent together, Lucy had come to appreciate he was a man of many moods. Reluctant to impose, although curious, Lucy kept the conversation light.

As they sipped their coffee, Moreau suddenly gave her an apologetic grin. 'Forgive me, I should have asked if you're happy with your accommodation. If not, I can recommend another hotel; there are several that would suit your needs. Or perhaps you would prefer to take a house?'

'Not at all; it is comfortable here, and I particularly like the gardens. Thank you for recommending it.'

'It is a great favourite with the English,' he remarked with a smile.

'Not just the English. So far, I have met the most fascinating mixture of people, and that was only at breakfast. I sat down with two American tourists, an Italian lady photographer and a Greek banker. I know you warned me, but I didn't fully appreciate how cosmopolitan Cairo would be.'

'There is an interesting enclave of foreigners here,' Moreau said. 'Many come here as tourists and love it so much they decide to stay permanently. Others like to overwinter and enjoy coming back to meet old friends. Others, of course, come for different reasons. They are probably *persona non grata* at home.

It may be best not to probe, if you understand me, although I hope you haven't been imposed upon?' Moreau wiggled his brows making her laugh.

'Not at all, everyone is so friendly, and I have had countless offers to take me out to Giza, or a tour of the city. Can you imagine that happening in London or Paris? I already feel at home here. Do you know the game of the moment is to guess the story of each new arrival? Poor lambs. They are scrutinised and interrogated, and within half an hour their history and plans are known by all. Thankfully, in my case, it does not appear to have put anyone off, though I may have left out certain details of my past.'

'A wise course of action, madame. And you do not mind this inquisitiveness?'

'Not here. There is camaraderie and an attitude I have never encountered before.'

Moreau smiled. 'Yes, many consider life here as an adventure. I had a suspicion you would enjoy that.'

'Is your hotel a similar melting pot?' she asked. Moreau and Hopkins were staying at a more modest hotel.

'Why, yes, though it is mostly archaeological teams who use it, not tourists. We always stay at the Montgomery. It is basic but suits us perfectly for the few days we need it, Madame Lawrence. As we hope to set up camp at the dig in a couple of days, I can't justify staying somewhere as expensive as this.' His gaze took in the beautiful surroundings. 'I'm answerable to my investors... to you, in fact.'

'I understand, but if it is a question of money—'

'Not at all! To be honest, if given a choice, I would rather be in Sakkâra at the dig. As soon as my concession location is finalised, we will leave Cairo.'

'Is there a delay?'

'The Director General is dragging his heels for some reason. But do not be alarmed; it will all be sorted out soon.'

'Is there anything I can do as your patron? Is he concerned about your funding? I would be happy to speak to him if you think it would help.'

Moreau gazed at her, a slow smile spreading over his face. 'I'll never cease to thank the gods I met you in Nice! What did I do to deserve such luck?'

'I have no idea!' she blurted out, embarrassed by the intensity of his gaze. Moreau took her hand and raised it to his lips.

'You're an angel,' he whispered.

Feeling uncomfortably warm, Lucy drew her hand away, all too aware of the other guests around them. The American Mrs Hamilton, seated across the way, threw Lucy a knowing glance. 'Please, M. Moreau, do not speak so.'

'Forgive me; it was not my intention to discomfit you.' Moreau settled back and took a sip of his wine. But his eyes gave him away, for they were brimful of laughter. Lucy suddenly realised he considered her a challenge. And she wasn't sure how she felt about that.

'I would like you to meet M. Joubert in any case. You will find him delightful,' he said.

Struggling to regain her composure, Lucy snatched at the straw. 'Why don't I host a dinner here in the hotel? Is he a sociable man?'

'Why, yes. Although not to the same degree as before. Since his wife died, he leads a quieter life. However, your idea is an excellent one, madame. He can't fail to fall for your charms.'

'Excuse me, M. Moreau?' a voice interrupted.

They looked around. One of the hotel waiters was trying to catch Moreau's attention.

'Yes?' Moreau asked.

'This was forwarded from your hotel, monsieur,' the waiter said, handing him an envelope.

Moreau frowned down at the letter. 'Forgive me, madame, this must be urgent for David to forward it.'

'Please, go ahead.' Lucy watched him pull a single sheet of paper from the envelope. But she was soon alarmed to see all his earlier good humour vanish as he read the note. His face was now deadly white.

'What is it?' she asked.

'*Mon Dieu!*' Moreau crushed the note and threw it down on the table. Breathing hard, he sat back. 'It would appear I have annoyed someone.'

'May I?' Lucy asked, glancing at the note.

Moreau pressed his lips together. 'Certainly!'

The single sheet of paper was typewritten and brief. It was in English.

Stop your meddling, Moreau. As you know, the desert can be a dangerous place.

Stick to digging in the dirt.

Lucy was horrified, the pit of her stomach suddenly leaden. 'Do you know what this is about?'

'I do!' Moreau cried, his face now flushed with colour.

Lucy put the sheet down with distaste. 'Have you received threats before?'

'No.'

'You must go to the police, M. Moreau. You can't ignore this.'

He gave a humourless laugh. 'It is *because* I went to the police that I have received this delightful note.'

'I don't understand,' Lucy said.

'Last season, there was a dramatic rise in the number of thefts from dig sites. The thieves grow more and more daring. I decided to take some action when a dragoman, who has a small antiquities shop, came to me when he was offered objects he knew had come from one of my digs. I run a tight ship and hand-pick the men I employ, so I was absolutely livid.'

'I'm sure you were. Did you discover who the culprit was?'

'No. David and I interviewed all the men, but I couldn't find any evidence. Before I left in March, I spoke to many of my fellow archaeologists, urging them to renew their efforts to stop the flow of items onto the black market. If we make a concerted effort, we can limit the mischief. They are as frustrated as I am, though one or two were markedly silent when I tried to push them.'

'But perhaps the temptation is too much for some if their funding is not adequate?' Lucy said.

Moreau nodded. 'Undoubtedly some are torn between their love of their work and the need to eat! But it is no excuse, Madame Lawrence. History is not a commodity.'

'I agree. And you shared your suspicions with the police?'

'Yes, but I accused no man. There was no evidence. Joubert and I went more to complain about their lack of progress in putting a stop to it, than anything else. They said they would investigate.' Moreau rolled his eyes.

'Did the dragoman tell you who tried to sell him the artefacts?'

'Unfortunately, he had never seen the man before nor did he ask his name,' Moreau answered. 'The networks these men use are vast. It would take a cleverer man than I to unravel it all. I do not have the time – or the patience.'

'What will you do?'

'Be extra vigilant on site to see if I can catch them in the act.'

'No, I mean about your own protection,' Lucy said with a stern glance.

'Do not concern yourself. I can look after myself,' he answered with a wink. 'You must understand, this country is not dissimilar to the Wild West in America.' He glanced around the room. 'Beneath the gloss of civilisation here in Cairo lies mystery, treachery and deceit.'

Lucy narrowed her eyes and smiled. 'That's part of what you love about it, I suspect.'

Moreau bit his lip, his eyes twinkling. 'Perhaps!'

Lucy sighed in exasperation. Typical man, playing down danger. How could he be so flippant about a death threat?

'Now, enough of this. While I'm still at your disposal, would you care to see something of the city this afternoon?' Moreau asked.

'Are you sure? You must be extremely busy. Though, I'll admit, I'd prefer if you were to accompany me so I might pick your brains,' Lucy quipped.

'It would be an honour to have them picked by you, Madame Lawrence. And, as it happens, there is someone I would like you to meet.'

'Who?'

'Wait and see,' Moreau said with an enigmatic smile.

'Very well, be mysterious if you must. Give me a few minutes, M. Moreau. I'd like my maid to come too. We both need to get our bearings.'

'As you wish.' He showed no surprise at her request.

When Lucy looked back from the doorway, Moreau was staring across the terrace, an anxious frown marring his features. He had played down that awful note in front of her, but he was obviously worried. Perhaps she should try to get to the bottom of the mystery? It wouldn't be easy in a strange city and country, but if she put her mind to it, she was sure she could find out something to help Moreau.

In her mind's eye, she could see Phineas shaking his head. It only spurred her on.

THREE

Whatever Lucy's expectations of the city had been, they were surpassed. She adored it. Moreau took her arm and led her through the ancient thoroughfares, Mary following close behind, apprehension on her pretty face. Shafts of sunlight penetrated the shade provided by the overhanging upper stories of the buildings, illuminating the constantly moving mass of people going about their business. Such crowds and such noise! Lucy couldn't help but stare at the mixture of locals, tourists and the ubiquitous donkey boys with their ornately decorated steeds. And all along the alleyways the shop merchants sat silently regarding it all, smoking, hermit-like on the front steps of their tiny shops.

Lucy felt a tug on her sleeve and turned.

'Who are all these people, ma'am? Are we safe at all, do you think?' Mary asked, her eyes on stalks. 'I've never seen the like in London or Dublin; not even at the Queen's Jubilee.'

Moreau smiled at Mary. 'Nor will you, Mademoiselle O'Reilly. Cairo is the melting pot of the East. You will find every nationality and creed here. Do you see the man over there?'

Lucy followed his gaze. A man in baggy trousers and a braided jacket, with a rifle slung casually over his shoulder, was standing chatting to an elderly man drawing water from a fountain.

'That man is a dragoman, and he's talking to a fellah – the old man dressed in blue with the jar.'

Mary blinked up at Moreau. 'I don't understand, sir, what's a... dragoman?'

'He's an interpreter. Most visitors hire one to make their visit more comfortable. They translate Arabic into English or French and negotiate where necessary on your behalf. The fellâheen are the Egyptian peasants – farm workers and general labourers. I employ them on my digs because they are hard-working. It would be impossible to do my job without them.'

'Thank you, sir,' Mary said, but she looked askance at the local men.

Lucy smiled at her. 'It is all new to me, too, Mary.' Lucy turned to Moreau. 'Where next?'

Moreau drew her hand back through his arm. 'We must now meet Rafiq!'

They stopped outside an establishment they'd reached through a warren of narrow alleyways, which Lucy was sure she couldn't find again if her life depended on it. Peering inside, she could see it was full of men smoking and drinking coffee, the aromas drifting out whenever the door opened.

'Ladies, if you would wait here for a moment? I won't be long,' Moreau said, before slipping inside.

A few minutes later, he reappeared, followed by a giant of a man who smiled broadly and bowed. He wore a scarlet jacket with gold braid and baggy cream trousers.

'Please may I present to you Rafiq Mostafa, Madame Lawrence? He has been my dragoman many times in the past, and I have engaged him for you for the duration of your stay, if you're agreeable?'

Rafiq bowed. 'It would be an honour to serve you, Madame Lawrence,' the man said with only a hint of an accent. Up close, Lucy saw he was older than he first appeared, with grey in his beard and at his temples.

'Thank you,' Lucy said to Rafiq, taking an instant liking to him. She would feel a lot safer with him by her side. The other hotel guests had that very morning advised her of the need of the services of a dragoman. For him to be recommended by Moreau was even better.

'Are you sure you can spare Rafiq, M. Moreau?' Lucy asked.

'Indeed I can. I'm glad to say my Arabic has improved greatly over the years to the point I no longer need this rogue's assistance.'

A belly laugh exploded from Rafiq. 'Yes! You can swear like a native now.'

Moreau grinned sheepishly at Lucy. 'I'm afraid it is true.'

'I'll be at your hotel first thing in the morning to receive your instructions, Madame Lawrence. Until then, *ma' al-salāmah*,' Rafiq said. He bowed to the ladies, then Moreau, and went back into the coffee shop.

Lucy turned to Moreau. 'I appreciate this very much. You've saved me a lot of trouble.'

'My pleasure. He's extremely reliable but unobtrusive and will protect you. This will ease my mind when you're in Cairo, and I'm at the dig. The Mostafas are an ancient Cairo family with extensive experience as dragomen and on site at digs. Both Rafiq and his younger brother, Ali, have been of great value to me. Ali is now my site supervisor at Sakkâra. A clever and stead-fast young man, just like Rafiq.'

Lucy consulted her watch. 'It is still early, and I would love to see more if you can spare us the time?'

'Of course. Would you care to go to the carpet bazaar? We are close,' Moreau said. 'It is just off the Muski.'

'Yes, please,' Lucy answered.

Some minutes later, they passed under a stone archway and into a network of narrow alleyways, fringed by houses with lattice windows and beautiful old doorways. Every possible colour and pattern of floor covering was on display, hanging from windows or piled high in the street. One fine oriental rug caught Lucy's eye and she stopped to admire the workmanship, while Moreau and Mary walked on ahead. Lucy spotted the merchant at the rear of the shop, sitting cross-legged. The interior was gloomy, but she could make out his white turban and a dark-coloured robe. The hairs on the back of her neck prickled. He was watching her steadily. No doubt he was weighing her up as a tourist ready to be plucked. Still, his gaze made her uncomfortable. As Lucy inspected the superb weave of the rug, she was aware of him coming towards her out of the corner of her eye.

'Lady like? You want buy?' the merchant asked, catching the edge of the rug and stroking it.

Lucy realised Moreau was out of reach, and she didn't want to try her hand at negotiating just yet. 'Not today.'

The man tilted his head and quirked a brow. 'Special,' he said, motioning her inside. 'Special for lady.'

What could he mean? With a quick glance at Moreau's retreating back, she stepped over the threshold and stayed just inside the doorway. There was barely room to stand for carpets and rugs. As Lucy waited, the merchant took out a wooden box from behind a pile of rugs at the back of the shop. It was the size of a hat box, the lacquered surface scratched and dented. The shopkeeper glanced over her shoulder out towards the alley, then beckoned her forward. Lucy's curiosity won out.

As she drew level with him, he removed the lid and tilted the box for Lucy to see. With a gasp, she stepped back, her heart thumping. Inside the box was a mummified hand: a gold ring with hieroglyphs sat askew on a black shrivelled finger.

The man screwed up his eyes and placed a finger against his mouth. Then he whispered. 'You want? Good price for lady.'

'Certainly not!' Lucy cried with a shudder, stumbling backwards before escaping the shop as quickly as she could.

The Excelsior Hotel, the Following Morning

Lucy had found a quiet corner in the guests' lounge, and was so engrossed in *The Times* she didn't realise she had company. She glanced up to find Isabella DeLuca smiling down at her. On meeting her the previous morning at breakfast, Lucy had taken an instant liking to the exotically beautiful Italian and had been only too willing to join Isabella's party for dinner the previous evening. Isabella oozed charm, confidence and wealth. Her lively brown eyes constantly twinkled with mischief. When Lucy had asked her about her near-perfect English, Isabella had informed her that a year spent in London accounted for it. But what was even more interesting was Isabella's sense of her own worth. Nothing appeared to faze her. She travelled alone, hiring a maid only if she needed one. Her description of some of her exploits had Lucy mesmerised. Lucy felt such a dull creature and a coward in comparison.

However, when Lucy had probed Isabella about her family, Isabella had turned the question and changed the subject. Lucy didn't pursue the topic for she could sympathise: she didn't particularly want to discuss her own family either. But it was obvious the DeLucas were a wealthy Milanese family and were happy to fund Isabella's independent lifestyle and career. If she were honest, Lucy was a trifle envious, but she admired both Isabella's skills and her pioneering nature.

'*Buongiorno, Signora Lawrence.*'

'Good morning, Signorina DeLuca. I missed you at breakfast. Won't you join me for coffee?' Lucy asked.

Isabella consulted her watch. 'I'm sorry, perhaps later. I must meet someone regarding a work opportunity in about ten minutes. If you do not mind, I'll wait here.' Isabella settled down opposite her with a smile. 'And please call me Isabella.'

'And me Lucy, if you will.'

Isabella nodded. 'Very well, Lucy.'

'So, tell me. Is it the kind of work you were hoping to do?' Lucy asked.

'Potentially. I'm meeting a Signor Whitmore – an archaeologist. He sent a message first thing this morning as he wishes to interview me for the position of photographer on his dig.'

'How wonderful! But you've worked at various digs before, isn't that so?'

'Yes; for several seasons now. Thankfully, archaeologists realise the benefits of photography. Sketching artefacts and interiors is far too slow in this modern age of technology. Can you imagine being stuck down in a dirty and dusty tomb laboriously drawing? Not to mention the heat; it can be exhausting.'

'I can imagine,' Lucy replied although the thought of being down in a tomb set her heart pounding with excitement. 'Photography must be a godsend to the profession.'

'And provides employment opportunities for poor photographers like me,' Isabella replied with a chuckle.

'Now that you mention this man, I recall someone mentioning his name at dinner last night. Is he staying at this hotel?' Lucy asked. 'I haven't met anyone of that name yet.'

'They arrived late yesterday evening, I believe.'

'They?'

'His sister Rosemary always travels with him.'

'Is she an archaeologist too? I understand some universities are allowing women to study the subject now.'

'No, Rosemary is not qualified, but she assists him in his

work and is knowledgeable in her own right. It is rumoured she has written most of his papers.'

'Miss Whitmore sounds like an interesting woman. Did you work for Mr Whitmore in previous seasons?' Lucy asked.

'No, and I'm not sure I want to.' Isabella leaned towards her and lowered her voice. 'I've heard he's a difficult man and extremely demanding of those he employs. Last season his photographer left after only a few weeks. There were rumours of a terrible row at the dig, unreasonable demands, expecting him to work half the night. Not very encouraging.'

'No, it isn't. I take it he's British with a name like Whitmore?'

Isabella nodded. 'He's Scottish and partly funded by the British Museum. I'll wait to see what he has to say and then decide. M. Joubert of the EAS has also asked me to help him catalogue the new exhibits out at Boulaq. That is a much more tempting offer.'

'I can understand why you would think so, if those rumours about Mr Whitmore are true.'

'Do not worry, Lucy, I'll do what's best for my career. I can't afford a stain on my reputation, particularly out here. M. Joubert is a gentleman, so sweet and old-fashioned. There would be no risk working for him.'

'I haven't met M. Joubert, but I understand he's an outstanding director.'

'They say he's good, but Mariette, his predecessor, was unique, and therefore it is impossible for Joubert to fill his shoes no matter how he tries. Forgive me, but it is all over the hotel—is it true that you're funding M. Moreau's dig this year?'

'Partly, yes. We met by accident in Nice, and before I knew it, I had agreed to help him.'

'Good for you!' Isabella said. 'Though I hope you realise, you're now in the middle of a war.'

'Whatever do you mean?' Lucy asked.

'Did no one tell you? The French and the English are great rivals in the field of archaeology as well as everything else. It does not help that the Antiquities Service is run by the French and the purse strings are held by the English. There has been trouble over licences with accusations of favouritism. The rivalry has caused a lot of tension.'

'Good heavens! I had no idea. Will my backing of a French team make matters worse?'

'Time will tell,' Isabella said with a flash of humour in her brown eyes. 'It will make life... interesting.'

No wonder Moreau had been so pleased to secure her patronage, Lucy thought, suddenly annoyed. Why hadn't he warned her about that particular situation? It made her a little uneasy. Was he more desperate for funding that he had originally implied? Hopefully, this wasn't going to make life unpleasant.

'M. Moreau has promised to teach me a little during my stay and has given me some books to get me started. I hope to join him at the dig, just to observe, even if it is only for a few days.'

'If you're funding him, I can't see why he would refuse. But be warned; there can be a lot of waiting around while they dig test trenches. Often as not, they find nothing but pieces of broken pottery. However, I imagine Moreau will want you to come out to experience the excitement. It is in his interest for you to become addicted to the thrill of it. That way, he's guaranteed repeat funding.'

'Your view of men is cynical, Isabella.'

Isabella grinned. 'Perhaps! But seriously, you may not be aware how difficult it can be to secure enough money for an entire season.'

'I am. Everyone has mentioned it. Are you acquainted with M. Moreau? Did you ever work for him?'

'Unfortunately, he has never had need of my services, but he's highly respected in the profession. M. Moreau has made some exquisite finds. If you visit the museum at Boulaq, you will see them. I have never heard a bad word said against him.'

'That is reassuring. Do you know anything about his American assistant, David Hopkins? He's a very different character.'

Isabella looked uncomfortable for a second, and Lucy wondered if that was a hint of a blush creeping into her companion's cheeks. But it was so fleeting, she could have imagined it.

'I have met him, of course... but I hardly know him,' Isabella answered.

Lucy was disappointed. She'd hoped to learn more about the American from others who knew him professionally.

Just then, Lucy noticed a woman weaving her way through the tables, her eyes fixed on Isabella's back. When she reached their table, she gave Lucy a curt nod before turning to Isabella.

'Miss DeLuca, my brother would like to see you now,' the woman said. Lucy could detect a Scottish twang to her low-pitched voice.

Lucy regarded the lady closely. She was an unusual-looking woman with the potential to be stunning. Her greatest asset was her pale skin which was almost translucent with a light dusting of freckles across her nose, most likely testament to her years in Egypt. Unfortunately, her dress was ill-fitting and plain, and she wore her strawberry blonde hair pulled back tight from her face in a matronly fashion.

Isabella looked up. 'Ah! Signorina Whitmore. You are so kind to come and fetch me. Let me introduce Mrs Lawrence to you. Lucy, this is Miss Rosemary Whitmore.'

Lucy held out her hand and received a cool shake and a glance which was cooler still.

'Mrs Lawrence,' Miss Whitmore said in a dry tone, her grey eyes raking over Lucy.

'Delighted to make your acquaintance,' Lucy replied, surprised she'd generated such animosity in a complete stranger. Had Isabella understated the enmity existing between the various factions? The months ahead would be interesting and, if Lucy wasn't mistaken, challenging.

With a sniff, Miss Whitmore turned back to Isabella. 'If you would care to come with me, please? My brother is extremely busy with his preparations. It would be best not to keep him waiting.' Her tone was reproving, and Lucy wondered how Isabella would react. But Isabella darted Lucy an amused glance before following Miss Whitmore from the room.

FOUR

Later that evening, Lucy watched Mary as she flitted about the hotel bedroom. Her blonde curls were escaping her pretty white cap and her cheeks glowed pink. 'Where did I leave it? Oh ma'am, I'm ever so sorry. It's your favourite.'

'Mary, calm down. It's only a fan. Another will do just as well.'

'Here it is!' Mary picked up the tortoiseshell and mother-of-pearl fan from the floor beside the bed. 'I knew it couldn't have gone far.' She handed it to Lucy. 'Gosh, you look grand, ma'am. Those Frenchies know how to make a dress!'

Lucy had to agree. The burgundy ribbed silk bodice fitted perfectly, setting off her auburn hair and blue eyes to perfection. The skirt of brocaded satin was luxurious to touch and was finished off with a short train. It was probably the most daring evening gown she'd ever worn, being off the shoulder with a deep décolletage. Lucy wasn't vain, but couldn't deny the boost of confidence the image in the mirror gave her. Hosting a dinner for Moreau and M. Joubert was a little daunting: a rather grown-up occasion compared to those casual soirées she and Charlie had held in St John's Wood.

'Which jewellery would you like to wear tonight, ma'am?'

'I think the opals, Mary.'

Mary grinned back at her. 'Good choice, ma'am. They'll go perfectly with the colour of your dress.' She skipped over to the wardrobe and took out Lucy's jewellery case, then brought the opal set over to the dressing table.

There was a tap at the door.

'That will be Signorina DeLuca, Mary,' Lucy said, as she quickly put in her earrings.

'*Sei bellissima!*' Isabella cried, clasping her hands together as she stepped over the threshold. 'Lucy, your dress is divine. I detect the hand of an expert seamstress.'

Lucy smiled back at Isabella as Mary fastened her opal pendant around her neck. 'Correct! While in Paris, I took advantage of what was on offer. However, I can return the compliment.' Isabella's green and cream evening gown was embellished with gold thread and shimmered as she moved.

'*Grazie!* The gentlemen will be eating out of our hands, my friend.'

Lucy rose up and took a final look in the mirror. 'Will I do, Mary?' The maid beamed back at her in answer. 'You need not wait up for me.'

'Very good, ma'am. Enjoy your evening.' Mary bobbed, before slipping out the door.

Lucy smiled at Isabella. 'Thank you for agreeing to join my party. I was afraid you would refuse now that you're working for the enemy.'

Isabella chuckled. 'Oh yes, I should not be consorting with the likes of you.'

'Seriously, will dining with Moreau this evening cause you trouble?'

Isabella tilted her head and smiled. 'I'll dine with whomever I choose. Hah! I do not intend to miss any of the fun. Whitmore is paying above the odds. How could I resist? But he does not own me. Besides, until he makes a find of some kind, I'll be waiting here in Cairo with next to nothing to do. Hopefully, it will not be too long before the work begins. I prefer to be busy and near the excitement.'

'I'm glad you aren't leaving Cairo straight away, for I'll miss your company.'

Isabella beamed back at her. 'And I, yours.'

'Where is Mr Whitmore's concession?'

'He hopes to win one of the Sakkâra licences,' Isabella replied.

'The same as Moreau,' Lucy exclaimed. 'That will make for an interesting few months. I wonder if they are searching for the same thing.'

'My dear Lucy, of course they are. However, what they really desire is fame and fortune, though they'd never admit it. Those two have always been rivals. Whitmore envies Moreau's success; he has yet to prove himself, which is why the British Museum are only partly funding him this year. Moreau, on the other hand, does not rate Whitmore's work. Last year there was trouble out at Sakkâra. There were rumours it involved a woman, but I never heard the details. I think it was more likely to do with artefacts.'

'I think I know what it was about.'

Isabella's fine brows rose. 'Really?'

'Moreau was only talking about it a few days ago. Last season, he approached many in the profession about the necessity to curb the black market. Perhaps Whitmore didn't take kindly to M. Moreau broaching the subject.'

'Not if Moreau was lecturing him. Whitmore would have taken exception to it, particularly with their history,' Isabella said.

'I wonder why men are so competitive. Would it not be better to co-operate?'

Isabella snorted. 'Egos in the way, my dear.'

'Well, now I'm even more determined to spend some time at Sakkâra. If you are there too, it will be such fun.'

'We wouldn't be the only women as Rosemary Whitmore will stay out at the dig too. She usually does.'

'For the entire season? The conditions can't be agreeable.'

'The conditions do not bother her; she seems to thrive on the hardship. Though she did leave early last year. I believe she fell ill just after Christmas. When I saw her here in Cairo, just before she departed, she looked dreadfully unwell.'

'The camps can't be healthy places.'

'It depends on whose camp it is,' Isabella said. 'Some are basic, while others have every comfort imaginable. It is amazing what you can manage to strap to a donkey's back if you are so inclined.'

'But Miss Whitmore must be fully recovered to come back?' Lucy remarked.

Isabella shrugged. 'I assume she is, as she looks well enough but ... she seems different.'

'In what way?'

'She's more serious, almost austere, and, if anything, even more controlling of her brother.'

'It is a wonder he tolerates it. Most men hate fuss,' Lucy said.

'Why would he mind? Rosemary is utterly devoted to him and keeps everything running smoothly. He's totally absorbed in his work and relies on her to look after all the practical matters. The partnership appears to work well.'

'Miss Whitmore didn't appear pleased to meet me this morning,' Lucy remarked.

Isabella nodded. 'She won't be happy that you're funding her brother's greatest rival. Do not be concerned; once the digs are underway, there is no reason for you to meet for Sakkâra covers a large area.' Isabella glanced at the clock. 'Now, let's enjoy our dinner, and with two charming

Frenchmen for company it promises to be an agreeable evening.'

Lucy took a deep breath. 'I certainly hope so.'

The grand dining room of the Excelsior had been modelled on the Langham in London. Opulent, with a gold and white colour scheme, it reminded Lucy of the one occasion she and Charlie had dined at the Langham as guests of one of his business associates. It had been one of the few times she'd been ill at ease, for their host that evening had flirted openly with her, while Charlie had sipped his wine apparently oblivious, and the man's wife threw her dagger-looks. Lucy had remonstrated with Charlie on the way home, but he had laughed it off, telling her not to be so stuffy. It was only after Charlie's 'accident' that Lucy had analysed some of the stranger events during their marriage and wondered if she'd ever really known her husband.

The maître d'hôtel greeted them solemnly and escorted them to their table. As they approached, Moreau rose up, a broad smile on his handsome face. An older man with a shock of white hair falling over his forehead and gold-rimmed spectacles stood up beside him. He was the epitome of a college professor, although a very well-dressed one. It had to be M. Joubert, the Director of the EAS.

An hour later, Lucy and Victor Joubert were getting along famously. Joubert was an interesting man and entertained her with stories of his own excavations and his sojourn at the Egyptian Antiquities Service. Lucy was impressed by the breadth of his knowledge.

'You have lived in Egypt for a long time now, sir. Would you ever consider going back to France and your old life?' Lucy asked.

Joubert's expression turned melancholy. 'Since my wife Rebecca died some years ago, I'm not interested in returning home. She's buried here in Cairo, and I couldn't bear to leave her. No, my life is here now.'

'I'm sorry to hear about your wife.'

'Rebecca was everything to me, but she died in a terrible accident. She was only forty-three. She was vivacious and always the centre of attention. Much like Miss DeLuca.'

Lucy glanced across at Isabella who was in full flight, regaling Moreau with some story or other. Moreau was gazing into her eyes, totally absorbed. It was a skill he had; no doubt part of his seduction armoury. He could be perfectly charming without resorting to these tricks, Lucy thought, with a hint of annoyance. Was it a compulsion to flirt with every woman he met? Of course, it was ridiculous to care one way or the other. It was most likely the French way. With an Englishman, one never really knew where one stood until he was pushed beyond his endurance and declared himself. At least a woman had the power when dealing with men like Moreau. If she wasn't interested, she could brush him off, and if she were...

Lucy dismissed Moreau from her thoughts and turned back to M. Joubert. 'How dreadful for you; you must miss her terribly.'

Joubert sighed. 'Best not to dwell on the past.' The director's face darkened momentarily, then he appeared to shake himself free of his ghosts. 'Life goes on, Madame Lawrence. We must live on our memories.'

Lucy felt so differently she almost laughed out loud. She was desperately trying to escape her past. Charlie had brought her nothing but heartache and Phineas, too, had hurt her. Hadn't he admitted a lack of trust in her when all the misunderstandings had led to her flight from London to Yorkshire during the sapphire case? And it was only when he heard she was leaving London that he had attempted a reconciliation. And where had that led? Exactly nowhere. And now he had disappeared and most likely with his ex-fiancée. Lucy squirmed. *Good God, I have appalling judgement.*

'I could not be more pleased for Armand to have found such a wonderful new patron,' M. Joubert commented, breaking into her misery.

Moreau suddenly swung around. 'What's this? I'm sure I heard my name.'

Joubert huffed. 'You're too full of yourself, Moreau. Attend to the lady!'

Moreau exchanged an amused glance with Lucy before resuming his conversation with Isabella. But Lucy was surprised by the undercurrent to Joubert's words. Weren't these men supposed to be great friends? Was Joubert upset by Moreau's attention to Isabella? It didn't make much sense. To her astonishment, M. Joubert scowled at Moreau, but Moreau was too engrossed in whatever Isabella was saying to notice. Joubert sipped his wine, watching the couple across the table for several moments, a frown creasing his brow.

Then, all of a sudden, Joubert turned to Lucy. 'Forgive me, dear lady, I was distracted. What were we talking about?'

'Patronage,' she said.

'Yes, indeed. I'm not sure if you realise how difficult it's become to secure funding. I often refuse licences to the worthiest of men. But if they don't have the funding, I can't let them work. They'll cut corners at the digs and not pay their men.' He grunted. 'It has happened too many times, and always it falls to me to clear up the mess. And now *this* season is proving more irksome than usual.'

'How so?' she asked, feeling sorry for him. It sounded as if his job was not easy.

Joubert sighed. 'Several Egyptologists are clamouring to dig in the same location. I do not understand why. Perhaps it is because Moreau is keen on the site.' He shook his head.

'They all want to excavate at Sakkâra?'

Joubert glanced over at Moreau. 'Yes!'

'Oh, dear! How will you decide?'

'The only fair solution I can find is to draw lots. We will hold the draw tomorrow morning, here at the hotel.'

'What a clever solution. Now, I understand why M. Moreau has been so preoccupied since we arrived in Cairo,' Lucy said. 'He must be worried which plot he will be awarded. There is a particular tomb he's anxious to find. Much will hang on the outcome of your draw, monsieur.'

'Yes, I'm aware of Moreau's wishes in the matter, but I have no choice. The allocation of plots must be transparent. Of course, as Moreau's patron you are welcome to attend, Madame Lawrence, to see all is done fair and square.'

'Thank you. Though, to be honest, I think this draw makes things a little more exciting.'

Joubert frowned. 'I wish there was another way, but there is always an element of luck involved in archaeology. Moreau knows this well.'

'Yes, he's a seasoned campaigner. I consider myself fortunate to have met him and to be involved in his work. Such a shame others may not be able to pursue their dreams if funding is an issue. I understand it is because of stricter rules on removing artefacts.'

Joubert nodded. 'It has contributed to the explosion of the black market. Every back street in Cairo is swamped with artefacts pilfered from digs and, I suspect, some are trafficked by the archaeological teams in a desperate attempt to fund their excavations. In those cases, they are mostly inferior artefacts, small statues or fragments of papyrus. However, it is still illegal, and it is my responsibility to curb the trade. I can't prove what they are doing, of course, but I'm sure of it.'

'Is there nothing you can do?' Lucy asked, thinking of her conversation with Moreau about the threatening note.

Joubert shrugged. 'It is an epidemic. There are too many

people involved. Poverty drives them to it, and some are too ignorant to realise they are selling their heritage. Of course, there are many who do know but are driven by greed. There is one particular village where the entire male population is engaged in nothing but tomb robbing!'

'Good gracious! Can't the authorities sort it out?'

'I have a path worn out to the door of Inspector Vauquelin, madame! Even Moreau has complained. I must give the police some credit, though. They try their best, but with so many digs in operation during the season, it is impossible to control. Most digs employ guards at night, but I suspect half of them are open to bribery, and under cover of darkness the robbers do as they wish.'

'I was offered something at the carpet bazaar the other day,' Lucy said. 'It looked like a mummy's hand with a golden ring on one of the fingers.' Lucy shuddered. 'It was horrible.'

'And most likely counterfeit, Madame Lawrence. While there are tourists willing to pay for these 'artefacts', the locals will provide what they think people want. Before the end of your stay you will be offered everything from a full mummy to a papyrus most ancient. However, if you're interested in seeing the genuine artefacts, you must come out to me at Boulaq, and I'll show you around the museum. Your dragoman will show you the way.'

'Thank you, monsieur, you're very kind. I would love to.'

FIVE

Some Hours Later

Lucy was too warm. She pushed the bedcover over the side of the bed and turned over, irritated that sleep was proving difficult tonight. This was the second occasion she'd woken up. But this time, it had been one of those disturbing dreams. She couldn't remember what it had been about as the details had dissolved like wisps of morning mist as soon as she tried to grasp them. Bother! She could just about make out the dark outlines of the furniture against the paler walls of the bedroom. It must still be night-time, she thought, and turned over onto her back. Eventually, she began to doze, but fitfully.

A floorboard creaked. The sound ripped through her consciousness. Instantly, Lucy was awake, her senses on high alert. *There was someone in the room!* Her heart raced and she broke out in a cold sweat.

Trying not to panic, she strained her eyes but, although it must now be nearer to morning, there was little light to see anything clearly. Then she became aware of another, more terrifying sound that made her shiver. It was the sound of a person's

rapid breathing, and it was coming from the end of her bed.
There could be no mistake; someone was standing there. Lurking. Waiting... As her eyes adjusted, Lucy could just make out a
dark figure. Her stomach contracted in horror. Why were they
standing there looking at her like that? Did they mean her
harm? Was she about to be attacked? Frantically, she tried to
think of a way to defend herself. But she had no weapon to
hand. A pillow. Could she defend herself with that? Slowly her
fingers curled around the edge of the pillowcase lying next to
her even as her mind screamed that it was pathetic. She thought
longingly of her pistol, wrapped up in linen, and, of course,
helpfully at the bottom of her trunk. But she had never dreamt
she was in any danger. If only she had been sensible and kept
the pistol under her pillow. Hadn't Moreau compared Cairo to
the Wild West?

Minutes ticked by and still the person remained standing at
the end of the bed. Surely, they would have attacked by now if
that was their intent? She needed to calm down and try to think
clearly. Maybe it was a thief who wanted to ransack her room
for valuables and wanted to be sure she was asleep? Should she
cry out for help? Would that scare them off? But who would
hear her cry of distress anyway? What was she to do?

The worst thing was feeling so vulnerable. Lucy tried yet
again to steady her own breathing, her damp fingers clenching
the sheets. She feared she was rooted to the spot. If the person
meant her harm, there was little she could do. But then, above
the pounding of her heart, Lucy heard the floorboard creak once
more. The shape was moving away and, if she wasn't mistaken,
they were heading towards the dressing table. So, it *was* a thief!
Oh no, Lucy thought; I left my opals on the table before retiring; they'd be easy pickings.

Suddenly angry, Lucy decided to act. As quietly as she
could, she pushed herself upwards into a sitting position. Now
she could see more clearly. Someone *was* standing before the

dressing table on the other side of the room, their hands outstretched. The figure was slight, probably a young boy, Lucy surmised. Could she tackle him? Then she heard the click of the jewellery box opening. She had to act now. Lucy leapt from the bed.

'Hey! Stop!' Lucy shouted. But somehow her feet were tangled in the discarded bedcover. Next thing she knew she was toppling down to the floor. The thief took fright and swept past her. Lucy reached out and grabbed the person's leg, but they were stronger and kicked out, shaking her off with ease. Helpless with rage, Lucy watched her burglar wrench open the shutters and leap out onto the balcony and disappear from sight.

Cursing her luck, Lucy managed to disentangle herself and follow. But it was too late. She was just in time to see the blackclad figure drop down from the balcony, before racing across the garden and disappearing from view.

Early Next Morning

'I can only apologise, madame, most profusely,' M. Bisset, the hotel manager said, having listened to Lucy's description of events during the night. 'We will call in the police immediately. You must believe me; this has never happened in our hotel before. In others, yes, but we pride ourselves on the safety of our guests.'

'Yes, well, last night someone did get in. It was a terrifying experience. I feared for my life,' Lucy snapped. 'What if it had been a murderer?'

The manager paled. 'Oh no, madame. Surely not.'

Lucy gave him an icy stare.

He cleared his throat. 'I can only imagine how frightening it must have been.'

'Yes, it was, but somehow, I managed to scare them off, but who's to say the thief wasn't successful in another room?' Lucy replied. 'They were very daring, you know. The door of my suite was locked, but they came in through the balcony shutters in my sitting room and from there crept into my bedroom. It was sheer luck I woke when I did. I checked this morning. It would be relatively easy for someone nimble to scale the supports of the balcony or even shin up that date tree, and from there gain entry to my suite.'

The manager shook his head. 'Please, madame, it would only frighten the guests if they were to hear of this. I would appreciate if this unfortunate occurrence could stay between us. Obviously, we will not be charging you for your stay.' An uneasy smile flickered across the manager's face.

'I don't see how you can keep this quiet. Once the police arrive, it will be all over the hotel.' Lucy was surprised by his offer and could only guess that the hotel market must be cut-throat. Did Bisset anticipate a mass exodus of guests just because an intruder had attempted to rob a guest? Or was the problem more pervasive than he was letting on? In such a poor country, Lucy reckoned wealthy hotel guests were easy targets for the desperate. Though she was mystified as to why she'd been targeted when there were far more ostentatious guests in the hotel. Lucy rarely wore much jewellery and had only been in the hotel for a few days. Had she been noticed when walking about the city and followed back to the hotel? Perhaps it was sheer bad luck and not design; after all, her room was accessible from the garden without too much trouble.

There was a commotion outside the door, and Lucy made out the familiar tones of Robert Hamilton, the American guest. 'It is an outrage, I tell you! I must see the manager at once.'

Lucy and M. Bisset exchanged a glance. 'Oh dear, perhaps our intruder was successful after all,' Lucy remarked, rising to her feet. 'Please have someone notify me when the police arrive.'

'Yes, madame,' the now subdued hotel manager managed to utter.

The door flew open just as Lucy was about to leave. 'Beg your pardon, ma'am, but I have to see Bisset right away,' Mr Hamilton blustered.

'What has happened, Mr Hamilton?' Lucy asked.

Hamilton started to explain, but spotted Bisset and rushed over to him. 'My wife's pearls were stolen last night. What are you going to do about it, eh? I demand the police are called in.'

Lucy slipped out of the room, happy to leave the unfortunate manager to deal with the irate Mr Hamilton.

Lucy returned to her room hoping the police wouldn't be too long. It was the morning of the draw, and she didn't want to miss any of the excitement. But it was an hour later when Inspector Vauquelin of the Cairo police was announced by Mary. A distinguished-looking man with a military style moustache, he shook Lucy's hand solemnly before taking a seat at her bequest. He removed his hat to reveal a head of grey curling hair. Lucy judged him to be in his mid-fifties with the air of a man who knew what he was about.

'An intruder stole from one of the guests last night. I understand from M. Bisset, madame, there was an attempt to steal from you too?'

'That is correct.'

The inspector grunted. 'Then, perhaps, you may be able to help us with our enquiries.' Inspector Vauquelin took out a notebook and pen from the inside pocket of his jacket.

'I'll do my best, Inspector.' Lucy described the events of the night before.

Vauquelin wrote it all down, then looked up. 'And you didn't see the intruder's face?'

'No. It was too dark, I'm afraid.'

'And your maid?' he asked. 'Could she have seen anything?'

He was obviously well informed, and had already investigated her circumstances: he knew she travelled with her own maid. Lucy was impressed. 'She sleeps in the servants' quarters on the top floor. I was alone.'

'Can you describe the person you saw?'

'They were slight, probably about my height, and dressed all in black. I'm sorry, that isn't particularly helpful,' she replied with a wan smile.

'No, it is useful. Would you say male or female?'

Lucy considered this. 'Again, it was difficult to see, but they were definitely wearing trousers as I grabbed their leg as they shot past, so I suppose it is most likely a young lad.'

The inspector huffed. 'And nothing was taken?'

'Luckily, I scared them off.'

'And gave chase, I understand. That, if you do not mind me saying, was extremely foolish. They could have been armed.'

Although miffed, Lucy saw his point. 'Perhaps, but my initial fear had turned to anger. One's room should be a sanctuary and I have an intense dislike of being a victim.'

Inspector Vauquelin raised a brow. Lucy returned his gaze unflinching. He stood with a grunt. 'I'll not detain you any longer, madame. Thank you for your help.'

'Have you any idea who the thief might be?' Lucy asked, just as the inspector reached the door.

Inspector Vauquelin paused with his hand on the door handle, his expression one of surprise. 'None, madame, as yet. This is the second season this burglar has been plaguing the up-market hotels.' He teased the side of his moustache with his fingers and frowned, perhaps surprised he had revealed the police's failure in the matter. His gaze hardened. 'But there is no need for you to be concerned about it. M. Bisset has assured me that he will be putting measures in place to ensure there is no reoccurrence. Besides, it is unlikely they'll come back to this hotel again, and, of course, it is only a matter of time before we catch them. Good day to you, Madame Lawrence.'

The air of excitement in the hotel was palpable with half of Cairo present to witness M. Joubert's draw. As she made her way through reception, Lucy noticed even the local morning papers featured the event on their front page. The babble of voices rose as she drew near the terrace. When Lucy stepped out, she was confronted by a wall of gentlemen's backs. Determined not to miss anything, she skirted around them and stepped down into the garden to join the crowd gathered on the lawn. Lucy soon realised the men on the terrace were the hopeful teams, waiting to know their fate. They stood out from the rest by their motley attire and sunburnt faces. At the edge of the lawn some newspaper men stood by, notebooks at the ready. Lucy spotted Isabella at the front, her camera set up.

Straining her neck, Lucy could discern M. Joubert at the back of the terrace, standing before a table on which two boxes and a stack of files were laid. Two high spots of colour on his cheeks and a harassed expression suggested he was not enjoying the occasion. The poor man, she thought; he's probably regretting his decision to hold the draw.

Behind him, pinned to the wall, was a large map, divided up into a grid with each section numbered. It was too far away for her to make out any detail. Fleetingly, Lucy wondered which plot Moreau wanted the most. He had mentioned wishing to work in the southern part of the site. Scanning the crowd, she made out his distinctive mop of curly hair. Hopkins stood beside him, looking as cheery as ever. Moreau turned at that moment and spotted her. A warm smile was the result.

M. Joubert stepped forward and a hush fell over the audience. 'Ladies and gentlemen, you're welcome here this morning. By agreement with the Board of the Antiquities Service, it's been decided to take the unusual step of drawing lots for this season's concessions located in Sakkâra. This is the fairest solution in light of the unprecedented level of interest in excavating there.' He turned to the waiting teams. 'I would like to make it clear, gentlemen, the draw result is final, and I'll not entertain any arguments. Do you understand?'

A murmur rose up from the group on the terrace. It didn't sound as if everyone was in total agreement. Joubert scowled at them, pushing his glasses up his nose. They fell silent. With a grunt, he beckoned to another man to come forward.

'M. Japp, my assistant, will draw the names from the first box, and I shall draw the lots from the other.' The fair-haired young man bowed, his cheeks suddenly suffused with colour. Head bent, he retreated to the table.

'Make a start, M. Japp, if you please,' Joubert commanded, 'We don't have all day!'

The assistant gave a nervous cough before drawing the first name. 'Reginald Whitmore,' he announced.

Joubert dived into the second box. 'Lot number seven,' he said, holding aloft a piece of paper. Whitmore stepped forward, and Lucy studied him closely, curious to see what Rosemary's brother looked like. They were alike in colouring but not much else. He was not the most prepossessing of men with his stocky build, ruddy cheeks, and round grey-tinted spectacles.

Joubert handed him the licence and ushered him away with an impatient gesture. Whitmore moved off the terrace and walked straight past Lucy. Half turning to see where he was going, she realised Rosemary Whitmore had been behind her. Lucy observed them as they moved away slightly to her left.

Rosemary snatched the piece of paper from him. 'Is the plot any good?' she asked, peering at it. 'Where is it, exactly?'

'Somewhere in the south. I'll have a better idea when I can study the map in more detail. I can hardly do so while the draw is taking place.'

Rosemary rolled her eyes. 'Joubert is a stupid man; what's he playing at? This draw may be rigged in favour of the French.'

'I don't see how.'

'You are far too naïve, Reg. I'm sure they could manage it. I only hope Moreau doesn't get a better plot. He's Joubert's favourite. Doesn't he always get preferential treatment? We should make a complaint to the Board if he does. Joubert must be senile. A draw indeed; whoever heard of such nonsense. He's clearly incompetent.'

'Och, Rosie, don't start!' Whitmore said before walking away, shoulders hunched. Rosemary caught Lucy's eye and treated her to a spiteful glare.

What a nasty woman, Lucy thought, and turned her attention back to the draw. A few minutes later, Moreau's name was called. Lucy held her breath and crossed her fingers.

'Lot number eight,' Joubert announced. 'That is the last concession, gentlemen. Thank you.'

The crowd began to disperse. Lucy strolled up to the terrace just as Moreau and Hopkins were posing for Isabella, Moreau holding up the licence in front of his chest. She waited for Isabella to finish.

'Well, M. Moreau, shall we be rich and famous?' Lucy asked.

Moreau laughed and looked down at the licence. 'My gut feeling is good, Madame Lawrence. Do not fear; we will find something wonderful. You will bring us luck.'

Hopkins moved across to scrutinise the map. Moreau held out his arm. 'Shall we take a peek, too?'

David Hopkins turned as they drew level. 'Not too bad, Moreau,' he said, tapping the map in the bottom left-hand corner. 'It wouldn't have been my first choice...'

Moreau peered at it. 'Hmm, it will do nicely, David. It's the right general area. See, it's not too far from where Lepsius was digging when he found traces of New Kingdom tombs.' A shadow crossed his features. 'Unfortunately, he was a little vague about where, exactly.'

'Your neighbour in lot seven is Mr Whitmore. Will that pose a problem?' Lucy asked.

Hopkins raised his eyes skywards, before strolling away. But Moreau tilted his head and frowned. 'Have you been listening to the gossips? You must ignore them. I have no issue with Mr Whitmore; he may dig where he wishes.'

But it is clear the Whitmores think differently about you, Lucy thought, though she refrained from voicing her concern. However, the viciousness of Rosemary Whitmore's earlier comments remained with her for the rest of the day.

SIX

Egyptian Museum, Boulaq, Cairo

Rafiq Mostafa answered Lucy's summons to the hotel early next morning. They set off on donkeys through the crowded streets towards the museum out at Boulaq, led by a young boy with a charming but roguish smile. Lucy found the journey amusing, but frustratingly slow, as many times the boy had to repel, with sharp rebukes, the encroaching donkey boys who insisted their steeds were far superior.

'What a confident fellow he is,' Lucy remarked to Rafiq.

Rafiq smiled broadly. 'Thank you. He is my eldest son.'

'Ah!'

When they reached the Nile and crossed over the bridge, Rafiq pointed out the museum close to the bank. The roof of the single-storey building was just visible above a high boundary wall. As they rounded the corner, Lucy saw a group of tourists gathered at the closed entrance gate. They looked aggrieved. Two beleaguered policemen, their faces stern, blocked their way.

'I'll ask what's going on,' Rafiq said, handing the reins of the donkey over to his son. Lucy watched him approach one of the officers. They spoke for a few moments before the policeman gesticulated and shrugged.

'His orders are to not let anyone in,' Rafiq explained when he returned. 'It would appear there was a robbery here last night. What do you wish to do, Mrs Lawrence?'

'Good gracious! How extraordinary and most unfortunate. However, M. Joubert is expecting me and we have come all this way. I shall try, Rafiq.' The dragoman bowed with an amused and doubtful glance back towards the entrance.

As Lucy advanced, one of the gentlemen tourists began to remonstrate with the officers. 'This is outrageous!' he exclaimed, his face reddening. 'I demand you let us past. Why do you deny us entry? We are British, you know. I expect you devils want payment; that's it, isn't it?'

A mulish expression spread over the policeman's face. 'No, monsieur, my orders are to keep visitors out. *No* exceptions. The museum is closed.'

The gentleman began to bluster. Lucy sidestepped and smiled at the other policeman. Pulling a letter from her bag, she lowered her voice so that he had to lean towards her. Lucy gave him a wide-eyed look, then glanced down at the letter.

'Please tell M. Joubert I have arrived. Mrs Lawrence is my name. He was anxious I come immediately to help him at this most difficult time.' The officer frowned but didn't ask to see the letter, which was just as well, as it was one she'd received that morning from her friend Judith. Lucy smiled as beguilingly as she dared.

His expression softened. 'Very well, madame, if you will come with me?'

Lucy followed him through the gates to howls of protest from the other tourists and Rafiq's hearty laugh.

Inside the museum was pandemonium. And in the middle of it all was the director. On spotting her, M. Joubert came forward. Taking her hands, his face pale and drawn, he exclaimed, 'My dear Madame Lawrence! It is so good to see you, but you must forgive me. We are in total disarray.'

'There was a robbery, I understand?'

'Yes, it is terrible, most terrible. Nothing like this has happened before. Please, come to my office.' He shook his head sadly, his voice shaking.

'Please do not concern yourself, monsieur. Would you prefer if I came back another day?' Lucy hoped he wouldn't agree: her curiosity was on fire.

'*Mais non*! You have come all this way,' he said, taking her arm. 'We must leave the police to do their job.'

Lucy regarded him with concern, for he was deadly pale, and his voice trembled. He was barely hiding his distress. When they reached his office, Joubert pulled out a chair for her, then skirted around the desk and sat down almost absentmindedly. Lucy feared he was going to weep, for his eyes were suspiciously bright. He laced his fingers upon the blotter, his face grim.

'For this to happen on my watch... I can't believe it.' he said. 'My only hope is the police find the missing artefacts before they leave the country.'

'I'm sure they'll do their best. What was taken, sir?'

Joubert placed his hand on a large leather-bound book on the desk. 'This is the museum catalogue. It was one of Mariette's innovations. He insisted on every single item being described in detail and photographed.' Pulling the book towards him, he opened it at a page marked by a loose sheet of paper. Joubert turned it around so that Lucy could read it. He tapped a particular paragraph. 'The cabinet contained the jewellery and funerary objects found in a tomb in Dashûr. It was an excavation of mine, as it happens, and Moreau was the one who found them. The objects belonged to a chief queen, much revered and loved by the pharaoh.'

Lucy scanned the paragraph quickly, then looked up at the Director. 'And?'

He sighed, pointing to some pictures on the opposite page. 'They took the necklace with the three golden cats, the bracelet of turquoise and a funerary dagger – a most exquisite gold piece. Ceremonial, of course – it wouldn't have been used in battle.'

'She was a warrior queen?'

'Yes. Her sword and battle dagger would have been of iron; gold is too soft for such use. If you look at the photograph, Madame Lawrence, you can see the handle is formed of four female heads, wonderfully worked and distinctive.'

'Priceless?'

'Oh yes! And, my dear madame, irreplaceable.'

Lucy frowned. 'And this was all that was taken?'

Joubert gasped, his eyes wide. 'All! Is it not enough?'

'No, you misunderstand me, M. Joubert. What I mean is why would someone go to the trouble of breaking in and only taking these particular items when the cabinets are bursting with precious objects?'

Joubert looked much struck by this. 'Now you say it... But perhaps the collector who put these vile men up to it wanted only these items.'

'The gangs steal to order?'

'It is not unknown. Only it is usually from the digs that arte-facts disappear. No one has dared to infiltrate this building before.'

'Is there no guard here at night?' she asked.

'Yes, there is a night porter. Poor Tarek! When M. Japp arrived this morning, he found Tarek, semi-conscious and in distress, writhing around on the floor.' Joubert swallowed and shook his head as if to dislodge the horrible image. 'The main door was unlocked.'

'Which suggests the porter must have known the thief, surely?'

'I do not know why Tarek would have opened the door or to whom, Madame Lawrence. He has been employed here for many years. He wouldn't have let this happen willingly.'

'Have the police questioned him?'

'Not yet, for he's still too ill. Inspector Vauquelin suspects he may have been poisoned for there was some half-eaten bread found beside him. It's been taken away to be analysed.'

Could the porter be faking illness, she wondered, for it sounded very much like insider mischief. But she doubted Joubert would want to hear that. 'Hopefully the police will be able to solve the robbery as soon as the man can speak to them.'

'Yes, I must trust in Inspector Vauquelin. However, how long will it take for Tarek to speak and tell us who is responsible? In the meantime, there is no clue as to who perpetrated this. If the items were to appear on the black market in Cairo, we would have some chance of recovering them, but I fear they are already on their way to foreign shores. And as a result, my reputation as guardian of Egypt's treasures lies in tatters. I have been informed some government ministers will be here presently, and the English will be only too happy to point out my shortcomings. They desperately want to usurp me and take control of the EAS.'

Lucy sat back and regarded him for several moments; it was hard not to feel sorry for him. 'Why not let me help you, M. Joubert? I have some experience in finding missing items.' Lucy briefly outlined her success in retrieving the maharajah's sapphires.

But Joubert didn't look impressed. He gave her a bleak smile. 'Surely, madame, you're joking?'

Lucy's exasperation rose. Why did men always underestimate her?

· · ·

As Lucy passed through the hall of the museum towards the main door, a familiar figure approached and partially blocked her exit.

'We meet again, Madame Lawrence.' Inspector Vauquelin looked none too pleased. 'You should not be here. The museum is closed today as it is the scene of a most serious crime.'

'As it happens, I'm an acquaintance of the director, and I'm here at his request,' she replied.

The man's eyes narrowed slightly. 'And what's your business here today?'

'As I said, visiting M. Joubert, by his invitation,' Lucy replied in her haughtiest tone.

The inspector's gaze hardened. 'Hmm. I can't have members of the public disturbing my crime scene.' Behind him, Lucy spotted a young officer sweeping up broken glass from the floor. The cabinet above his head must have been the target for its timber frame was cracked and shards of glass were sticking out at odd angles. Someone had taken a hammer to it, she reckoned. Not very subtle, but then there was no one about to hear, except the unlucky porter.

'I do not envy you your task, sir. A strange business. The director tells me your only witness is in no fit state to be questioned.'

He huffed. 'M. Joubert had no right to share that information with you, madame. But, yes, the poor man is lucky to be alive. However, he's too ill to be of any help, and the doctors at the hospital won't let me near him yet.'

'And time is slipping by. At least the objects stolen are distinctive if they should turn up in Cairo.' The inspector's brows shot up. 'The director showed me the items in his catalogue.'

Vauquelin grunted. 'I doubt they'll be seen again. The local thieves wouldn't have risked such a daring robbery. They tend to be more opportunistic. I would hazard this was a professional undertaking. Some collectors will go to any lengths to get what they desire.'

'But, Inspector, as I pointed out to the director, why go to all this trouble only to steal a handful of artefacts?' Lucy's gaze flicked across the sarcophagi and other objects adorning the room behind him. Even the smaller items must be worth hundreds of pounds.

Vauquelin gave her a sharp glance. 'How observant of you, madame. This was meticulously planned, there can be no doubt. Perhaps their goal was to get in and out as quickly as possible. Now, if you will excuse me, I have a robbery to solve.' The inspector bowed and walked away.

Lucy couldn't help herself and called out: 'And how are your enquiries progressing regarding the theft of Mrs Hamilton's pearls?'

The inspector stopped in his tracks before slowly turning back towards her. 'I appreciate your interest... madame, but that information is confidential,' he snapped.

Lucy tilted her head. 'That's hardly an answer, Inspector; after all, it is only luck my jewels were not taken as well.'

'It's the only answer you will get from me,' he said with a grunt. 'Good day, madame!'

Just as Lucy reached Rafiq and his son outside, she heard her name called by a shrill female voice.

'Mrs Lawrence? Is that you?' Lucy turned around to see Rosemary Whitmore advancing at a brisk pace, a tentative smile playing about her lips. The smile didn't quite reach her eyes. Reluctantly, Lucy handed the reins of the donkey back to Rafiq, muttering under her breath. She wanted to return to the hotel to think about the strange break-in, not engage in idle chit-chat with the less than charming Miss Whitmore. Even if Joubert wasn't keen, Lucy would love to have a crack at solving the robbery. Cairo was turning into a hotbed of crime, Lucy thought, with no small degree of satisfaction. Just in case she should become bored.

'Whatever is going on? Someone said there has been a robbery, and the museum is closed,' Rosemary said. 'This can't be.'

There was no escape; Lucy gave Miss Whitmore what she hoped was a reasonably polite smile and stepped forward. 'Yes, indeed; it is true and quite shocking. Poor M. Joubert is distraught. Several artefacts have been taken, and the unfortunate porter was attacked and is extremely ill.'

'Oh! *You* have been inside?'

'Yes. I had an appointment with M. Joubert.'

Rosemary just about controlled a scowl and turned to her brother who was following slowly. 'It is confirmed, Reginald, there has been a robbery. This is terrible! Isn't it, Reginald?' Mr Whitmore kept glancing over his shoulder to the main entrance of the museum. 'Reginald?' He turned back to them, his brow creased with a deep frown. 'Let me introduce my brother, Mrs Lawrence; I don't believe you've been introduced... properly.'

Lucy, resigned to her fate, endured a half-hearted handshake. Whitmore's eyes bored into her, but his voice was surprisingly gentle with its Highland twang much like his sister's. 'My pleasure, Mrs Lawrence. I understand this is your first visit to Egypt?'

'Yes, Mr Whitmore. I have fallen for its many charms already. I plan to spend the winter here.'

'There are few places as pleasant to do so. I'm lucky enough to spend each winter here working. I'm an Egyptologist, you know. Is it the climate that draws you, Mrs Lawrence, or an interest in antiquities?'

Lucy guessed what he was up to, but she was determined not to be steered into a conversation about digs. 'I must admit I find the climate wonderful. Compared to winter at home, so dreary, dull and damp, this is a pleasant surprise,' she said. A deft change of subject was required. 'Had you planned to visit the museum this morning? I do believe it will be closed all day, unfortunately.'

The frown reappeared on Whitmore's brow. 'I was particularly keen to visit as I understand M. Joubert has finished the display of artefacts from my dig last year. Have you any idea what was taken, Mrs Lawrence? I do hope it wasn't anything from my display.'

'I have no idea.' Lucy prevaricated, taken aback by his childish comment. He didn't appear concerned that precious artefacts had been taken or that a man was fighting for his life. How obnoxious he was!

Rosemary stepped up beside him and tucked her arm through his. 'How would Mrs Lawrence know what was stolen or indeed know the value of the treasures in the museum? This is her first visit to Egypt. Never mind, my dear. There is no shortage of other places for us to visit. We can come back here tomorrow.'

'But I wanted to see it today! And now I'm worried my display was the target; it can't be a coincidence that this should happen just as it was about to be unveiled,' Whitmore growled. 'Besides, I do not have time to go gallivanting; I must leave for Sakkâra in two days, and there is still much to do.'

Rosemary rubbed his upper arm. Lucy suddenly felt sorry for Rosemary if her main role in life was to smooth the feathers of this moody man-child. 'Don't fret, Reginald, if anything of yours was taken the director would have sent a message. Your finds were exceptional, and I'm sure the museum has done an excellent job with your display. M. Joubert will let us see it tomorrow. Now, why don't we go out to Giza instead? It always cheers you up.'

Reginald shrugged and a sullen expression settled on his features.

'Have you been to Giza yet, Mrs Lawrence?' Rosemary asked.

'No. But I hope to do so this week.'

'Why don't you join us this afternoon? My brother is very knowledgeable and would be delighted to show you around.' Rosemary's hand tightened where it lay on her brother's arm.

The signal wasn't lost on Lucy. She could discern the conflict in them. On the one hand, they saw her as a potential money-pot and, on the other, Mr Whitmore clearly considered playing tour guide as beneath his dignity.

'Yes, I'd be delighted,' he answered in a flat tone, chewing the inside of his mouth.

Oh joy, Lucy thought, could he be less gracious?

'Do say you'll come. It's frightfully interesting,' Rosemary said. 'No matter how many times I have seen it, I can't wait to explore the site again.'

Lucy struggled. As much as she wanted to visit the pyramids, she didn't want to do so in their company. Whitmore didn't look enthusiastic either. But Moreau was leaving for Sakkâra that afternoon and wouldn't be able to accompany her to Giza anyway. It would be far better to visit the site with an archaeologist than to traipse about on her own with only her Baedeker guidebook, with its dry descriptions.

'How can I resist such a tempting offer? Thank you,' Lucy said, catching a knowing smile from Rafiq before he lowered his gaze to the donkey's ears. The man appeared to be able to read her thoughts.

How disconcerting!

SEVEN

Giza Plateau, Cairo

The little expedition set out from the Excelsior after luncheon. With some reluctance Lucy dismissed Rafiq, for the Whitmores had use of a carriage for the trip and their own dragoman in attendance. For the first part of the journey, Reginald, encouraged by Rosemary, launched into a monologue on the history of Giza. As Lucy had spent the previous evening reading about it in one of Moreau's books, she already knew most of what he had to say. Politeness meant, however, that she had to listen. It was unfortunate Reginald possessed such a dry flat tone. Whereas Moreau made the subject come alive, Reginald smothered it with detail. It was all she could do not to nod off.

Eventually, his facts and figures were exhausted, and he sank back against the squabs, absorbed in his private thoughts behind his extraordinary glasses. Rosemary then took up the mantle with a stream of chatter. Lucy did her best not to show her frayed nerves to her travelling companions and stole glances out of the carriage window between nods and appropriate comments. The landscape fascinated Lucy, and she would have preferred silence in which to contemplate it. The road out of Cairo was lined with acacias and, the pyramids glowed golden in the afternoon sun, their magnetic pull undeniable.

Lucy was relieved when the carriage came to a stop, and the steps were let down. Before Reginald had time to act, she alighted, stepping out with relief.

Giza at last! A far cry from London's grey and damp streets. It was hard to believe she was actually here.

As more and more of the pyramid Bedouins milled about the carriage, Lucy moved away, unable to pull her eyes away from the monuments so tantalisingly close, just over the ridge of a large sand dune. As she watched, she spotted movement at the top of the Great Pyramid. Lucy was astonished. Those tiny specks had to be people. The realisation of the scale of the pyramid was almost overpowering. She gulped, her fear of heights sending a shiver of apprehension down her body. Hopefully, the Whitmores wouldn't expect her to climb up there.

All too soon the brother and sister joined her. 'Quite a sight, is it not, Mrs Lawrence?' Rosemary gushed. 'Nearly there.' Miss Whitmore took off up the slope of the sand dune like a gazelle.

Reginald took Lucy's arm, and she was soon glad of it. Her boots sank and slid on the silky surface as they followed his sister. At the top, they stepped out on to a plain scattered with rocks and pitted with holes. Bedouins, camels and tourists were milling about.

Rosemary turned to Lucy, her face alive with excitement. 'Behold the Sphinx and the pyramids!' Turning to Reginald, she continued: 'Do enlighten Mrs Lawrence, if she has any questions.'

'You're too kind,' Lucy murmured, her heart sinking at the thought of another lecture.

Rosemary's answering smile was sickly sweet. 'There is nothing quite as agreeable as having an expert with you on these visits, I can assure you, Mrs Lawrence. These foreign chaps are all very well, but isn't it far more pleasant to have one of your own as a guide? Reginald is too modest to say it himself, but he's considered one of the foremost authorities on this site... and other ancient sites too, including Sakkâra.' Rosemary's stare was defiant. Reginald grunted.

How foolish they were, Lucy thought. If they wanted funding, why not just be forthright about it? Silly games and impugning Moreau's credentials would only raise her hackles.

As Reginald launched into another discourse, Lucy pasted a smile on her face and began to move forward, forcing the pair to keep up with her. As they neared the base of the north face, they were swamped by pyramid Bedouins fighting for the chance to be their guides. Lucy took an instant liking to the men. They were full of smiles and laughter. Their billowing cloaks, some plain, some striped, caught the breeze, giving them a slightly rakish look. Reginald's dragoman stepped in and a few sharp comments sent the majority away.

'Would you care to climb to the top, Mrs Lawrence?' Reginald asked. 'The view is spectacular.'

Lucy craned her neck and looked up. 'It's very high.' She tried to keep the panic out of her voice.

'It's nothing. Why I have climbed it many times,' Rosemary said with a pitying glance.

'I'd much prefer to see inside,' Lucy said turning to Reginald. 'Would that be possible?'

'Of course,' he replied.

'It's rather horrid; slippery, cramped and smells quite foul,' Miss Whitmore cut in, wrinkling her nose. 'Once was enough for me.'

'There is no reason why we can't do both,' Reginald remarked with a touch of impatience and a meaningful look at his sister.

'I shall wait for you out here then. The dragoman will stay with me.' Rosemary glared at Reginald before walking away.

Rosemary then sat on a rock facing the pyramid, her posture stiff. With a snap of her wrist, she opened a parasol.

Seemingly oblivious to his sister's mood, Reginald instructed his dragoman who then negotiated with four young men. The deal was closed, and coins exchanged.

'We must climb up to the entrance. Your guides will help you,' Reginald said, pointing upwards. Lucy wondered if she would regret the impulse: clambering about in long skirts would be tiresome. Too proud to admit her doubts, she followed Reginald a little further along towards the eastern end. Her guides smiled kindly and with a combination of pushing, pulling and encouraging words in a mish-mash of English, French and German, she'd soon scaled several rows of blocks. Lucy waved down to Rosemary who was staring up at them, her hand shading her eyes. Miss Whitmore didn't respond.

Reginald stopped at the entrance, tucking his spectacles into his jacket pocket. 'It will be extremely hot inside. If at any stage you wish to abandon this, just say so...'

Lucy smarted. 'I enjoy a challenge, Mr Whitmore. Lead on!'

The first thing to hit her was the smell. Ammonia and lots of it. Lucy's eyes began to water. The passageway was rough and narrow, and she decided it was best not to examine the sliminess of the floor too closely.

About twenty yards down the passageway, they reached a junction and came to a stop. Something small and dark flitted close to her face. Startled, she stepped back against the wall, her heart pounding hard.

'Bats,' Reginald explained. 'Place is full of 'em.'

That also explained the odour, she thought, willing her breathing to calm.

He pointed upwards. 'Shall we proceed up to the King's Chamber? It is the most interesting part of the tomb.'

'Yes, please.'

The climb was steep, and soon Lucy was gasping for air, feeling a trickle of perspiration down her back and her gloves becoming sticky and damp. The humidity increased as they progressed. But a rising excitement took hold of her.

'This is the Grand Gallery,' Reginald said at last as they emerged from the narrow tunnel.

'And well named it is!' Lucy exclaimed. 'What a wondrous place!'

The guides stood to the sides, holding up their small oil lamps. The light was scant but enough. The ceiling soared above, rising upwards gradually towards an opening she could just make out in the faint light. As Whitmore described the space, Lucy realised she'd underestimated him completely. He was just as obsessed with this ancient land as Moreau. He might come across as rather dull, but his fervour for his subject could not be denied.

'Come, let us go up to the King's Chamber – the very heart of the pyramid,' Reginald said. When they reached the top of the ramp, he turned to her. 'You will have to duck down and crawl to get through, I'm afraid.'

True enough, Lucy had to creep through the confined space of the passageway on her hands and knees, until she came out into a large room. The guides held up the oil lamps for her to see. The chamber was tall and rectangular with a flat ceiling. Huge granite slabs, impossibly smooth, lined the room and in the far corner was a red granite sarcophagus, its surface glinting; beautiful in its simplicity. One corner was cracked and damaged.

'Where is the lid?' Lucy asked as she stared down inside.

'No one knows. It was missing when the French first entered the chamber in Napoleon's time. The grave robbers used fire and water repeatedly to fragment the stone. Once it cracked, they hacked it away in pieces. Their only interest was the mummy within.'

Lucy looked back towards the entrance. 'I don't understand. How did this sarcophagus come through that narrow opening?'

'Well spotted, Mrs Lawrence. One of the many mysteries of this place.'

'And no mummy?'

'No trace whatsoever. No funeral goods; just an empty chamber. Such a disappointment. It seems we are never destined to find a pharaoh's tomb that hasn't been disturbed in some way. Even in antiquity, these places were not sacred. Curses and spells were no hindrance when such wealth lay within reach. When times were bad, the locals took to grave robbing to feed their families.'

Lucy scanned the walls and the sides of the sarcophagus. 'There are no hieroglyphs; how do we know for certain it was Khufu's tomb?'

Reginald looked upwards. 'Above us are four chambers which help to take the load off this flat ceiling. Vyse and Perring blasted their way up in the late '30s with gun powder.'

'How barbaric!' Lucy exclaimed.

'Yes, thankfully Egyptology has moved on from such methods. However, in the highest chamber, known as Campbell's Chamber, named for Patrick Campbell who was a British agent and consul general in Egypt at the time, a cartouche bearing a pharaoh's name was found.'

'Khufu?'

'Yes.'

'I'd like to see that, please,' Lucy said.

An hour later, they emerged out of the stale humid air of the pyramid, blinking and coughing. A slight breeze touched Lucy's face, blissfully cool. She soon spotted Rosemary walking back across the plain towards them. With dismay, Lucy twitched at her skirts, now dusty and stained. A quick glance confirmed her boots were scuffed at the toes, but it had been worth every nerve-wracking minute.

Reginald turned to her. 'You can't leave without seeing the view from the top, Mrs Lawrence. The worst of the heat has passed; it will be quite pleasant up there.' He pulled out his glasses and popped them on before leaning towards her. 'The trick is not to look down.' He had guessed her fear.

Lucy's stomach plummeted at the idea of the climb. Without waiting for her reply, he called down to Rosemary. Within minutes she'd joined them, and they began their ascent. Resigned to the possibility of an embarrassing and nasty death, Lucy let herself be hoisted upwards. But the Bedouins' assistance, carried out with a lot of cajolery, had her laughing along with them. Their natural good humour lifted her spirits almost as much as the achievement of stepping out onto the platform at the top twenty minutes later. It was about thirty feet square and impossibly high. A couple standing at the far side hurriedly dropped each other's hands, the lady blushing. With a nod, they moved down a tier and started to descend. Lucy wondered if they were newlyweds. Such a shame they'd disturbed the couple's romantic moment.

The guides sat down at the edge, unfazed by the height. Hot and flustered, Lucy sought the shade provided by the remains of two incomplete tiers. Her legs were shaking and her dress clung damply to her back, but at least she'd made it. Lucy tried not to think about the journey down.

'Well done, Mrs Lawrence. We can rest here a while,' Reginald said before sitting down at the edge, facing south.

Rosemary leaned against the tier which formed Lucy's seat. 'Some people come up here for picnics. Can you believe it?' she remarked.

'That seems almost sacrilegious,' Lucy muttered.

'I've seen and heard much worse,' Rosemary replied. 'Some lose all sense of propriety here when they should be leading by example. How will the natives ever learn to be civilised if Europeans lose control? I blame the French. I'll never understand how they got a foothold in this country. As for them having jurisdiction over antiquities; why it is outrageous! How did the British government allow it?'

Reginald swung round, frowning at his sister. 'Leave it be, Rosie!'

'No, Reg. This is too important, and Mrs Lawrence needs to know how things stand. Joubert and his cronies have done nothing but slight you and your work.' Rosemary turned to Lucy, her face flushed. 'They always award the best concessions to the French and the Germans and give preference to displaying their finds at the museum.'

'That isn't quite true, Rosie. My finds from last year are on display at Boulaq,' Reginald chipped in.

'Huh! Only because I created such a stink at the reception at the khedive's palace last year to honour Moreau and his chums! Anyway, we don't know for sure, do we? We couldn't get in to check today. We will have to go out there again tomorrow.'

Reginald let out a slow breath. 'Do come and take in the view, Mrs Lawrence,' he said. 'It is perfectly safe.'

Lucy jumped down and stepped past Rosemary before making her way to the edge, her mouth suddenly dry.

Reginald greeted her with a smile. 'You mustn't mind Rosemary. She takes it all very seriously, don't you know,' he said sotto voce, as she sat down beside him.

'It's wonderful she's so supportive.' What else could she say? Slowly, she let her eyes take in the view, her heart thumping in panic.

Reginald glanced at her. 'The best vista in all of Egypt.' There was an echo of reverence in his voice.

Gripping the edge of the block on which she sat, Lucy tried to relax. From this vantage point, she saw each pyramid was surrounded by lesser tombs, some being small pyramids, others hewn from the bedrock. Taking a peek to the north, she could make out the verdant glow of the Delta as it melted away towards the Mediterranean. To the south, the Sphinx faced east, forever destined to greet the rising sun.

'How old is the Sphinx, Mr Whitmore?' she asked, doing her best to distract herself from the hollow feeling in her stomach.

Reginald followed her gaze. 'Ah, a very good question. Some believe it was built by Pharaoh Khafra about 2500 BC; he built that pyramid over there.' He inclined his head towards the second largest of the pyramids. 'But the causeway for Khafra's pyramid skirts the Sphinx.'

'Therefore, the Sphinx must pre-date it,' Lucy said.

Reginald shrugged. 'That is my theory. We may never know for definite, but it is certainly one of the oldest monuments in Egypt.' He pointed to the mountains rising up in the east. 'Those are the Mokattam hills from where the limestone for this tomb was quarried. Over there is Cairo, and the Nile forms the silver ribbon of light which disappears towards the south. If you follow the course of the Nile, you can see the cliffs of Tura where they quarry white marble. Opposite is Memphis, the old capital, Mrs Lawrence. And the pyramids in the distance?' Lucy nodded. 'They are located in Sakkâra where M. Moreau and I will spend the winter.'

'Thank you. It is much easier to visualise it all now. Maps do not do the landscape justice,' Lucy remarked.

'It is my pleasure. I would be happy to show you the sites down at Sakkâra. Do you plan to visit the dig?'

'Most certainly. I hope to make my first trip next week.'

'I would be honoured if you would visit my dig too,' he said.

'I would like to very much,' she replied.

Lucy squinted and could just discern the forms of the pyramids she'd read about only the night before. Bands of light and shade defined the unique shape of the Step Pyramid, and nearby she saw the famous Bent Pyramid of Dashûr. It only made her impatient to see them at close hand.

'Thank you for persuading me to come up; this is a special place,' Lucy said, her throat tight with emotion. He nodded slowly. They sat in companionable silence, watching the shadows of the pyramids creep across the plateau below.

But at last Rosemary broke the spell, her voice an intrusive whine. 'I'm famished. Shall we go down?'

Rosemary swept past, hopping lightly down to the next tier, ignoring the guide's proffered hand. Lucy stood still for a few minutes more and took in the vistas one last time, her only disappointment the fact she was not experiencing this amazing landscape with someone special by her side. With reluctance, Lucy nodded to the guide and began her descent.

EIGHT

Sakkâra, a Week Later

Lucy stepped down onto the train platform at Bedrashên to join the many groups of tourists disembarking from Cairo. Mary and Rafiq followed with the bags. They were immediately surrounded by donkey boys and beggars. Lucy left Rafiq to deal with the pandemonium and wandered further down the little platform, searching the crowd for Moreau's distinctive form. But to no avail. A little disappointed but not too concerned, for Rafiq knew the route to Sakkâra, Lucy rejoined her party just as their bags were being secured to the backs of several donkeys.

'M. Moreau is not here, Rafiq,' Lucy said. 'Shall we make our own way?'

'Yes, Mrs Lawrence, there is no difficulty.' He flashed her one of his brilliant smiles and hoisted his rifle further up on to his shoulder.

Mary stood by, looking at the donkeys with suspicion. Beads of perspiration stood out on her forehead.

'Mary, have you ever ridden a donkey?' Lucy asked her.

Mary's face reddened. 'Well, no, ma'am, not as such. Sure I grew up in Dublin; I'm no clodhopper!'

'There is no other means of transport, Mary,' Lucy told her, trying not to laugh at her outraged expression. 'Unless you wish to go by camel?'

Rafiq opened his mouth as if to protest, but she caught his eye and winked.

Mary shuddered and treated Lucy to a pained glance before approaching the nearest donkey. 'Camel, indeed!' Mary muttered under her breath as she drew alongside. Rafiq helped her mount the side saddle and gave her a reassuring smile and some soft-spoken instructions.

They set off, crossing the railway line and heading through a hamlet of mud houses which stood amongst lofty palms. Children ran along beside them, laughing and joking and asking for bakhshîsh. All the while, the local dogs skittered about and yelped, only to be shooed away by the donkey boys.

On the outskirts of the settlement, Lucy spotted David Hopkins's tall form, and told the donkey boy to stop. Three men were with Hopkins in the shade of some palm trees, and they appeared to be embroiled in a heated discussion. One of the men was almost nose to nose with the American and was gesticulating wildly. Hopkins happened to glance up and met Lucy's gaze. He turned to his companions and dismissed them with an angry gesture. They moved away but kept looking back at him as he took up the reins of his horse and made his way towards Lucy. Now, Lucy wondered, what was that all about?

'Good morning, Mrs Lawrence,' Hopkins said as he pulled up beside her. 'M. Moreau sent me to be your guide.'

'Good day. I thought M. Moreau was going to meet us,' Lucy replied.

'That was his plan, certainly, but at dusk yesterday we made a discovery.'

Lucy's heart rate shot up. 'Really? What did you find?'

'We aren't sure yet. One of the men saw a fox scrambling in the sand. The creature then disappeared. It was too dark to investigate last night. We marked the location and Moreau started digging at first light.'

'How exciting. I do hope it is the tomb he's hoping to find. I'm sorry you're missing out. Rafiq knows the way, we would have found you.'

Hopkins's eyes flickered over Rafiq and back to her. 'Moreau wouldn't like it. Besides, it's no trouble, ma'am,' he said with a tight smile.

How well he lies, she thought. 'How long will it take us to get to the dig?' she asked as he turned his horse to the west.

'About two hours. If you wish, we can stop off to look at the colossus of Ramesses II. Little remains of Memphis except his fallen statue.'

'I'd like to, if it doesn't delay us too much,' she replied and Hopkins nodded.

Lucy manoeuvred her donkey alongside Hopkins. The difference in height made conversation difficult, which suited Lucy. There was something about the man she found unsettling, and his set features and hooded eyes didn't encourage even polite chit-chat. They continued on through the palm groves before coming out onto a plain that stretched for miles.

'This was Memphis,' Hopkins said. 'Hard to believe it was once a magnificent city.' Apart from some low ruins and half-buried stones, not one building stood. Hopkins pointed to a grove a little way off. 'The statue is over there. Originally, there were two of them marking the entrance to the Temple of Ptah.'

It was the sorriest sight Lucy had ever beheld. The huge granite statue lay face down in a dark muddy pool. The head and torso were intact, but most of the limbs were gone or badly damaged.

'In a few months, when the water has receded, it will be

possible to see the underside. The features are exquisitely carved,' Hopkins remarked.

'Such a shame! Could it not be moved further from the river?'

'It belongs to the British Museum,' Hopkins said, 'but your government can't afford to ship it back. They are happy to leave it here, like this.' The sneer in his voice was unmistakable.

'But it is a good thing it remains in the country,' Lucy said. 'The days of stripping Egypt of its heritage are over. Certainly, that is what M. Joubert wants.'

Hopkins raised a mocking eyebrow and pursed his lips. 'The French are idealists; however, the reality is there is a market for antiquities, and poverty drives the market.'

'As an Egyptologist, you can't condone it – the black market – no matter what the reasons for it?'

'I do not. It is a plague and one we have tried hard to eradicate,' he retorted. 'Even with guards, we can't stop the pilfering.'

'It has happened on Moreau's digs, I understand.'

Hopkins's laugh was without mirth. 'It happens on *all* digs.' He pulled his watch out then snapped it shut. 'We should continue on our way.'

'Of course,' Lucy said, tugging the reins of her donkey and smothering her irritation.

Two hours later, Lucy was relieved to see the camp come into view: a tiny village of canvas in a semi-circle with a grove of palms giving some much-needed shelter. She was hot and tired from the long ride through the desert and, from the expression on Mary's face, her maid was in some distress. Rafiq helped Mary dismount and began to organise their belongings. A tall man emerged from a tent and called out to him. The men embraced. It was then Lucy remembered Rafiq's brother, Ali, was the site supervisor. In the far distance she saw the pyramids of Giza to the north and Dashûr to the south. But on the horizon dominating all was the Step Pyramid, quivering in the heat and dust, but there was no sign of Moreau. He must still be at the newly discovered site.

Mary was hustled into their tent by one of the men and Lucy followed. The canvas tent was no more than eight feet square with two piles of blankets for beds and a small petroleum stove. Their two bags were tucked into a corner. Lucy had to smile; it was pretty basic. It only added to her sense of adventure, but from her maid's white face and doleful expression she knew Mary didn't share her enthusiasm. She slumped down on one of the blanket piles, the picture of misery. Lucy asked the servant to fetch some water and made soothing noises while Mary gulped it down when he returned with a flask.

'Best you stay here, Mary,' Lucy said when she was satisfied the poor girl wasn't going to expire.

Mary raised a woebegone face. 'Oh, no, ma'am. That wouldn't be right.'

When the maid tried to stand up, Lucy pushed her down gently. 'No. I won't be long.'

Once back outside the tent, Lucy looked around the surrounding area, searching for Hopkins. On the far side of the encampment, she spotted him and walked towards him. If she didn't know better, he scowled before turning and beginning to walk away from her.

'Mr Hopkins, would you take me to the dig, please?' she demanded.

He stopped and turned to her with a surprised expression. 'If you wish. I should warn you; it is about fifteen minutes' walk... and it's the hottest part of the day. Perhaps you would prefer to stay here and rest—'

'No. Thank you for your consideration, but I'm fine. I'd like to know what's happening at the dig. As I'm sure do you,' Lucy replied.

'Very well. I just need to fetch my things.' He disappeared into one of the tents.

Lucy turned to Rafiq. 'Take care of Mary, please, Rafiq. She's finding all of this overwhelming. I'll be fine with Mr Hopkins.'

Rafiq bowed. 'Of course.'

Some minutes later, Hopkins reappeared, holding a leather-bound notebook. With a grunt, he set off at a brisk pace. Really, the man was so churlish, Lucy thought, as she traipsed after him, pulling her hat down to shade her eyes. She had to tread carefully. All around them were half-crumbled blocks, pieces of glazed pottery and what looked suspiciously like bleached bones and scraps of linen. Lucy soon realised, with dismay, they were walking through centuries of violated graves.

Soon a dark shape shimmered on the horizon. Was it real or a mirage? Moreau had spoken of such things in the desert. Without waiting for her to catch up, Hopkins increased his pace, his long legs covering the ground far more quickly than she with her heavy skirts. When she got back to Cairo, she would have to invest in some lighter attire and better boots. Lucy trudged after him, periodically lifting her head and squinting, trying to make out what it was they were heading for.

The mirage now took on more definition. It was a group of men with a hoist made up of timber beams and a metal pulley. A few feet away a small tent had been erected. The men were milling about, and Lucy heard snatches of excited conversation in Arabic, drifting across the sand. It was contagious; her heart began to pound. Could Moreau have been so lucky, so quickly?

The men made way as Hopkins approached, falling back into a huddle, except for two who were holding onto a thick rope which was attached to the hoist. A muffled shout came from below, and the men started to heave. Lucy kept back, straining to see where the rope went, but all she saw was a gaping hole, a yard wide, in the sand. All of a sudden, a head popped up. It was Moreau. His clothes were filthy, but he was beaming. As he was being hauled out, he spotted Hopkins and stretched out his hand. In his palm lay a small blue statue.

'Shabti!' exclaimed Hopkins, reverently taking the figurine and turning it over repeatedly, an expression of delight spreading over his face.

'Yes!' Moreau said, 'And there are plenty more of them down in the tomb.' Turning, he caught sight of Lucy. 'Ah! Madame Lawrence, you've chosen a momentous day to join us.'

Lucy nodded and returned his smile. 'Yes, my timing couldn't have been more perfect. What is this *shabti?*' she asked, taking in the plain little figure, and wondering why it was causing so much excitement. It looked crude and rather dull. Hopkins was using the sleeve of his jacket to rub away the dirt on it as you would a child's mucky face.

'Moreau, there is no name,' Hopkins said, his voice full of disappointment, before Moreau could answer her.

'Yes, I know, but it does carry spell 472 from the Coffin Texts. I could not examine all of them. I'll leave that to you, my boy. We will find out whose tomb it is in due course.'

Moreau brushed down his jacket, the ancient sand and dust billowing out in the breeze. 'Shall we return to the camp and get you settled in? Also, I'm famished; it is hot work down there.' Moreau took her arm. A part of Lucy wanted to stay and go down into whatever lay below. With reluctance, she nodded.

'Now, madame, you were asking about the figurine. It is from the funerary goods of a high-ranking person, perhaps even a pharaoh. During the First Dynasty, the pharaoh's servants would have been sacrificed and buried with him, so they'd be on hand to help him in the afterlife.'

'How barbaric!'

'Yes, to our modern way of thinking, but you must remember the afterlife was most important to them. If the pharaoh failed to reach it, it meant disaster for the entire population. They believed the sun wouldn't rise and chaos would ensue. However, sense prevailed and, in later tombs, we find these shabti which were replacements for the sacrificial servants.'

'Therefore, if you find one—'

'Oh, there are many!' Moreau said, squeezing her arm, his eyes alight.

'You've found an important tomb as you hoped?'

'It is possible, yes,' he said. 'The shaft leads down to a passageway. The statue was found in a nook in the wall. Further along we gained access to an antechamber with many more.'

'And?'

Moreau's face fell. 'That was all, and the passageway is blocked just beyond. It will take many weeks to clear. But I'm hopeful, Madame Lawrence. It may not be a New Kingdom tomb, the crudeness of the shabti casts some doubt, but it is a tomb all the same. The shabti are identical as far as I can tell, but unfortunately the tomb must be of someone who died unexpectedly. Usually, the name of the deceased is on the figurine. As David pointed out, it is missing.'

'But it would have been important for the shabti to be in the tomb?'

'Absolutely crucial. How else was someone of high rank to survive in the afterlife with no servants to do the menial chores? It would be unthinkable.'

Lucy couldn't help smiling. 'How lucky to have found the tomb so soon.'

'Yes. However, tomorrow I'll return to Cairo, as I must speak to Joubert urgently.'

'Why so? Is there a problem? Do you need more funds?'

Moreau grimaced. 'No, dear lady, not money. A technicality, I'm afraid. The rest of the tomb runs under the area which is part of another concession.'

'Oh dear! Do you know whose concession it is?'

'I do! Young Whitmore,' Moreau said with a grimace. 'And he won't be pleased.'

Lucy silently agreed, her memory of the overheard conversation at the draw foremost in her mind. 'I'm sure some kind of arrangement would be possible. M. Joubert strikes me as a reasonable man.'

Moreau shrugged and patted her hand where it lay on his arm. 'He is, but Whitmore is a disagreeable young man. Joubert has become weary of the squabbling of late, and I can't blame him. I find it tiresome myself. Do not let this overshadow this experience for you, madame.' Moreau smiled warmly. 'Now, I hope you will not find camp life too difficult. Not every lady can cope with the conditions.'

'But I'm not every lady, monsieur, let me assure you,' Lucy replied.

Moreau chuckled. 'Of that, I'm aware!'

NINE

As they approached the camp, Lucy caught sight of Rafiq sitting under the shade of a palm, talking to a group of men. As soon as he spotted her, he hurried over.

'Mrs Lawrence, your maid is ill. I believe the desert does not agree with her. I have given her more water and told her to rest.'

'Thank you, Rafiq, you are very good. Most likely the journey was too much. I'd best go to her.' Lucy turned to Moreau. 'Forgive me, monsieur.'

'Not at all,' he replied with a bow. 'I understand. You will join us for dinner later?' He pointed to the largest tent, set in the middle of the campsite. 'If your maid remains unwell, the men will serve her or both of you at your own tent, if you prefer?'

'Hopefully that won't be necessary. I'm sure Mary is only suffering from the heat. She will be fine once she rests.'

Lucy found Mary exactly as she had left her; sitting on the blanket heap with her head in her hands.

'What ails you, Mary?' Lucy asked gently. 'Are you still sore from the donkey ride?'

'A little, ma'am. All that jostling and the heat. Sure you'd burn alive out there. And as for this tent; I've never seen the like. Just look at it. How am I to take care of you and your things in a cramped, dirty place like this? And, I'm sure there are all kinds of dangerous creatures lurking about. One of them Arab fellows spoke of snakes and scorpions.'

'Yes, isn't it fun?' Lucy pulled off her hat and blew the sand off the rim. If she stayed chipper, perhaps Mary would come around. 'Everything is so new and different. It's an exciting place, and to think we have arrived on the day they may have discovered a tomb.'

Mary's eyes popped. 'Fun?'

'Why, yes, Mary. This is a grand adventure. Something you can tell your grandchildren about someday; you know, like our little... excursion to Yorkshire in the spring.'

Mary looked at her with a horrified expression. 'I'm not likely to forget that! I thought we were goners!'

'We survived, Mary, and won the day. Just think how impressed Ned will be when you tell him all about this when we're back in London.'

'London? We'll be lucky to get out of here alive!'

'Mary, don't exaggerate so. We are perfectly safe. Rafiq will make sure of it. Now, let's rest before dinner,' Lucy said, stretching out on the opposite makeshift bed. 'This is much more comfortable than it looks.' Lucy closed her eyes with a contented sigh.

A snort of disbelief was the only response.

Lucy awoke from her nap, shivering. The sun had set. In the dim light, she made out Mary's sleeping form, nestled in a blanket, her breathing slow and regular. The temperature drop was extreme here. It hadn't seemed as dramatic in Cairo, but perhaps that was because there was only a piece of canvas between Lucy and the cold desert air. Sitting up, she listened to the sounds of the camp for a few moments. The men were talking and laughing amid the banging of pots and pans. Curious, she pulled back the flap of the tent. Across the open space, she saw a few of the men huddled around a large pot suspended over a fire, and was delighted to detect the smells of cooking food wafting her way. Lucy's stomach rumbled in response.

She quickly found a heavy woollen shawl in her bag and wrapped it round her trembling shoulders.

'Wake up, Mary.' Lucy gave the maid's shoulder a gentle shake. 'Dinner will be ready soon. We haven't eaten since breakfast. You must be famished; I know I am.'

Mary sat up, bleary-eyed. 'I'm hungry, ma'am. What sort of food will there be? I'm not eating snake!'

'It might not taste that bad,' Lucy replied. 'Oh, Mary! I'm only teasing. Moreau is a civilised man with refined tastes. Dinner will be quite ordinary. Do come along and see.'

'I can't eat with you, ma'am,' Mary said, her eyes wide. 'It wouldn't be proper.'

'Of course you must, unless you wish to eat with the local men, cross-legged in the dirt. This is a camp, Mary. There is no standing on ceremony. If you wish to eat, you must come along with me.'

'I never heard the like,' Mary muttered, slowly rising to her feet. 'I don't know what me ma would say!'

Moreau and Hopkins were at the far end of the large central tent, with Moreau standing over his deputy who was delicately brushing one of the shabti statues with a small brush. Several more of the figurines lay on the table, along with more brushes and a magnifying glass.

'Good evening,' Lucy said.

Moreau turned around and smiled. 'Good evening, Madame Lawrence, Mademoiselle O'Reilly.'

What a gentleman, Lucy thought. An Englishman would

never acknowledge a servant like that. Lucy nodded at the figurine Hopkins was holding. 'Have you found a name for the tomb owner?'

'Unfortunately not, ma'am,' Hopkins said, glancing up from his task.

Moreau picked up another shabti and showed it to her and Mary. 'We do know these were made by the same craftsman. See the little notch here on the back? There is an identical one on each one examined so far.' He placed the shabti back on the table and put his hand on Hopkins's shoulder. 'Enough work for today, David. It is time to eat, now the ladies are here.' Hopkins grunted.

Moreau took Lucy's hand. 'Why you are frozen! We should have warned you the temperatures drop dramatically in the evenings. I'll order the men to light the stove.' He pulled out a chair for Lucy at a smaller table near the entrance. 'Here is where we work and eat. All a bit rough-and-ready; I hope you don't mind.'

Lucy shook her head. 'I wasn't expecting fine dining!'

When Mary and Hopkins were seated, Moreau took the seat beside Lucy. 'You would be amazed to see what some tourists bring out here. All home comforts. We can't lumber ourselves with such unnecessary things. I have even slept in a tomb.'

'What was that like? Were you afraid?' Mary asked, wide-eyed.

Moreau winked at her. 'What of? If a dead pharaoh visited me, I was too tired to wake. The heat down in the tombs can be exhausting. When you work all day in such conditions, trust me, you sleep like a baby. Now tell me, ladies, today was your first day in the desert; how do you like it?'

Mary gave a shrug, looking askance at the dish being laid before her.

It smelt delicious to Lucy who was ravenous. 'I enjoyed it

very much, and it is so exciting to be here the day you found the tomb.'

'Let's hope it turns out to be a significant find. All will be well once I sort out the problem with Whitmore.'

'Could he have your dig stopped?' Lucy asked.

'He can try,' Hopkins said with a scowl.

'Yes, he could make life difficult, if he chooses,' Moreau said before giving her a measuring glance. 'In that light, I wonder if I might impose on you, Madame Lawrence?'

'Certainly. What can I do for you?'

'Would you mind coming back to Cairo with me tomorrow evening? As my patron you would lend considerable weight, and elegance of course, to my case for full access to this site.'

'Use my womanly wiles on M. Joubert, you mean?'

Moreau laughed. 'Something of that nature.'

'Of course, I would be happy to help,' Lucy said. She noticed Mary stiffen. The poor girl would be thinking about the donkey ride back to Bedrashên, but there wasn't anything Lucy could do about that. Smiling sympathetically at Mary she continued, 'I should warn you, I did indicate to Mr Whitmore I might be willing to help him financially. He was exceedingly kind in showing me around Giza. His knowledge of the site is extensive.'

Moreau pursed his lips. 'It should be; he worked there long enough. Well, I can't blame the young buck for trying to charm you. No, it wouldn't be a problem if you were to assist him. In fact, it might smooth things over considerably. Very magnanimous of you. But soon every Egyptologist will be at your door, and you will forget about me. It is rumoured Petrie is at Dashûr this season; no doubt we will see him at first light, cap in hand.'

Lucy laughed. 'M. Moreau, I can assure you, my loyalties will not be swayed even if the great Mr Petrie does honour us with his presence.'

Moreau raised a brow and poured the wine. Then he raised his glass. 'To Egypt!'

'And her mysteries,' added Lucy. They all clinked glasses.

'Speaking of M. Joubert, I wonder if the stolen artefacts from the museum have been found yet,' Lucy said, eagerly accepting a second helping of stew.

'A strange and bad business. If the museum is not safe, then where is? Those items are irreplaceable,' Moreau said, glowering down at his plate. 'I was rather proud of those finds – the stuff of every Egyptologist's dreams. My career blossomed afterwards and, the following year, Joubert persuaded Mariette to let me lead my first excavation.'

'Yes, Joubert told me about that particular dig, and I saw the photographs of the artefacts. They were incredibly beautiful. Unfortunately, the policeman I spoke to didn't seem hopeful,' she said. 'I offered to help investigate, but M. Joubert wasn't enthusiastic, to say the least.'

Hopkins threw her a quizzical glance, while Moreau began to chuckle. 'No, I'm sure he wasn't. He's old-fashioned in his ways. Since his wife died, he has become even more strait-laced.'

'I understand she died in an accident.'

Moreau set down his glass and gave her a bleak smile. 'Yes. A very beautiful woman and much younger than he. Her death was a great tragedy. Rebecca always accompanied him on his excavations, but she slipped and fell down a shaft, hitting her head. There was nothing to be done.'

'The poor man!' Lucy exclaimed.

'Yes, he was devastated, of course. He was the one who found her the next morning, lying lifeless in the dark.' Lucy shivered. Moreau continued. 'He has always blamed himself for allowing her to stay at the dig site. As I said, he has some antiquated ideas about women's roles here in Egypt, and they have become even more so since Rebecca's death.'

'What's *your* opinion on the subject?' Lucy asked.

Moreau laughed. 'I can hardly object with you sitting beside me, can I? You're my patron. But seriously, I do not see why women should not get involved if they are truly interested and have something to offer. In my experience, gender does not guarantee intelligence or application. No, I'm all in favour of the fairer sex gracing us with their presence. Isn't that so, David? Wouldn't you agree?'

Hopkins replied with a half-hearted smile and kept eating.

'Joubert is a different generation, that is all,' Moreau said.

'Miss DeLuca is working for him while she waits for Whitmore to call on her, so he can't be that prejudiced,' Lucy remarked. Hopkins glanced up from his plate, an eager expression flitting across his features.

'There you are. Mind you, Miss DeLuca is special. Brains, beauty and skill, combined with lethal Italian charm. Not even Joubert can resist. Don't judge Joubert too harshly for not engaging your sleuthing skills, Madame Lawrence, for he is a great director. I would imagine your suggestion probably horrified him.'

'It did, indeed, despite my telling him of my previous success.'

'The sapphires? I'd almost forgotten about them.' Moreau grinned across at Mary, his eyes twinkling with mischief. 'Your redoubtable mistress, Mademoiselle O'Reilly; you must count yourself most fortunate to work for her.'

Lucy had to bite her lip as Mary struggled to answer. Moreau was a terrible tease.

TEN

As the convivial meal came to a conclusion, Lucy sensed Mary's unease in the company. When Mary cast her an anxious glance, Lucy suggested the maid might wish to retire as she didn't require her services for the rest of the evening. With a grateful smile, Mary excused herself and disappeared into the night. Hopkins stayed only a few minutes longer, then departed, pleading an early start the next morning. Lucy wondered, with Moreau's earlier gallantry fresh in her mind, if Moreau had asked Hopkins to leave them alone. All the way back from the dig site Moreau had walked at a slow pace to allow for the terrain, keeping her arm tucked tightly through his. His glance had been warm, and Lucy had found herself responding to his bonhomie. She felt so comfortable in his company and liked the fact she knew exactly where she stood with him. Unlike some gentlemen who disappeared off the face of the planet without explanation...

Of course, there was the possibility that Moreau was merely flattering her to ensure she kept her promises regarding funding. Lucy gave herself a mental shake. That was the kind of theory Phineas would voice in that annoyingly practical way of his.

Well, he can keep his nasty thoughts to himself, Lucy thought, and turned her most winning smile upon Moreau as he rose up from the table.

'Grab your shawl, Madame Lawrence, and let's sit outside under the stars,' Moreau said. One of the servants brought out some chairs, then melted away into the darkness. All was quiet in the camp. On the far side, Lucy saw Mary's shadow reflected on the canvas of the tent as she readied for bed. She would make things up to Mary when they got back to Cairo. Such a pity Mary wasn't suited to this rough-and-ready life. Lucy, on the other hand, loved it. To be free of the restraints of society, to explore and visit such places, was the kind of independence she had longed for all her life. And she might have missed out if she hadn't met Moreau. Life was definitely taking a new and exciting turn. Didn't she deserve an adventure? Not the dangerous variety like earlier in the year, obviously. Though, dabbling in romance might be just as perilous.

Moreau handed her a glass of brandy. 'This will warm you up. A rather special bottle my father gave me. I have been saving it for a special occasion.'

'Do you really believe this tomb is special?' she asked. 'The one you've been looking for all these years?'

'It is promising, though the shabti are a puzzle. But over the years I have learnt to be cautious. More than likely the tomb has already been discovered and robbed. The blocked passageway may well be the result of mischief.'

'Does the blockage look recent?'

Moreau started to laugh. 'Recent is a confusing concept out here! In terms of Egypt, a few thousand years is relatively recent.'

'Well, modern then?' Lucy asked.

'Hard to tell, but I do believe in luck, and I consider meeting you extremely fortunate.' He took the seat beside her, his gaze dark and intense.

A little thrill went through Lucy, but being slightly embarrassed, she could think of no response. Moreau was unlike any man she'd encountered before. He was so... direct. Did he mean what he said or was it mere flirtation? Uncomfortable but intrigued, she sipped her brandy enjoying the sensation of warmth it created, fixing her eyes on the edge of the campsite. 'You know, M. Moreau, it is not always easy to know if fate is being kind or not.' She was thinking of Charlie and Phineas: two instances where fate had dealt her vastly different hands. How different her life would be if she hadn't met either of them.

'Perhaps,' he answered, 'but I prefer to be optimistic. Life is so very short, is it not?'

'Unless you're a pharaoh and have gained eternal life,' Lucy quipped.

Moreau chuckled, and Lucy relaxed once more. 'By the way, have you received any more threatening messages?' she asked.

'No, and if I did, I would consign them to the fire. It was childish nonsense.'

'I'm glad to hear it. But you will be careful?'

His eyes shone. 'Your wish is my command!'

Lucy spluttered and shook her head reprovingly. Leaning back in her chair, she contemplated the night sky. There was no moon, but the heavens twinkled with stars; tiny points of light in the velvety blue-blackness.

'It is rather special. I find it mesmerising,' Moreau said after a few moments. 'The same sky the ancient Egyptians stared at thousands of years ago and dreamed of the afterlife.'

'The sky is wonderfully clear, and there are so many stars. I haven't seen anything like it before, not even at home in Yorkshire.'

Moreau turned towards her. 'Everything about Egypt is unique. There is magic here and, trust me, it will cast its spell on you; before you know it, you will want to come back every year.'

Lucy smiled. 'Of course, you have an ulterior motive for wishing me to return, but you may be right for I'm more content here than anywhere else on my travels, so far. Widowhood hasn't been easy, particularly when my husband left such a trail of misery.' Lucy turned away. 'I need to find my place in the world again. Most of all, I want a purpose. I drifted for far too long as a married woman, depending on Charlie to give my life meaning. It didn't feel that way in the beginning, but as the years passed, I accepted life would always be quiet and uneventful.' She chuckled. 'At least that is no longer the case!'

Moreau leaned towards her, his voice low. 'You will find a role, madame. When beauty and brains are combined, it is easy.'

Lucy tilted her head. 'Particularly as I'm now wealthy?'

'Ah, a curse indeed! But seriously, you will come back to this country, and not just because you're helping with my funding. I can sense you're genuinely interested in this place and the work we are doing here.'

'I am.' After a pause, Lucy looked at Moreau's profile as he gazed upwards. It was refreshing; he didn't talk down to her but treated her as an equal. 'M. Moreau, I want to learn more. I'd actually like to be involved in some practical way, not just reading the books you gave me, fascinating as they are.'

Moreau gave her a measured look. 'Nothing could be easier. You shall accompany us tomorrow, if you wish.'

Lucy twisted around in the chair to face him as a surge of adrenalin coursed through her. 'I can go down into the tomb?' She was already mentally going through the few items of clothing she'd brought with her. Was any of it suitable to wear?

'Yes. At first light when it is coolest. It will be dirty and hot down there, I must warn you. The conditions are challenging.'

'I don't mind! How can I help? I still know so little.'

'David's camera is broken so until the part arrives from

Cairo, it can't be used. Do you draw? The antechamber's walls are covered in hieroglyphs and images, and I would like to start recording them. If you were willing to do it, it would free up David for other tasks.'

'I would love to try, but I must admit my drawing skills are at best poor,' Lucy answered, thinking of all the times she'd disappeared out into the park at Somerville at the first hint of an afternoon spent sketching or painting. It had been a matter of pride to avoid reaching the level of accomplishment her mother had considered suitable. The idea of being *prepared* for the marriage market had made her rebel. All her parents' attention was focused on her brother Richard, for all the good that had done! But now she realised with dismay, her lack of skill might preclude her from helping Moreau.

'That is a shame,' he said, rubbing his chin. Lucy's heart dropped. 'You don't happen to carry a camera in your luggage?' he asked at last.

'Alas, no,' she said. 'Miss DeLuca has one... but she's engaged to work for Whitmore, and to be honest I've never used one.' It was embarrassing; she needed to rectify all these short-comings.

'Hmm. Well, poor sketching it will have to be.' He reached across for her hand, drawing it close and kissing it. The gesture caught Lucy off-guard. Suddenly, it was as if the rest of the world had melted away. His gaze deepened with unmistakable warmth and a question: one she'd been half hoping for, half dreading all day. But was she ready for that level of intimacy? At best, Lucy realised it would be a brief affair, but she couldn't deny it was a tempting notion. Out here in the desert, who would care what she did?

Moreau leaned closer. Lucy felt his breath caress her cheek as she closed her eyes. His kiss was gentle and undemanding at first. Lucy returned it with ease, relaxing into his embrace. But minutes later, the sound of laughter from the far end of the camp broke the spell. With difficulty, she broke away from Moreau, not particularly easy to do when someone is regarding you as if you were a goddess. 'You are a rogue, monsieur!' Lucy said, half laughing.

Moreau's eyes shone with humour. 'Take pity; I'm only human.'

'It is late. I must retire now if I'm to be of any use to you tomorrow,' Lucy said as lightly as possible. 'I bid you good night.'

Moreau released her hand, a flash of disappointment in his eyes. 'Ah, oui! Tomorrow is another day,' he said softly.

From the prickle at the back of her neck, she sensed his gaze follow her across the camp until she slipped inside her tent. When Lucy peeped out before retiring for the night, he was still sitting there in the darkness, his face upturned to the stars.

A hurried breakfast was consumed just before sunrise, and soon the company trekked out towards the dig site. Hopkins supplied Lucy with a canvas bag in which he had put a sketching pad and pencils. She smiled when she spotted two brush erasers at the bottom; Moreau must have told Hopkins her skill was wanting.

The journey was far more pleasant in the early morning as the air was still fresh with a light breeze. Lucy reckoned there were at least twelve fellâheen in the group and all were in good spirits, their light-heartedness making her soon forget her night of tossing and turning, not to mention Mary's despondent expression as she'd left her. Rafiq had agreed to stay at the camp, more to give Mary reassurance than to stave off any possible danger.

But to Lucy's surprise as they approached the dig, Moreau became silent, with his head down. What a strange man he was, she thought, and how complex. Were the problems of the site worse than he had admitted to her? Was he still worried about the threat to his life? Perhaps he was afraid Lucy would withdraw her funding if Whitmore kicked up a fuss or it turned out to be an empty tomb. It was disappointing he might think so little of her loyalty to the project. Lucy had hoped her presence and willingness to get involved would be enough to convince him. Or had her hesitation to take things further the previous evening offended him in some way? She, however, did not regret it. This morning, she was thinking more clearly. Any liaison with Moreau would only result in complications.

'Damnation!' she heard Hopkins exclaim as he stopped dead in front of her. Surprised, she almost ran into him. Cautiously, Lucy peeked around the American. A group of unfamiliar men stood at the tent Moreau's men had rigged up at the entrance to the tomb. They didn't look welcoming. 'Stay here!' Hopkins snapped at her, before joining Moreau and advancing to meet the men.

Ali, Rafiq's brother came and stood beside her. Worryingly, he had swung his rifle off his shoulder. 'Lady stay here,' he said quietly. Lucy nodded, and turned her attention to the situation up ahead. The men's reactions concerned her, the tension in those around her almost palpable.

But to Lucy's frustration, Moreau and Hopkins were too far away to hear what was being said. She could, however, make out Whitmore now in the welcoming committee. Matters were developing far more rapidly than any of them had feared. Somehow Whitmore must have found out about their discovery. Who could have told him? One of Moreau's men?

Lucy watched as Moreau and Whitmore moved apart from the others. A heated discussion took place for several minutes. Beside her, Ali tensed up. He stood stock-still, putting her in mind of her old cat, Horace, ready to pounce. Suddenly, Moreau stood back with his hands up. Whitmore lunged at him, knocking him off balance. Moreau stumbled but righted himself with ease. He was a much bigger man than Whitmore; it was as if Moreau was letting Whitmore take out his frustration. Hopkins took a step towards them, but Moreau waved him away.

But Lucy was frustrated too. This impasse might mean she wouldn't get down into the tomb. 'I'll sort this,' she said to Ali and, before he could protest, she set off.

'Mr Whitmore, that is enough!' Lucy said, stopping a few feet away.

Whitmore swung around and gaped. 'Mrs Lawrence!' he said, breathing hard. 'What on earth are you doing here?'

'Visiting *my* dig. If there is a problem, Mr Whitmore, I suggest we discuss it like civilised people. There is no need for violence.'

Whitmore went redder than he already was and started to splutter.

Moreau's lips twitched. 'An excellent idea, Madame Lawrence. Shall we?' He gestured towards the inside of the tent.

Lucy led the way inside. Whitmore took off his hat and wiped his brow with a handkerchief. 'I apologise, Mrs Lawrence,' he mumbled as Moreau pulled down the flap.

'That is all well and good, but it is not the way to behave, now is it?' Lucy demanded. 'I understand your frustration, as I'm sure does M. Moreau. However, the fact is the entrance to this tomb is within our concession area.'

'Only the entrance,' Whitmore protested. 'Most of it is within *my* concession.'

'Tell me truthfully, did you intend digging in this area?' she asked.

'Well, no, there was no reason to suspect there was anything here,' Whitmore said sulkily.

'We, however, did,' Moreau said, his face impassive.

Lucy sighed. He wasn't helping much. 'Can't we come to some agreement, Mr Whitmore?' she asked.

Whitmore straightened up. 'Only M. Joubert has the authority to settle this.'

'I'm more than happy to let him decide,' Moreau said.

'Of course you are. You Frenchies will stick together!' Whitmore shouted, throwing his hands up in the air. 'Good day to you.' He pushed the tent flap out of his way and stalked out.

'Oh dear, we have upset your countryman, Madame Lawrence,' Moreau said with a mocking grin.

'It isn't funny, Moreau; I would like to avoid any trouble.'

'There is history between us. Unfortunate history.'

'Would you care to elaborate?' Lucy snapped, her temper now frayed.

'No. It is in the past,' Moreau said. 'And irrelevant.' He looked out of the tent, then turned back to her. 'Now, since our Scottish friend and his little party are gone, let's get on with the day's work.' He quit the tent as if nothing had happened.

Lucy stood for a moment wondering what on earth was going on. An uneasy feeling came over her, taking the shine off what should have been one of the most exciting days of her life. Why was Moreau so reluctant to explain the animosity between himself and Whitmore? Granted, she had no right to pry if the matter was personal, but she couldn't fathom what it could be. If it was a professional issue, then surely as his patron she had a right to know? Moreau was hiding something from her, and she didn't like it.

The worst part was stepping away from terra firma and floating above the hole in the ground. Despite Moreau's reassuring smile and the harness around her waist, panic rose in Lucy's throat, her fear of heights making her perspire. As she was lowered slowly down into the darkness, she smelled decay –

and something else which made the hairs on the back of her neck prickle. It didn't help that it was oven-like below ground. The shaft was about thirty feet deep and just wide enough for one person. Notches in the walls, at regular intervals, must have been used by the tomb builders to get up and down. As Lucy reached the bottom, she was relieved to see Ali waiting. With a smile Ali undid the harness, gave it a tug, and it disappeared upwards.

Once Lucy's breathing had slowed, and she had stopped shaking, she took a look around. The walls of the passageway were smooth and unadorned, and continued off into the blackness beyond. Soon Hopkins and Moreau joined her.

'This way,' Moreau said, taking the lamp and turning down the passageway. Hopkins gestured for Lucy to go ahead with a smile that bordered on insolent. Lucy bristled, but she was determined to not let the annoying man get under her skin.

The room Moreau brought her to was extraordinary. As he held up the lamp, fabulous figures loomed out of the darkness. The bizarre thing was they looked as though they'd been painted yesterday. Awestruck, Lucy reached out and touched one of the walls, outlining the figure before her with her finger. It was a strange mummy-like creature with a white crown, fringed with feathers and a crook and a flail in his hand.

'That gentleman is Osiris,' Moreau said.

Lucy glanced at the other figures, then frowned. 'Why is his skin green? He looks ill.'

Moreau chuckled. 'It symbolises rebirth. He was the god of death and the afterlife. Sometimes referred to as the Lord of Silence.'

What an extraordinary moniker, eerie in the extreme. Lucy turned away from the figure, uncomfortable. 'Where would you like me to start?'

'David will explain it all to you,' Moreau said, quitting the antechamber, his mind obviously elsewhere already.

. . .

Two hours later, Lucy's fingers ached. No matter how she tried, the sensation of a presence in the small room lingered: someone watching as she worked. It was silly, and the men were only a few feet away down the passageway working on the blockage. Chiding herself, Lucy clutched the pencil tightly and tried to concentrate on the figure and symbols she was drawing. The oil lamp flickered, and the figures before her danced. Lucy squeezed her eyes shut for several moments, only too aware of the pounding of her heart. If she called out, the men would consider her a simpleton and ban her from the tomb. There was no way she could let that happen. Slowly, she opened her eyes. All appeared to be normal again. Perhaps it was the heat or tiredness.

Stretching her shoulders, Lucy scrutinised the drawing she'd made. Thankfully, Hopkins had drawn a grid on the page which made transferring the images a lot easier. It wasn't a bad effort at all; in fact, she was proud of it.

'How are you getting on?' Moreau asked, popping his head in the door. Lucy held up the sketch. 'Excellent. I may hire you after all,' he quipped. Lucy made a face at him and tried not to smile. 'Come along, that is enough for today. We need to leave now if we are to make the train to Cairo this evening.'

With relief, Lucy stuffed the sketching pad back into her bag. 'I'd nearly forgotten.'

Moreau leaned against the doorframe. 'It will be late when we reach the city, unfortunately. Now that Whitmore is aware of this find, it would be wise for us to go and see Joubert first thing in the morning.'

'Before Whitmore has a chance to?'

'Well, yes,' he replied with a grin.

Lucy dusted down her skirts and stood. 'We should send a telegram to Joubert from the train station at Bedrashên, apprising him of the situation.'

'A very good idea,' Moreau replied before standing back to let her pass.

At the bottom of the shaft, Lucy watched as Ali strapped Moreau into the harness, then Hopkins. Silently, they slipped away into the darkness of the shaft, and soon it was her turn.

'There, lady safe now,' Ali said. Lucy stared at him; such a strange comment to make. Had he sensed a strange presence down here too? Suddenly, Ali smiled before tugging on the rope. Lucy strained her eyes towards the light as she slowly left the depths of the tomb. But the image in her mind was that of the Lord of Silence below in the velvety darkness. Waiting.

ELEVEN

Lucy shifted in her seat and tried to find a more comfortable position.

'Madame Lawrence, you are very quiet,' Moreau remarked. 'Is anything the matter?' He tilted his head, looking at Lucy with concern from across the railway carriage.

Aware of the curious glances of Mary and Rafiq, Lucy smiled. 'Nothing, I'm a trifle tired that is all. It was quite a day.'

'Yes, it was certainly eventful. And take heart; it takes everyone time to get used to the conditions working in a tomb. Hopefully, the heat and dust hasn't put you off?' he asked with a grin.

Lucy straightened up. 'Certainly not! I enjoyed every minute of it and hope to return soon.' Moreau smiled at Lucy but made no comment and returned to his note-taking. Lucy was sure she heard a groan from Mary, but the maid covered it up with a cough and slumped further into her corner of the carriage. Where had the plucky Mary of their last escapade gone? Was she pining for her Ned?

Lucy turned back to the passing scenery. Her mind was racing after such an unsettling day. Blast Whitmore and his meddling. Every time she began to like the man, he did something maddening to change her opinion. Lucy closed her eyes and tried to relax to the rhythm of the train. Gradually, the tension in her body eased, and her thoughts turned to more practical matters.

'Will M. Joubert halt work at the dig when he receives your telegram?' Lucy asked Moreau. Conscious that Whitmore might attempt to gain access to the dig, they'd left Hopkins behind to ensure there was no mischief in Moreau's absence.

'Most likely Joubert will insist upon it until he makes a final decision,' Moreau said with a sigh. 'Politically, Joubert must be seen to be fair. And don't forget, although we control the Antiquities Service, the English hold the purse strings. I don't suppose you have any contacts in the Treasury?'

'Unfortunately, no,' Lucy replied. It was so unlucky the way matters had transpired, for she'd hoped to spend most of her time during the winter at the dig helping, but if the situation became politically charged, the site might remain closed for the entire season, and she would be stuck in Cairo.

Soon villages of mud houses began to appear; they'd reached the outskirts of the city once more. One look at Mary's face confirmed she was relieved to be back. Wasn't it strange how Cairo was like home already?

The Excelsior Hotel

The next day proved a frustrating one. Mid-morning, Lucy and Moreau travelled out to Boulaq only to discover Joubert was visiting a friend in Alexandria and wouldn't return until the following day. Their telegram had not even been read. Despondent, they returned to the city, resigned to wait it out. Moreau departed for his hotel, promising to keep her informed. There was no hint of his amorous approaches being repeated, and Lucy began to wonder if she'd imagined it all. Clearly, Moreau's mind was preoccupied with the problems at the site, which was as it should be, so why, now that she had more time to think about it, was she disappointed? Had she been reckless in allowing herself to be charmed by him? However, it wasn't something she could discuss with anyone, so she kicked her heels in frustration for most of the day, then dined with Isabella. To Lucy's consternation, the Whitmores entered the dining room shortly after they sat down. Reginald had the gall to nod to her; Rosemary treated her to a sneer.

Lucy's hastily written warning note to Moreau brought him to the hotel early the next morning. Straight away, Lucy sensed he was in a foul mood.

'I can't believe it!' he exclaimed, after kissing her hand and sitting down. 'Whitmore followed us. They must have been on the next train.'

'You can hardly blame him; he has come to plead his case with Joubert, too. Admit it, in his shoes you would do the same. We must be reasonable, for there is a lot at stake if the tomb is intact. I'm sure he craves success just as much as you.'

Moreau ran his hand through his hair. 'Yes, yes, but he isn't experienced enough. He may do more damage than good if he were to be given permission to take over. Why do you think the British Museum has only partially funded him? Whitmore is an amateur!'

'Do you really believe that, M. Moreau, or is it your frustration talking? The fact you discovered it and opened it up on your licenced site should give you the advantage over Whitmore. It is hardly fair to penalise you. When the plots were being divided up, no one could have known a tomb was located in two adjacent ones.'

Moreau jumped up and began to pace. 'Even a day's delay is intolerable. Excavating such sites can take years. The season is short, and the work is slow. The blockage in the passageway might only be a few feet deep or it could be hundreds. We may need to come back each season to pick our way carefully through the next few yards. There is no way of knowing for sure. Joubert may delay making a decision for appearances' sake, for he will not wish to be considered partisan. But I'll lose precious days, perhaps weeks.'

'You must be patient, Moreau.'

'As it happens, Joubert sent me an instruction first thing this morning to close the dig.'

Lucy was astonished. 'But how did he find out about the problem? He hadn't read our telegram.'

'Our friend Whitmore must have found out where Joubert was and sent him word.' Moreau growled. 'I'd hoped Hopkins would continue the work, but he will not risk his reputation by disobeying Joubert's orders. So cowardly!'

'Moreau! You didn't ask him, surely? We agreed to stop work until Joubert was consulted. Besides, as your patron, I wouldn't wish you or Hopkins to break the law.' Lucy's anger started to bubble up.

Moreau blew out his cheeks. 'You think that crazy Scot obeys the law? Ha!'

Moreau resumed his pacing.

'When can we see Joubert?' Lucy asked, just about managing to keep her irritation in check.

Moreau pulled a telegram from his inside pocket and handed it to her. Due to commitments, Joubert wouldn't be able to meet them until late afternoon. 'Hmm, I suppose we can only hope one of these commitments isn't Whitmore,' Lucy remarked.

'Did you see *le mouchard* this morning?'

'Try to be kind, Armand. No, only his sister was at break-fast,' Lucy replied. 'And she didn't look like she wanted to indulge in conversation with *me*.' Moreau groaned. 'Please sit down, and let's consider what we're going to say when we do meet Joubert. We may only get one chance to convince him to let us proceed.'

Moreau shrugged and sighed but remained standing. 'Forgive me, perhaps I'm being unreasonable, but I have had one frustrating season out at Sakkâra, and my gut instinct is this tomb is the one I have dreamed of. I should be down there now, not wasting time in Cairo.' He paused and gave her a self-effacing smile. 'Though if I must waste time, I would rather do so with you.'

'Flatterer!' she scolded. 'Now, to work!'

Early Evening

Once Joubert and Moreau left the hotel, Lucy walked out to the garden. The sky was streaked with gold and pink as the sun set, and a gentle breeze shook the palm leaves above her as she ambled along the path. Lucy sat down on a bench and relived the whole debacle of a meeting once more. It had been short and disastrous. Joubert demanded the site stay closed and insisted he wouldn't make a decision until he had visited the site and then consulted the Board of the Antiquities Service. Moreau had been apoplectic, and Lucy was only glad her grasp of French did not include the ability to translate the stream of expletives he let fly. Joubert's reaction was enough to tell her how insulting the tirade was. The poor man had left in a huff, and Lucy couldn't really blame him.

'Why are you sitting out here? It will be dark soon.' Lucy looked up to see Isabella strolling along the path towards her. 'Your maid told me I'd find you out here. May I join you?' Lucy moved over, and Isabella sat down beside her on the wooden bench. 'Rough day?'

'Why is it men let their egos destroy everything?' Lucy asked.

'That is a bit deep and philosophical for me,' Isabella remarked. Lucy sighed and shook her head. 'May I ask if there are specific egos involved or are you generalising?'

'Unfortunately, very specific – M. Moreau and M. Joubert. And I'm stuck in the middle of the resulting tangle because two men can't see beyond their own importance.'

'I take it your meeting did not go well.'

Lucy nodded.

'So, we are speaking of French egos.' Isabella smiled. 'I have it on good authority they are the largest known to mankind.'

'It's not funny, Isabella. I don't know what to do next,' Lucy replied. 'Neither will listen to reason. And now we must wait for Joubert to make a decision. Moreau flew into a rage and insulted the poor man.' Lucy threw her hands up in the air. 'I had not realised how volatile Moreau can be.'

Isabella leaned back and regarded her with a serious expression. 'A tangle, indeed. Moreau's temper may cost him what he holds dear. You must persuade him to apologise, but I'd wait until tomorrow. Let him cool down. Approach Joubert alone.'

'And use my womanly wiles?' Lucy huffed. 'That was Moreau's great plan.'

'That aside, you're the only one who can intervene on Moreau's behalf.'

'Moreau will not like it if I grovel. I'm not sure I'd like it either.'

'Hopefully, it won't come to that. Use the arguments you had prepared for today's meeting. I'm sure they are sound. I don't doubt you can be very convincing when you put your mind to it.'

'Unfortunately, Whitmore will be attempting to do the same.'

'Ah, but you know well you have the advantage. Joubert and Moreau go back a long way,' Isabella remarked.

'I suppose it is worth a try. I might ask Joubert to a private dinner here tomorrow evening. Would you join us?'

'Safety in numbers?' Isabella laughed.

'Something like that.'

'Do you think they'll resort to violence? If so, it holds the promise of being a very entertaining evening.'

'Oh, Isabella, do not even joke about it.'

Isabella shook her head. 'Scratch the surface, and these men are all the same. Resorting to fisticuffs is hardly gentlemanly, but there is a lot at stake – reputations, funding, and egos, as you said. It is unfortunate you find yourself caught up in it.'

'Yes, but I don't regret coming to Egypt. In fact, I'm impatient to return to the dig. The place draws me in, and I'm doing something useful at last.'

'Once the present difficulty is resolved, I don't see any reason why you should not continue to be involved; after all, your money is funding Moreau's work.'

'Exactly! But some would frown upon my participation,' Lucy said. 'It is one thing to fund the work, but to get my hands dirty... My mother would be horrified if she knew what I was up to down in that tomb. Not that her opinion matters, of course.'

'Lucy, why do you torture yourself so? You're a young woman, and fate has thrown this amazing adventure your way. Enjoy it. My advice for now is to stick with it, but if the difficulties should escalate, remove to a safe distance and let the men fight it out. Try to look on it as a business transaction. Unless, of course, it is more than that?'

'You think I'm too emotionally involved?' Lucy couldn't keep the worry from her voice.

'Moreau has a reputation, my dear friend. You can't be unaware of this. I see the way he looks at you, and I do not believe you're immune to his charm. Perhaps a romantic adventure is just what you need?'

'Well, my friend, I can tell you one thing I *do* need.'

'What's that?'

'Since coming to Egypt I realise just how unaccomplished and uneducated I am, and I find it rather depressing.'

'But the skills and knowledge you lack aren't things a woman of our class requires. You, like me, were raised to be married off for the benefit of the family coffers.'

'True, but even the basics elude me,' Lucy said. 'If I wasn't interested in something, I ignored it. And if my mother was particularly keen I accomplish something, I deliberately made a mess of it. Miss Greyling, my governess, despaired of me.'

'Why did you act so?'

'To get attention, I suppose. Mother only graced the nursery to impart a lecture to me or a blistering scold to Miss Greyling. Richard, my brother, was the golden child and a complete bore.' Lucy wrinkled her nose. 'He never gave my parents a day's worry.'

'This Richard doesn't sound much fun.'

'Well, you can be sure where he is now is no fun at all!' Lucy gave Isabella a watery smile.

'I think you're very hard on yourself, Lucy. If you lack education, read. Hire a tutor. There are many ways to rectify these things.'

Lucy turned to her with a smile. 'That is an excellent idea; I'll do just that when I return home.'

'Good for you. My eldest brother sparked my interest in photography when he brought a camera home. I was instantly fascinated, and my life changed forever. Photography became my obsession. My family laughed at me when I said I wanted to be a photographer. When I persisted, Father threatened to marry me off. I refused and was sent away to stay with my grandmother in Milan. What my father didn't anticipate was her determination to undermine him, for they'd fallen out years before. Grandmother was happy to support me and, through a friend of hers, I found my first position in a tiny studio located in a back street near the Duomo di Milano. There I learnt my trade and used an inheritance to set up my own studio a few years' later.'

'Did your father leave you money after all that had transpired?' Lucy asked.

'No. Again, it was my grandmother. She left me her house and some money. My father did not like it, but there was nothing he could do.'

'Families!'

'And from what you tell me about yours, Lucy, we seem to be similarly *blessed*!'

'At least yours didn't have you arrested for a theft you didn't commit. If it is a competition for whose family is the worst, mine wins.'

Isabella laughed. 'Agreed.'

TWELVE

The following morning, Lucy headed out to Boulaq with Rafiq, determined to set things right with Joubert. But to her consternation, she saw Whitmore approach from the museum side as they crossed the bridge over the Nile. He must have paid Joubert an early morning visit. How cunning!

Rafiq gave Lucy a knowing look. 'The gentleman is an early riser,' he remarked.

'And up to mischief, Rafiq, I'll wager,' Lucy replied.

Whitmore drew up and doffed his hat. 'A fine morning, Mrs Lawrence.'

'Indeed, it is,' she replied coolly. 'I wish you a pleasant day.' Lucy nudged the donkey into motion. Whitmore bowed and set off back towards the city.

Joubert was in his office and looked up with surprise when Lucy was announced by M. Japp.

'An unexpected pleasure, Madame Lawrence.' He pulled out a chair for her.

'I was unhappy about the way we parted yesterday. It was most regrettable,' Lucy said. 'I hope we can come to an understanding regarding the site. Alas, M. Moreau's behaviour, though understandable, was inexcusable. I wanted to assure you I do not condone it.'

Joubert chuckled. 'Ah, Madame Lawrence, you do not know Moreau as well as I do. When it comes to business he can be, how shall we say, difficult. First thing this morning, I received a note from him, profuse with apologies. Do not concern yourself, dear lady; it is not the first time he has exploded in my presence like a volcano. He's quick to anger but always quick to be amenable again. To be honest, I rather expected it. It is because he cares so much. Egypt is his life.'

What a relief, Lucy thought. There was hope of retrieving the situation. 'Yes, I understand that now, but I wanted to be sure it had not damaged *our* relationship,' she offered with a smile.

'That would be impossible,' Joubert said. 'However, regarding the difficulty out at Sakkâra, I'm afraid nothing has changed. The site must remain closed.'

'That is a shame. The season is so short—'

'No matter. Everything must be above board, or the English will be complaining as usual. Since the theft here, they have been making a fuss and questioning my professionalism.'

'I don't see why. How can they blame you?'

'Tensions have been bubbling away for some time. The opportunity to cast – how do you say... aspersions? – was too good to miss by some. Yesterday I received a nasty telegram from a researcher in the British Museum, and when I consider the number of times I have facilitated their demands...'

'I'm sorry to hear that. However, you know as well as I how precious time is,' Lucy insisted. 'Notwithstanding, the men still have to be paid, and yet they can't work.'

'I fully understand your frustration, madame. Such things happen frequently. I myself often had difficulties on digs. M. Whitmore is impatient too, and pleads his case most convincingly.'

'I do not see what grounds he has, M. Joubert. Moreau found the tomb in his allocated area and has opened it. Whitmore is trying to steal his glory.'

'And yours, madame?' Joubert said, eyes glittering. 'Forgive me, but you're hardly impartial.'

Lucy sighed. This was futile; they were going around in circles. 'My point is, M. Joubert, Whitmore had no way of knowing of the tomb's existence. Everyone knows exploring these sites is a game of chance. He's upset because Moreau found it first.'

'Be that as it may, I can't make a decision without seeing the site for myself and listening to both sides of the argument.'

'Agreed. All I ask is you give me a reasonable opportunity to state our case, M. Joubert. Like M. Moreau, I believe this tomb is a significant find which will greatly further our knowledge. It would be a shame if it were to fall victim to politics.'

'I couldn't agree more, madame,' Joubert said. 'And you have put your case most eloquently.'

'As I'm sure Mr Whitmore did earlier this morning,' Lucy replied.

Joubert had the grace to appear uncomfortable. 'You must understand what passed between M. Whitmore and me is confidential.'

'Of course.'

'But I assure you I'll do my best to find a fair solution. I travel to Sakkâra later this week, Madame Lawrence. Once I'm satisfied I have all the facts, I'll endeavour to resolve the problem as quickly as possible.'

Lucy was disappointed, suspecting he might revert to drawing lots again. 'I would appreciate a speedy resolution, M. Joubert. I'm sure you will agree there is little point in having Moreau stuck in Cairo with nothing to do. He is like a caged animal.'

Lucy stood, and Joubert struggled to his feet.

'I'm hosting a small dinner party this evening at the hotel. Perhaps you would care to join us?'

Joubert's eyes lit up. 'Thank you! I would be honoured, madame.'

The Shubra Avenue, North Cairo, that Afternoon

The lightly sprung open carriage bowled along the broad avenue beneath the sycamores and lebbeks which formed a cool green tunnel of shade. Much to Lucy's surprise, it was far more crowded than she'd expected. Whether carriages or the ubiquitous donkey, every mode of transport had been employed, and half of Cairo appeared to have had the same idea of an afternoon drive.

'It is just like Rotten Row in Hyde Park,' Lucy remarked to Mary. 'I understand it is a favourite haunt of the tourists. Rafiq told me it is *the* place to be seen, particularly on Fridays and Sundays. Even the khedive likes to take the air here. Oh look, Mary,' she said as a carriage passed by with a veiled lady inside. 'I wonder if she's from one of the harems.' Lucy raised her parasol, trying to catch another glimpse.

'What's a harem?' Mary frowned at her. Lucy quickly explained.

'Good gracious! It is all wonderfully exotic, ma'am. I'm not sure me mother would approve.'

Lucy snorted. 'Or Father O'Brien?'

'Oh lord, ma'am, it would kill him entirely!'

'Best not tell them so, Mary. Stick to snakes and scorpions and your impossible mistress.'

Mary gave an exaggerated shiver. 'I don't know how you can joke about those creatures, ma'am. Cairo and Egypt suit you, but I'd rather be at home.'

'I'm sorry you feel that way, Mary, but it's only for a few months, and you'll soon be back with your Ned.' This brought a smile to Mary's face. Lucy continued: 'Perhaps I fit in here because I'm in my natural habitat. I'm among rogues, charlatans, thieves and chancers. The most fascinating group of people I have ever encountered.'

'Ah, ma'am. I know you're joking. You are none of those things. However, I've no doubt you will sort each and every one of them out if you can.'

Lucy replied with a smile. 'I shall try. It would appear we are all stuck here in Cairo for the present, and I need something to keep me occupied.'

'That's a shame, ma'am. I know how much you liked the desert. What do you have in mind?'

'I think a little detecting may be in order.'

Mary blanched. 'But look what happened the last time! Best not.'

'But, Mary, the theft at the museum hasn't been solved. Nor my middle of the night visitor, though I think that one is best left to the police. However, there is something very peculiar about the burglary at the museum, and it is niggling away at me. Why did they not take the opportunity to steal more than a handful of items? It does not make sense.'

Mary shrugged. 'It's a very poor country. People do what they need to do to survive and feed their families. Perhaps the burglar realised what he had was priceless and was happy enough, or was disturbed and made a run for it?'

'Hmm, well, I'm not convinced. Something about it does not feel right.'

'I'd leave it alone, ma'am. How could you possibly solve it? And those thieves may be highly dangerous. They'll not take kindly to you poking your nose in.'

Lucy gasped. 'Poking my nose in!'

'Sorry, ma'am, but yes. Let the police do their job,' Mary replied with a stern gaze. 'They probably suspect who did it and only need to catch them trying to sell the items to a dealer.'

Lucy narrowed her eyes. 'You seem to know a lot about how these things work.'

Mary sniffed. 'I hear the talk amongst the other servants, ma'am, at the hotel.' She leaned forward. 'I think one or two of them might be trying their hand in the black market. Very lucrative, from what I hear. Some of them plan to bring items home to sell on.'

'Indeed. That's interesting, Mary. Keep your ears open, and let me know if you hear anything else. Just think, we might try to crack it, just the two of us. It would be such fun.'

Mary didn't look convinced. 'Fun, is it? And what about me, when I have to return to England and explain to your grieving family and friends that your nasty death was down to *fun*?'

'It won't come to that. Don't I have you to watch out for me?'

Mary rolled her eyes skyward.

'You know if I get bored, I'll only make your life miserable. Come, what do you say, Mary? It won't be too difficult. I already know where to find one rogue who deals in stolen goods – the fellow who tried to sell me the mummy's hand. All I need to do is question him and try to trace his source. He was a slimy fellow. I'm sure for the right amount of money he would give us some names or useful information.'

Mary sniffed. 'More likely, a passport to heaven, ma'am!'

THIRTEEN

Isabella grinned as Lucy handed her a drink. They'd agreed to meet in Lucy's suite before dinner in the hopes of coming up with a successful strategy for the evening ahead.

'The British should employ you in the diplomatic service,' Isabella remarked. 'I'm amazed you have managed to entice all the parties in this catastrophe to dine at the same table this evening.'

'To be honest, Isabella, neither can I. I really expected the Whitmores to turn me down, but Rosemary sent an acceptance after lunch. The note was curt, but at least they have agreed to come. A compromise may be possible.'

Isabella's fine eyebrows shot up. 'Ah-ha, you are now in favour! I was sure they'd refuse.'

'Do you suspect they are up to something? It is all so tiresome. Rosemary makes me uneasy... I can't quite define it.'

'Rosemary is strange, certainly. One minute she's friendly, the next she's making nasty remarks and glaring at you as if you crawled out from under a rock. And, she's far too protective of her brother. Some would say it is strange.'

'But understandable to some extent. Rosemary has invested

her whole life in his work. Perhaps it was her choice to stay with him rather than marry,' Lucy mused.

'Pooh! I do not believe any man has ever proposed to her. The woman is so dull,' Isabella said, with a toss of her head.

'You are harsh, Isabella; we can't all be as beautiful and alluring as you.'

Isabella laughed as she sat down beside her. 'Flatterer!' Then she tilted her head and narrowed her eyes. 'You know, my friend, you've changed since your return from Sakkâra. These last few days you have a – what is the English word – bloom? Is there anything you wish to reveal to me?'

'No, nothing,' Lucy prevaricated. 'Despite all the trouble and delays, I'm enjoying myself; that must account for it.'

Isabella gave her an amused glance. 'And so it has nothing to do with the handsome M. Moreau?'

Lucy felt the heat rise in her face but shook her head. 'I'm his patron, Isabella, nothing more.'

Isabella didn't look convinced. 'Very well, I'll swallow this falsehood. It must be the country that has brought the sparkle to your eyes, then. I admit it can be mesmerising. It draws you in with the charm of a lover. But be careful; it can be as fickle as one too.'

Lucy glanced at her, wondering what Isabella was hinting at. Was she warning her against Moreau again, or men in general? 'Don't concern yourself. I'm careful. Tell me, are you speaking from experience? Have you lost your heart to someone here?'

Isabella chuckled. 'Many times! I fall in and out of love easily. I enjoy the attention, I have to admit. But when a man begins to make demands...' Isabella shrugged and smiled.

'Is there someone special here at the moment?'

Isabella shook her head. 'No, my dear friend. I may love, but I do not commit. I value my freedom far too much. I have found no man I'd wish to be tied to for life.'

'Not even in Milan?'

'Especially not in Milan. My family is well known and their wealth and position envied. How can I be sure it is not that which attracts a man? Lucy, you must have experienced this too, now you are a wealthy woman?'

'Well, no, not yet,' Lucy said, envisaging Phineas in her head for one fleeting moment. 'The irony is, I suspect it may have scared someone away instead. My mourning is over, and yet he does not court me despite a brief period when I thought – I'd hoped – he was merely giving me time to get through my period of grieving. We parted in London on such odd terms.'

'He must be a fool, this man you speak of. My advice is to forget him.'

'Well, he appears to have forgotten about me.'

Isabella narrowed her eyes. 'Did you let this gentleman know how you were feeling?'

Lucy spluttered with laughter. 'Phineas would have been horrified, and I would have died of mortification. It's not done in English society. Besides, it was all so... uncertain.'

'You English are so cold – like the fish. Unlike Italians – we are all emotion!' Isabella laughed and wagged her finger.

'Sometimes I wish we were more like you. It must be so much easier to be able to say how you feel.' Lucy then gave Isabella something of her history with Phineas. 'Perhaps we were both scared. We hurt each other very much. Misunderstanding and a lack of trust nearly undid our friendship.'

Isabella gave her a pitying look. 'So you left it all to chance, and nothing has come of it. Are you a coward, Lucy Lawrence?'

'I am not! But, as I said, he has vanished and possibly with another man's wife. I'll always be grateful to him for helping me, but romance was not to be.'

Isabella tucked her arm through Lucy's. 'But I can see this makes you sad, my dear.'

'A little, but since I have come to Egypt, less so.'

Isabella snorted. 'Ah, yes. M. Moreau has taken his place?'

'No, no.'

'Lucy, you must heed me. This small archaeological community we are now part of is... how do you say? Intimate. Over the years one hears things about others. Some of it good, some of it not so good. I do not like to gossip, but you should be aware of something. M. Moreau is a well-respected Egyptologist, but he has a penchant for dalliance with the fairer sex.'

'You've said this before, and I have seen for myself how he flirts,' Lucy murmured, her heart sinking.

'Yes, I hinted at it before, but I do not want to see you hurt. If you wish for a brief liaison, then Moreau would be perfect, but do not expect commitment from him. His work is his life. Many women have loved him and rued the day. I suspect it is the chase that interests him the most.'

Lucy squeezed her arm. 'Your concern is appreciated but, truly, I haven't fallen in love with Moreau. If I'm honest, I'm in love with the idea of him. Can you understand that?'

'Of course I can. You have had a horrible time of it with your husband, and along comes this romantic figure, and such a man as he you do not find on the streets of London. Who would not be beguiled?'

Lucy smiled, but she was crestfallen. She knew well that Isabella was right, but it was sobering to realise how close to disaster she had been prepared to sail. If she had let that kiss lead to its natural conclusion, it would only have added to the current mess. 'Well, now I have more important matters to worry about than trysts with interesting suitors.'

'Yes, you do. Let's hope the dinner this evening helps that situation,' Isabella said. 'I'm getting bored out at Boulaq and long for more exciting work.'

'It may be possible to sort it out, but my fear is Joubert will take weeks to resolve this. However, if I can broker a compromise, we might all be back to work much sooner.' Isabella looked sceptical. 'It has to be worth a try. Good food, good wine and good company – what Frenchman is able to resist such things?'

Isabella chuckled. 'Or any man for that matter. What do you wish me to do? Am I to flirt and flatter them into submission?'

Lucy smiled. 'I don't doubt you are capable of it, if it were just Moreau and Joubert we had to persuade. The problem is Whitmore, and as he has employed you, I can't use you as a weapon against him.'

Isabella pulled a face. 'You have far too many scruples. Technically, as he hasn't made a find for me to photograph yet, I'm not in his employ.' Isabella gave her a wry smile. 'Until such time as he does need my services, I'm working for M. Joubert. I can't bear to be idle. However, your problem is more complicated than you realise. No womanly wiles will bring Whitmore to do your bidding. He is the coldest fish of all.'

Lucy was surprised. 'Whitmore didn't give me that impression. Once he realised my interest in ancient Egypt was genuine, he was both informative and helpful.'

Isabella sniffed. 'There was trouble at Sakkâra last year. My understanding is Whitmore and Moreau fell out over a woman.'

'You said that before. Who was she?' Could this have been the 'history' Moreau had spoken of?

'I have no details, Lucy, as I was at Karnak,' Isabella replied. 'But perhaps it is information you might use to your advantage in your present difficulties?'

Lucy frowned and shook her head. 'Then it is only a rumour, and I do not see how it will help. Besides, I'd rather not be underhand, especially as it may not be true.'

'Then you are a better person than I.' Isabella glanced at the clock. 'Now, shall we join this party of yours?'

Lucy stood and glanced nervously in the mirror. 'So much hinges on this. I won't be able to eat a morsel.'

Isabella's face lit up with mischief. 'Yes, you will. Watch

me. I'll have Joubert eating out of my hand by the end of the evening.'

By the time dessert was served, the conversation at Lucy's table was flowing and the company, bar Reginald and Rosemary Whitmore, were relaxed and enjoying the evening. Joubert, in particular, appeared delighted to be seated beside Isabella, if the laughter was anything to go by. But Reginald Whitmore, for the most part, sat in stony silence beside Lucy while, in contrast, on Lucy's other side, Moreau was his usual flirtatious self.

Looking up at one point while giggling at one of Moreau's comments, Lucy caught a fleeting glance from Rosemary. Miss Whitmore quickly looked away to resume her conversation with her brother. Was that a flash of jealousy Lucy had seen in her expression? How odd. Under her lashes, Lucy studied the woman closely. If only she smiled instead of scowling so much. It was Rosemary's dress sense that undermined her looks the most. The woman had made no effort this evening and compared to the lusciousness of Isabella, in her purple gown and her glossy black hair intricately dressed, Rosemary was drab. Her dun-coloured dress with its high neck was nondescript and unflattering. Throughout the evening, Lucy had been aware of some other sharp glances from Rosemary, particularly when she and Moreau had conversed. Perhaps she's High Church and strongly condemns gaiety in any form, Lucy thought. Or perhaps she disapproves of Moreau's behaviour as much as his nationality? If Lucy wasn't mistaken, Rosemary had deliberately taken a seat far away from him on joining the party earlier.

Moreau nudged Lucy, glancing at the Whitmores. Then he leaned in close. 'What's wrong with them, do you think?'

'Whatever do you mean?' Lucy asked.

'They sit there like blocks of ice, barely speaking to anyone.'

'This isn't an easy situation for any of us, Armand. They must feel at a disadvantage.'

'I do not understand it. With two of the most beautiful women in Cairo at the table, Whitmore does not even try to engage you or Isabella in conversation. And as for Rosemary – why she's as dry as a sack of bones!'

'That is unkind! Besides, he's very clever, and she is...' Lucy trailed off in a desperate attempt to defend the Whitmores.

'What?'

'Loyal.'

Moreau harrumphed. 'Yes; I'm aware of his reputation and her *devotion*. But life is not all about work. On an occasion such as this, particularly with so much at stake, they should make the effort to be sociable.'

'Like you?'

Moreau smirked. 'I think you will find a Frenchman always remembers his manners.'

Lucy shook her head. 'You are incorrigible!'

'But it is easy to get along with people and the fairer sex even more so. To understand a woman, a man must trust his instincts,' Moreau said loudly. Lucy stiffened, acutely aware of Whitmore listening on the other side of her. What was Moreau up to?

'I don't really follow, Armand,' Lucy said, intrigued despite the tension emanating from Whitmore, who was now so rigid she feared he would snap in two. 'However, it is true we British tend to be reserved.'

'Reserved? Mais non! It is more than that, and I find it both fatiguing and dull.' It suddenly struck Lucy that Moreau might be deliberately trying to force out Whitmore's boorish tendencies in front of Joubert.

'*Perhaps*,' Whitmore piped up with a scowl of indignation, 'it is because we are deep thinkers and are happy to leave the

French to their *frivolity*. If a man can't take his business seriously, he should give it up.'

Moreau's laugh was harsh. 'Business? I was talking of love and the finer feelings.' Moreau leaned in closer to Lucy and lowered his voice, but not enough. 'The more experience with the fairer sex a man has, he comes to realise the difference between mere lust and a true connection with the other person's soul.'

'Outrageous poppycock!' Whitmore muttered under his breath. Lucy noticed Rosemary was siting as if frozen, her face ashen.

'You should write poetry, M. Moreau,' Lucy said, desperately trying to diffuse his mischief.

'I do... but few see it,' Moreau said with a wink. Now she was sure Moreau was deliberately trying to infuriate Whitmore.

Reginald, stiff with rage, turned away towards his sister. Moreau looked towards them and smirked. 'I doubt she ever enjoys herself; such a dull woman.'

Lucy sighed. Moreau was in a strange mood and was sabotaging her efforts. She didn't understand why. Lucy turned to him and hissed. 'Why did you provoke Whitmore? It will hardly help our cause. Would it not be a good idea for Joubert to see you two getting along? He might suggest a compromise of some sort as opposed to shutting the entire operation down.'

'Joubert wouldn't be fooled for an instant. He knows my opinion of that oaf well enough.'

Lucy was exasperated by Moreau's stubborn streak. Whatever had happened between the men in the past must have been very serious for them to act this way. All of a sudden, she wished the evening would draw to a close. Lucy decided this would be the right moment to ask the ladies to join her in the salon for coffee. Hopefully, Joubert would take charge once the men were alone and try to reach a settlement with Moreau and Whitmore.

But before she could speak, Reginald coughed to catch her attention. 'It was very gracious of you, Mrs Lawrence, to invite us to join you this evening.' Reginald looked sincere, or as sincere as it was possible to determine with his eyes obscured by his grey spectacles. But beside him, Rosemary's hard gaze disconcerted Lucy, her dislike only too plain to see. If Lucy wasn't mistaken, the woman's cold stare took in most of the people at the table. A model for Medusa? Lucy quickly dismissed the wicked thought.

'I was delighted you accepted,' Lucy answered quickly. 'We never had an opportunity to further our discussion on your work after your kindness to me at Giza. It was a wonderful day, and an experience I'll never forget. It was delightful to see it with someone who is so knowledgeable about the site. Perhaps we could discuss your situation in the next few days?'

'I would like nothing better,' Reginald said, but his tone was not encouraging. He wouldn't meet her eye.

'The state of affairs we find ourselves in is unfortunate,' Lucy continued. 'I would love to be in a position to help you along the lines we outlined at Giza.'

'But?'

'My first loyalty is to M. Moreau, as I'm sure you can understand. However, I would like to think we all have the same aim.' Frowning, he looked at her but made no comment. 'A compromise *must* be possible.'

'Most of the tomb is located in my concession. Under the terms of my licence, I have every right to excavate. I, therefore, do not see why I should compromise. Indeed, the British Museum was delighted to learn of the discovery and sent me a very encouraging telegram this afternoon. They informed me they'll be pleading my case with the director' – he nodded towards Joubert – 'quite vigorously.'

Lucy's heart sank, but she had to keep trying. 'Does it really matter who carries out the work? Whatever the tomb contains

will eventually be available for everyone to see at Boulaq,
furthering everyone's knowledge.'

'Please don't be naïve, Mrs Lawrence. The French will
never share what they find,' he hissed, catching her off-guard.
Colour rose in his face. 'It will end up in private collections or
the Louvre. They want all the glory for themselves, always
have. Napoleon and his cohorts plundering this country was
bad enough, but *that* man is the worst!' Whitmore's voice rose to
a shout as he pointed across her to Moreau. 'Always taking
credit for other people's hard work.'

The table fell silent.

Then the entire dining room.

Moreau picked up his glass and took a sip. The only thing
betraying his reaction was a slight shake in his hand as he
lowered it again. 'Whitmore, you forget yourself. There are
ladies present. I care not what you think of me, but I suggest you
apologise and temper your language.'

Whitmore shoved back his chair as he stood, his face livid.
'To hell with you, Moreau! Come along, Rosemary, I've had
enough of this farce.'

Rosemary glanced from him to Moreau, who was staring
down at the tablecloth, his lips tightly clamped. The most
malevolent expression crossed her features, making Lucy flinch.
Then Rosemary looked as if she might burst into tears. Lucy
was baffled and watched in dismay as brother and sister stalked
from the room, arm in arm, every person in the dining room
following their progress, open-mouthed.

Moreau continued to glare at the tablecloth.

Isabella smiled weakly across the table.

M. Joubert pursed his lips and shook his head. '*Quel
dommage!*'

PART 2

THE RECKONING

FOURTEEN

Egyptian Museum, Boulaq

Lucy brooded over the dinner fiasco for most of the following morning. Her great plan was in disarray. Foolishly, she'd pinned her hopes on persuading Whitmore to compromise, but how could she have anticipated the devilment Moreau would indulge in? Lucy had managed to extract a promise from a sullen Moreau the night before that he would call on her that morning to discuss the situation. But he hadn't turned up. Lucy was angry with him. He had deliberately provoked that outburst from Whitmore. Was the man now sulking in his hotel room? It took much restraint not to order a cab and confront Moreau at the Montgomery.

Thank goodness things hadn't progressed romantically. The better she knew Moreau the more she realised she'd had a lucky escape. Yes, he loved women, but it was their adulation he wanted, not commitment. She suspected he never really returned the feelings of the women he wooed. Armand saw himself as the great romantic figure: the intrepid archaeologist who deserved to be worshipped. To lose your heart to such a

man could only have one rather painful outcome. Their relationship would have to be on a more professional footing from
now on. How else could she continue to work with him at
Sakkâra? That was, of course, if they ever got back there.

Lucy was certain Moreau was hiding something important
from her now. He had mentioned an 'unfortunate history'
between himself and Whitmore that day at the dig, but didn't,
indeed *wouldn't*, expand on it. And then Isabella had suggested
an unknown woman was at the centre of everything. Initially,
Lucy had dismissed this as idle gossip, but the more she thought
about it, the more likely an explanation it could be for both
men's behaviour. Moreau couldn't help himself where women
were concerned. Perhaps he had stolen someone from under
Whitmore's nose just for the hell of it. It would also explain
Rosemary's attitude to Moreau. She would hate him for hurting
Reginald. But how on earth was Lucy to find out? Perhaps some
of the regular guests at the Excelsior might have heard rumours.
Morning coffee and afternoon tea would have to be on Lucy's
agenda for the next few days. As Isabella had claimed, the
community might be slightly bohemian but, like any group of
people stuck together for extended periods, they loved to gossip
about each other. And, as Mary spent a lot of time with the
other servants, she might dig up some interesting information
from them too. At least it would be something else to do while
Joubert mulled over the Sakkâra problem. But could she risk
Joubert procrastinating for weeks? They would all go mad.
There was only one thing to do and that was to go out to Boulaq
and try to force Joubert's hand.

But on arrival Lucy was informed M. Joubert was in a meeting, and she would have to wait. With no option but to kill time,
she decided to explore more of the museum. As she stood just
inside the rose-coloured granite door, which led from the Grand
Vestibule to the Salle du Centre, her mind returned to the day
of the robbery. That French inspector hadn't made any progress

on it as far as she knew. Or indeed on poor Mrs Hamilton's missing pearls. It didn't inspire much confidence in the Cairo police. Really, it was the outside of enough! Men were impossible. Here she was, although not quite as experienced as say *Mr Phineas Stone*, but she was ready, willing and able to help Joubert. Not that she needed anyone's permission. In fact, she decided, she would go to the bazaar that very afternoon to begin her enquiries.

Having decided on a course of action, she felt a lot better and turned her attention back to the room. It was packed with sarcophagi and statues between the display cabinets which were brimful of artefacts. Lucy wandered around. At last, against the far wall, she found the cabinet which had held the stolen artefacts. It stood empty. The glass lid had been replaced, and a crisp white card rested on the velvet inlay. *This display is temporarily closed* was all it said. Temporarily? It was unlikely those objects would be seen again. The photographs in Joubert's catalogue were the only evidence they'd ever existed. The loss of such precious objects denied future generations the chance to see the fine workmanship, to imagine the great queen in all her glory holding the dagger or wearing the beautiful jewellery. That particular queen's golden mummy case was set against the wall beside the cabinet, the queen's expression inscrutable as she looked down on Lucy. Lucy turned away, unsettled.

As she made her way back to the entrance hall, Lucy spotted Inspector Vauquelin coming in the front door. Thinking he might be here with news about the burglary, she headed towards him, determined to wheedle some information from him. Vauquelin's gaze swept around the various rooms as if he was searching for someone, and alighted on Lucy as she entered the hallway. The inspector's expression hardened but, to her surprise, he came straight over. He frowned down at her as if trying to decide something.

'Inspector,' Lucy greeted him.

'Good afternoon, Madame Lawrence,' Vauquelin replied, as formal as ever. 'Is the director here today? It is most urgent I speak to him.' He took out a linen handkerchief and wiped his brow. Over his shoulder, Lucy saw two more police officers enter and stand just inside the main door. Their expressions were as grim as their inspector's. Whatever was going on, it must be serious. Her heart began to race. Had he made an arrest in relation to the robbery? Had the stolen items been found? Lucy almost felt disappointed to be thwarted in her sleuthing plans quite so soon.

'M. Joubert is in his office, Inspector, with M. Japp, I believe. I'm waiting to see him myself. Is something the matter? You do look unwell.'

'I'm perfectly well, I thank you. But I'm the bearer of bad news.' Vauquelin cleared his throat, then gave her an odd look. 'You're M. Moreau's patron, are you not?'

'Why yes, I have that pleasure,' Lucy answered, starting to feel uneasy.

'Ah! I thought so. Perhaps you had better accompany me to M. Joubert. My news is relevant to you, madame,' he said, gesturing for Lucy to go before him.

Mystified, Lucy led the way down the corridor. Joubert's door was closed. Lucy knocked before entering with Vauquelin close behind. Japp and Joubert rose to their feet.

Joubert's colour rose. 'Madame Lawrence, Inspector! Whatever it is, it must wait.' He treated Lucy to a hard glance. 'I'm discussing museum business with my assistant.'

'M. Joubert, *my* business can't wait. I'm sorry to intrude but I have just come from Giza. I have some distressing news,' the inspector said, his eyes flicking between Joubert and Lucy.

Joubert's eyebrows snapped together. 'Very well, Inspector, you may speak freely. Not more thefts, I hope,' he continued with a scowl. 'I'm already dealing with the consequences of the previous one. The English are jumping up and down and baying for my head. I do not need another crisis.'

The inspector cleared his throat. 'I'm afraid it is far more serious than theft, sir.' Vauquelin glanced at Lucy. 'It would be best if Madame Lawrence were to sit down.'

The pit of Lucy's stomach dropped, and a prickle of anxiety settled in her gut. She exchanged a worried glance with Joubert then sat down quickly on the chair M. Japp pulled out for her.

'Well, what is it, Vauquelin?' Joubert demanded. 'I don't have all day.'

'The Bedouins opened up the Great Pyramid as usual this morning and escorted their first party of the day inside. However, when they reached the King's Chamber, they were in for a nasty shock.'

'And what was that, Inspector?' Joubert asked, barely hiding his irritation.

'There was a body in the sarcophagus, sir.'

'A body? Are you mad? We never found Khufu's mummy. Are you telling me it has suddenly turned up?'

'No, sir, you misunderstand. Not an ancient body, but a very recent one. It was the corpse of a man stabbed through the heart, and I would estimate he was not there more than a couple of hours.'

Lucy gasped. Joubert clutched the back of his chair, his face ashen. 'A murder!'

Vauquelin glanced down at Lucy. 'Madame, the details are not appropriate for a lady to hear. Would you care to wait outside?'

Lucy glared up at him. How dare he dismiss her. He had indicated this had something to do with Moreau; there was no way she was leaving. A horrible thought struck her. Could the dead man be Whitmore, and Moreau was responsible?

'On the contrary, Inspector, I insist you give us all the

details right away,' she said, half dreading what she was about to hear.

The inspector's lip quirked. 'Very well, madame, if you insist.'

'I do!'

Vauquelin reached inside his coat and pulled out something wrapped in a linen cloth. 'This was the murder weapon.' He stepped forward and laid the bundle down on the desk before carefully unwrapping it. The inside of the cloth was smeared with blood. Resting on it was a golden dagger, with a handle formed of four female heads.

The missing funerary dagger.

Lucy blew out a slow breath, and Joubert's eyes popped as he took a step backwards. '*Mon Dieu*! It can't be!' Joubert remained transfixed, staring down at the dagger.

'Did you recognise the victim, Inspector?' M. Japp enquired.

'Unfortunately, sir, I did,' Vauquelin said catching Lucy's eye before turning back to Joubert.

'Oh, no! It's Moreau,' Lucy whispered, gripping the edge of the seat, her throat constricting.

The inspector's expression was grim. '*Oui, madame. C'est vrai. Armand Moreau est mort.*'

FIFTEEN

A gateway from the museum garden brought Lucy through to the river. She sat down on a large flat-topped boulder and removed her hat with unsteady hands. Out mid-stream, a solitary ibis stood on a half-submerged branch waiting to catch its dinner. Near the bank the waterside reeds bent their heads, rustling and shaking in a light breeze, and the distant song of a bird was all that was to be heard. Glancing upstream, Lucy saw the moored dahabeeyahs, their sails tied up, waiting to carry their parties of tourists up the Nile on great adventures. The scene barely registered.

How was she to mourn Armand Moreau?

The question had echoed in her mind as she made her way down through the museum garden, almost blinded by tears. But here seemed the most appropriate place to grieve.

Moreau dead!

And in such a manner. Stunned into silence, Lucy had listened aghast as Joubert and Japp questioned the inspector, whose answers revealed grisly details she would rather not have known. The scene Vauquelin described in the Great Pyramid was nauseating, and she escaped the room to seek fresh air, refusing offers of accompaniment. At the door Lucy hesitated for one brief moment. Joubert was sitting with his head in his hands. Her instinct was to comfort him, but her own needs won out. She needed to escape, to make sense of it. And most of all, to cry.

The gruesome details brought Lucy back to the bleak day she identified Charlie in the morgue in London. At first that appeared to be an unfortunate accident, and it was only later, through Phineas's investigations, they discovered he had been murdered. But this was different. In this case, there could be no mistake, and there was cruelty and vindictiveness behind it. The manner of Moreau's death suggested someone hated him and wanted him to be found in a position that mocked everything his life stood for.

After the Whitmores' departure and the breaking-up of the dinner party the previous evening, Moreau had lingered for about half an hour but refused to discuss what had happened. If only she'd insisted on an explanation, but instead she'd pinned her hopes on seeing Moreau the next day, when hopefully he would be more forthcoming. In anguish, Lucy sucked in a sharp breath as the realisation dawned: she would never see him again.

'Madame?'

Lucy turned and spied Vauquelin coming through the gate. She should have anticipated he would want to ask her questions. Turning away, Lucy wiped her tears and tried to gather her thoughts. But there were fireworks going off in her head, and her stomach was twisting like a Catherine wheel.

Vauquelin stopped beside her, giving her a look filled with concern. 'Are you well, madame? I'm sorry you had to learn of M. Moreau's murder in such a way... but—'

'Yes, I know, Inspector, I would insist on staying. It's been a terrible shock. He didn't deserve to die like that. I am... struggling to comprehend.'

The inspector walked past her to the edge of the bank and stood looking out over the water. 'No, indeed, madame, no one deserves to die in such a way. In all my years, I haven't come across such a callous crime. It will shake Cairo society to its core.' He stood in silent contemplation of the great river for a few minutes, and Lucy suddenly realised what a huge case this would be for him. However, when he turned back to her, Vauquelin's gaze had softened. 'Madame, you're upset. Let me take you back to your hotel.'

It sounded like a command but unable to think of an excuse not to go with him, Lucy agreed.

The police carriage rattled over the bridge heading back towards the city. Lucy was numb. Hoping the inspector would leave her be, Lucy deliberately kept her gaze on the passing scenery. However, it didn't keep Vauquelin at bay for long.

'Forgive me, Madame Lawrence, but it would help me if you could answer some questions about M. Moreau.' His gaze was disconcerting as Lucy turned back to him. He produced a notebook from his pocket. 'You've been in the gentleman's company much of late.' There was an echo of distaste in the inspector's tone.

Now who had planted that nasty idea in his head? Was he insinuating something about her relationship with Moreau? A horrible thought struck her. Perhaps the gossips had been spreading rumours. They'd been in each other's company a lot, particularly at the Excelsior. Could that have been construed as more than a professional relationship? It was the kind of nasty innuendo Lucy could imagine Rosemary dropping into conversations over afternoon tea.

'I'm not sure what you're trying to imply, Inspector,' Lucy snapped. 'Our relationship was beyond reproach—'

'I wasn't suggesting there was anything inappropriate going

on, madame. But I should warn you there will be gossip. M. Moreau...'

Her throat tight, Lucy could only take a shuddering breath. 'Had a reputation. Yes, I'm aware of it,' she replied, utterly miserable.

Vauquelin frowned. 'It was well known he was ambitious. The kind of man who saunters through life using people to his advantage then discarding them when they cease to be useful. And when it came to women—'

The inspector appeared to be suggesting Moreau had used her, and it was an uncomfortable notion. At the back of her mind that niggling voice was wondering about it too. Lucy drew herself up.

'You underestimate me,' she replied. 'I can assure you I'm an excellent judge of character. M. Moreau impressed me with his professionalism, courtesy and willingness to share his vast knowledge. I'm not sure I like what you're implying, Inspector. Yes, he could be a charming devil, and I'm also aware of his reputation as a lady's man. But I'm *not* as green as you seem to think.' Lucy recalled the evening at the dig with Moreau. She could so easily have surrendered to it all: the stars, the exotic location and his charisma. However, the inspector hardly needed to be informed of that. 'M. Moreau did not take advantage of *me*. Our business arrangement suited us both very well. He sourced the funding he required, and in return he was willing to share his insights into the ancient world. Tell me, why did you dislike him?'

Vauquelin's eyebrow shot up. 'What on earth gave you that impression, madame? I only met him a handful of times. However, from what I have learnt of the man over the years, there was ruthless ambition hidden beneath his charm. There was something rotten in M. Moreau's world. Why else would he have met such an end? I'm sorry, this must be distressing for you, madame, but these are the questions I must ask.'

'I'll help you if I can, of course, but I can't make sense of this, Inspector. I find it difficult to imagine he engendered enough hate in anyone to have warranted such a ghastly end.'

Vauquelin regarded her, his expression sombre. 'And yet he did, without doubt, push someone so hard they carried out this vile act.' Vauquelin leaned towards her. 'Therefore, I must ask do you suspect anyone or have any idea why someone wanted to kill him?'

'I'm probably not the right person to ask; his assistant Mr Hopkins, or indeed M. Joubert, are better placed to help you. I've only known M. Moreau a short time.'

'Perhaps, madame, but I find a woman's insights are usually more profound. Ladies tend to notice a person's state of mind, whereas men take things at face value. Also, I'm only slightly familiar with M. Moreau's world. You are uniquely placed to help me. The main suspects are liable to be people you're acquainted with.'

It was a horrible idea, but likely. 'But am I not also a suspect?'

A smile flashed across the inspector's face. '*Mais non*. I do not consider you capable of such a crime, mainly because I'm aware of your history.'

'You've been checking up on me?' An uncomfortable sensation uncurled within her.

'Naturally, when you turned up at the museum on the morning of the burglary, I was curious about you, particularly when my men explained how you gained entry.' Lucy gave him an apologetic smile. 'So, I made some enquiries. My contacts in the British police informed me of your recent... adventures.'

'Is that so?' Lucy glared at him.

'I was impressed by your resourcefulness,' he said with something akin to respect in his gaze. 'You're a fascinating woman, madame, with an unusual past.' Lucy wasn't quite sure, but decided to take it as a compliment. 'Would you care to share your insights with me? Was M. Moreau worried about anything in particular?'

Despite her grief, a tiny flame ignited. He genuinely wanted her help. Moreau's murder was ghastly but could she possibly help avenge it?

'Well, there was a problem at the dig, and a nasty run-in with a fellow archaeologist,' she said slowly.

Vauquelin glanced down at his notebook. 'Ah, yes, M. Joubert mentioned this.'

'In fact... Oh dear, I wish I didn't have to tell you this because it makes someone appear guilty. Half of what I know is rumour.'

'This is a murder. I insist, Madame Lawrence.'

Lucy briefly outlined what transpired at Sakkâra and the trouble at dinner the previous evening.

'I do not know this M. Whitmore, but it sounds as though I ought to make his acquaintance immediately,' the inspector said.

Then Lucy gasped. 'Oh no! There is something else. I almost forgot.'

'What is it?'

'Moreau's life was threatened. Shortly after we arrived in Cairo, he received a note. I told him to go to the police about it, but he dismissed it.'

'Did he say who sent it? Was it from this M. Whitmore?'

'M. Moreau didn't say, but he indicated to me it was to do with the black market and his efforts to curb it.'

Vauquelin nodded. 'What did the note say? Did he tell you?'

'Better than that – I read it. It was typed and brief, telling him not to meddle, and the implied threat was something along the lines of the desert being a dangerous place. Moreau was upset on reading it, but quickly dismissed it. It didn't specifically mention the black market, but it was clear enough to him that that was the meaning.'

'He considered it an idle threat?'

'That, or he didn't wish to concern me,' Lucy said sadly, twisting her fingers in her lap. 'I should have insisted he went to the police.'

'This may be significant. Thank you, Madame Lawrence. As it happens, he did come to see me along with the director, but it was last spring. He had nothing to offer in the way of evidence and was unable to name any suspects in relation to the dig thefts. I suspected he was trying to impress M. Joubert.'

Lucy stared at him in disbelief. 'Moreau was an honourable man and cared deeply about what was going on. In his opinion, the police were not doing enough to curb the illegal trade in artefacts.'

Vauquelin raised a brow but made no comment. Lucy looked away, suddenly very angry indeed.

'Madame Lawrence, you must understand I can't act on rumour. Without evidence, there was nothing I could do, and both gentlemen appeared to accept this at the time. M. Moreau should have come to me with this note instead of ignoring it.'

Lucy knew he was right. Perhaps if Moreau had gone to the police, he wouldn't have met such an end.

The inspector pulled at the side of his moustache. 'Of course, there is another possibility. Perhaps M. Moreau's predilections led to his murder... a vengeful husband, for instance.'

Lucy shook her head. 'I don't think so, Inspector. The use of one of his finds as the murder weapon, the location of his death, all point to professional envy.'

'Or, it was planned to look that way so that I wouldn't pursue a line of enquiry of a more personal nature? You see, madame, I must consider all possibilities.'

SIXTEEN

The Excelsior Hotel, Later that Evening

Lucy paced the floor, her mind reeling. Desperately, she tried to be calm and logical, but it was all still too raw. Who killed Armand Moreau and why, were the questions dominating her chaotic thoughts.

Mary stood by, watching. 'Ma'am, you really should eat. I'm awful sorry about M. Moreau. Such a nice and kind gentleman, but you must keep your strength up.'

Lucy stopped and squeezed Mary's hand. 'No, impossible. I can't bear the thought of food. Is the news all over the hotel?'

'Indeed it is, ma'am. Place is buzzing with it, even down in the servants' quarters.'

Lucy shuddered. Moreau's murder would send Cairo society into a spin. 'Have you heard if anyone has been arrested?'

'Not that I know of. However, the police are still in the hotel. The servants are fed up with them, I can tell you. Sick of the sight of them, in fact.'

'Why so?'

'The jewellery theft, ma'am.'

'Oh, yes, I'd forgotten about that. So much has happened since.'

'Well, ma'am, as is often the case in these situations, the police are convinced it's one of the servants that's responsible. It's led to a lot of bad feeling below stairs.'

'I'm not surprised. It speaks of lazy police work to me,' Lucy said, then quickly dismissed the matter; it hardly had anything to do with Moreau's murder. She was finding it difficult to think clearly, and yet she must. She hadn't parted from Inspector Vauquelin on the best of terms. No doubt he would want to question her again if he was still in the hotel.

Mary tilted her head, her blue eyes full of poorly disguised hope. 'Ma'am, will we be heading home now?'

Lucy couldn't believe what she was hearing. 'Certainly not! My friend has been brutally murdered. I'll not run away.'

'It's hardly running away, ma'am. You might be in danger too. No one would expect you to stay. The police will solve it.'

Lucy glared back in reply. 'Well, if Vauquelin can't solve a simple burglary in the museum or catch a young jewel thief, I don't hold out much hope of his finding M. Moreau's killer. I'll not leave Cairo until this dreadful crime is solved and the murderer brought to justice.'

'I was afraid of that,' Mary muttered.

'I'll need your help, Mary.'

'Gawd, ma'am, you're never thinking of trying to solve this yourself?' The horror was only too evident in Mary's tone.

Lucy didn't trust herself to reply, and returned to her pacing.

Minutes later, there was a knock at the door. 'I just heard about M. Moreau,' Isabella cried, as she rushed past Mary. 'Is it true?'

'Yes, I'm sorry, Isabella. M. Moreau has been murdered.'

Lucy hugged her and led her friend over to the sofa. 'Thank you, Mary. That will be all for now.'

Isabella sat shaking her head. 'It is too dreadful.'

Lucy poured two glasses of sherry from the bottle on the sideboard. 'Something strong is in order,' she said, handing one glass to Isabella.

Isabella took a sip of the sherry, then placed the glass on the table. 'Poor Moreau!' She pulled out a lace handkerchief and dabbed her eyes with it. 'Why would anyone want to kill him?'

'I have no idea and, as yet, the police don't either. But I'll not rest until I find out who did this. I want justice for M. Moreau and his family.'

'You're not considering investigating this yourself?' Isabella asked, eyes wide, echoing Mary's sentiments minutes earlier.

'Why not?'

'You're a woman!'

Lucy frowned at her. 'What has that got to do with it? It doesn't mean I'm incapable of solving this. If anything, I'm perfectly placed as both his friend and patron. Even that inspector admitted as much and asked for my help.'

Isabella stared at her open-mouthed. 'But it might place you in danger if the murderer should become aware of it. Please don't get involved.'

'But I must. This must be solved quickly. Why, we still haven't figured out the museum theft.'

Isabella frowned at her. 'What has that to do with Armand Moreau's murder?'

'The stolen dagger was the murder weapon,' Lucy replied. 'Vauquelin must merge the two cases now.'

'How ghastly! That is shocking.' Isabella crossed herself. 'But... but might it not be a coincidence? The dagger came into the murderer's possession for some reason, and then he decided to use it in the murder?'

'Unlikely, Isabella. Although, if the crimes had been months apart, I might agree,' Lucy said.

Isabella sighed. 'How will this ever be solved? It is so complicated.'

Lucy swirled the sherry in her glass. 'Obviously, I had to tell Vauquelin about the dinner last night. He will want to question everyone who was there. You are warned, Isabella; he will come calling on you too.'

Isabella blinked rapidly and licked her lips before smiling. 'Thank you for the warning, but I have nothing to hide.'

'I'm certain you do not, my dear. Just be prepared. The inspector is very forthright and may put some uncomfortable questions to you. Personal questions.'

Isabella's fine brows drew together, and it was several moments before she answered. 'Why would he think this had anything to do with me? Moreau and I were acquaintances, but I had no interest in him romantically, Lucy. I never had the opportunity to work for him, which is a matter of regret. As for last night, if I recall, I spoke briefly to Joubert and Moreau after Whitmore broke up the party... then I retired for the night and slept right through to morning.'

'As did I. But will Vauquelin be satisfied with our answers? No one can vouch for us as we slept alone in our beds.'

'But your maid can vouch for you.'

'Only until I got into bed. She spent the night in the servants' quarters.'

Isabella shook her head. 'It wouldn't have been easy to over-power Armand Moreau. I'm not strong enough to do such a thing.'

'Nor I. Most likely it was a man... although... it might be a woman if she caught him off-guard. He wouldn't have expected a woman to be a threat.'

Isabella frowned, a look of distaste flashing across her features. 'But who?'

'No idea.' Lucy took a deep breath. 'I haven't seen Moreau single any lady out since we arrived in Egypt. Unless, it had to do with a liaison during a previous season. Do you recall seeing him with anyone last year?'

'On the few occasions I saw him, he was either alone or with Mr Hopkins,' Isabella answered.

'Of course, it could have been a secret affair few knew about. But I'm determined to find out. Moreau was not just in my employ – he was my friend.'

'The inspector will not take kindly to your interference, Lucy. The French do not like the English meddling in their business.'

Lucy huffed. 'Well, he will soon learn his mistake! Besides, he has already admitted I might be of help.'

The door opened, and Mary came in. Behind her, looking very dishevelled and travel-stained, was David Hopkins. Isabella stiffened, looking disconcerted.

Moments later, Hopkins stood before Lucy. 'Is it true? It is all over Cairo – Moreau is dead?'

'Yes, Mr Hopkins, I'm afraid it is so. But tell me, how on earth did you get here so quickly? I only sent a telegram to Sakkâra an hour ago.'

'To inform me about Moreau?' Hopkins asked, looking confused.

'Why, yes, of course,' Lucy said.

He shook his head. 'You were not aware Moreau had summoned me to Cairo?'

'No, he never said a word to me,' she answered.

Hopkins glanced at Isabella and nodded. 'Miss DeLuca, my apologies... my manners desert me.' Hopkins shook her hand. 'How are you? We haven't met since we both worked at Karnak a few years' ago.'

'Yes, how the time has flown, Mr Hopkins,' Isabella said.

'Do sit down, Mr Hopkins, and have a drink. I'm sure you

could do with one,' Lucy said. 'I'm not sure I understand why you're here.'

'Moreau insisted I come to Cairo to help bolster our claim to the site. I only arrived about an hour ago. I can't believe it. Poor Moreau! This is a disaster.'

'Yes, it is. My condolences, Mr Hopkins,' Lucy said.

Hopkins poured a glass of whisky and downed it in one, before sitting abruptly. 'Thank you. As you know, I worked for him for several seasons, both at Karnak and Sakkâra. He was a teacher as well as a friend. Now, what am I to do?'

'Everything will be in disarray for a while, but we must hope this is solved quickly. Until such time, we must be patient,' Lucy answered. 'Obviously, the site will remain closed.'

What looked like a flash of anger momentarily ignited in Hopkins' eyes. He puckered his lips. 'Of course.'

To Lucy's surprise, Isabella stood up and moved over to the window as if she didn't want to be a part of things. For several moments, she stared out the window, but then she suddenly piped up. 'Mr Hopkins, I'm concerned for Mrs Lawrence's safety, particularly if this murder has anything to do with the Sakkâra site.' Lucy scowled at her, but Isabella ignored her. 'Indeed, anyone involved in the dig might be at risk. Until such time as the police can find out why Moreau died, you too should be careful.'

Hopkins recoiled and looked to Lucy. She nodded. 'Miss DeLuca may be correct. Do take precautions. Also, it might not be a bad idea for you to contact Inspector Vauquelin of the Cairo police. He's investigating the murder, and I'm sure he would wish to speak to you. But do tell me, Mr Hopkins; you worked alongside M. Moreau for some time. Who would want to hurt him?'

'Only one man comes to mind, Mrs Lawrence. Whitmore!' Hopkins exclaimed. 'Damn his eyes!' he growled, looking down at the floor. With a start he looked up and began to apologise.

Lucy waved her hand and smiled at him. How could she reprimand him when he was obviously distressed?

'Is Whitmore capable of such an act?' she asked.

'Of course he is!' Hopkins answered. 'You witnessed the confrontation at the tomb?'

'I did, indeed.'

'Whitmore is deranged. He has always made trouble for Moreau. Ali, our site supervisor, told me the rumours are flying around Sakkâra. Whitmore was delighted he had a hold over Moreau. And I don't care what anyone says – he never intended to compromise. By getting Moreau out of the way, he could then easily convince M. Joubert to let him take over the dig. He has everything to gain from Moreau's demise. But I won't stand for it!'

Lucy was taken aback at the man's vehemence, but naturally he was upset. She glanced at Isabella who was watching Hopkins closely. 'I would agree that it doesn't look good for Whitmore as he has a strong motive,' Lucy replied. 'I assume you have been informed of the circumstances of Moreau's death?'

Hopkins gave a mirthless laugh. 'Oh yes, I heard he was killed out at Giza.'

'But does it not strike you as odd that Moreau would willingly meet Whitmore there or anywhere, knowing his volatility?'

Hopkins shrugged. 'Maybe Whitmore enticed him to a meeting promising to come to some agreement. If he thought Whitmore was sincere, he may have gone along for the sake of peace. Who knows?'

But in the middle of the night? Lucy doubted it, especially so soon after the flare-up at the dinner. That was a bit of a stretch.

'Look, Mr Hopkins, I'm determined to unravel this if I can. If you think of anything at all, please let me know.'

Hopkins shrugged. 'I don't see how I can help. I was not *here*. Of course, I'll tell the police about what happened at Sakkâra.'

'Good. However, for the sake of argument, let's assume it wasn't Whitmore. Is there anyone else who might want Moreau dead?'

'Moreau got on well with everyone,' Hopkins said. 'He was extremely popular among his peers... Well, except for the British.'

'No jealous husbands, here or in France?' Lucy asked, trying to steer him away from his pet theory.

Hopkins smirked. 'He was always discreet.'

'Were there many ladies in his life?'

'It was not something he discussed with me, Mrs Lawrence. Besides, there aren't many women out in the desert. It was none of *my* business. You're chasing the wrong hare there. This had to be about Sakkâra and jealousy. It had to be Whitmore.'

'Could there be some significance to his murder taking place in the Great Pyramid?' Isabella asked.

'That is the most bizarre thing, Miss DeLuca, I have no idea. Why would someone choose it? Moreau never worked in Giza to my knowledge.' Hopkins turned to Lucy. 'Whitmore has, of course. About three years' ago, if my memory serves me correctly. We were at Karnak that season and didn't encounter him at all.'

'But last year, both Whitmore and Moreau worked at Sakkâra?'

'Yes, but our plots were at either end of the site. There was little or no interaction.'

'But I've heard there was some kind of trouble,' Lucy said remembering Isabella's words.

'I was not aware of it,' Hopkins said. 'We had a fruitless season and found nothing. Whitmore made some finds which he boasted about, ad nauseam, to whoever would listen. They are now at the museum.' He sighed heavily. 'What will happen about Armand's funeral?'

'I received a telegram from M. Joubert about an hour ago. He has informed Moreau's family of his death and asked if they want his body returned to Nice, but his parents wish him to be buried here in Cairo. The funeral will be later this week, I understand.'

'I'm glad. It is only fitting he's laid to rest in the place he loved. I'll send a message to the men at the camp. Some will want to attend,' Hopkins said. 'I'll stay in Cairo until the funeral. If you should need my services, Mrs Lawrence, you will find me at the Montgomery.'

SEVENTEEN

The Next Morning

After a hurried breakfast, Lucy and Mary set off in a carriage to the Montgomery Hotel. Lucy hoped that by getting there before eight in the morning, they might beat the police to it. They were greeted at the door by a sleepy-looking porter, who was none too pleased to find two ladies greeting him cheerfully and quizzing him at that early hour.

The duty manager, M. Ibrahim, was summoned and took Lucy into his office. After a few minutes of polite conversation, during which Lucy explained who she was, she broached the tricky topic of seeing Moreau's room. 'Poor dear M. Moreau has died in such tragic circumstances and, as his friend and his employer, I'm anxious that his effects are retrieved and sent back to France to his distraught family. Certain items are of great sentimental value to his parents. I'm sure you understand.'

M. Ibrahim frowned, giving Lucy an anxious moment thinking he might refuse, but slowly he began to nod.

'This is a difficult time for all of us who knew M. Moreau,' Lucy said. 'Did you know him well?'

'Yes, madame. M. Moreau stayed here every year before setting up camp. He was a kindly man, tipped well. The hotel employees are much affected by the sad news.'

'When did you see M. Moreau last?'

The manager scratched his chin. 'I bid him good night as he left the hotel, the night before last. I didn't see him again.'

'He didn't return to the hotel that evening?'

'No. The porter locks the doors at midnight. The bed was untouched when the maid went in to clean the room yesterday morning.'

'Did M. Moreau have a key? Could he have let himself in unseen?' Lucy asked.

'No, madame. It is not our policy to hand out keys to the main door.'

'Thank you, M. Ibrahim.' Lucy threw a significant glance at the row of hooks on the wall from which dangled room keys.

Taking the hint, the manager plucked one, and handed it to her.

'Top floor, room twenty,' he informed her as they went back out into the hall.

As Lucy made for the stairs, an idea struck her. 'Oh, M. Ibrahim, has Mr Hopkins checked in yet? I understand he's in Cairo again.'

M. Ibrahim smiled. 'Yes, indeed, madame, he checked in late yesterday evening. Do you wish to see him?'

'No, no. I was concerned he might have been too late to obtain a room, that is all.'

M. Ibrahim nodded and returned to his office.

'But you knew he arrived yesterday, ma'am. Why did you ask that?' Mary enquired as they climbed the stairs.

'Just checking his alibi, Mary. Who's to say he didn't arrive a day earlier.'

'Blimey, so he's a suspect?'

'They all are, Mary; every last one of them.'

. . .

Moreau's room was a spartan space under the eaves with a single bed, a small table-cum-washstand and a wardrobe. At some point the walls had been painted white but now were grey with age. Lucy thought it the most depressing room she'd ever seen.

'Mary, keep watch at the door. We don't want Vauquelin or his men to find us snooping around.'

'Yes, ma'am.' Mary closed over the door leaving just a small gap.

'I'll make a start over here,' Lucy said making for the bed. She pulled back the threadbare blanket on the bed before poking the pillows. Nothing. Then she moved on to the bedside table, pulling out drawers and lifting the ewer out of its matching but chipped bowl.

'The fact M. Moreau didn't come back here that night suggests he either met his killer on his way here or had already arranged to meet him after the dinner.'

Mary looked back over her shoulder. 'Who's to say he didn't just fancy a walk, ma'am, to clear his head and had the misfortune to meet some blackguard?'

'Impossible to know,' Lucy answered, as she lifted Moreau's travelling bag down from the top of the wardrobe and placed it on the bed. 'If only we could find someone who saw him after he left the hotel.'

'I don't think that would be easy, ma'am. The city is alive with people, day and night. Them crowds never seem to go home to their beds like decent Christian souls would.'

Lucy glanced at Mary, slightly disturbed by her prejudice, but this wasn't the time or place to have that particular conversation. 'But Moreau was well known in the city, Mary.'

'Don't be fretting, ma'am. Sure the police will find the rogue who done him in, and then the whole sorry affair will be sorted out,' Mary replied.

Lucy didn't share Mary's optimism. Moreau's murder had not been mischance or a random attack. Whoever the killer was, they'd planned the killing meticulously. They'd no intention of being caught. Lucy opened the bag, but there was nothing inside. Then she spotted a small pocket on the inside. A leather-bound journal lay within. Pulling it out, Lucy sat down on the edge of the bed and flicked through the pages. Moreau's entries appeared to be a mixture of some kind of shorthand and hiero-glyphs. 'Bother!'

'What's wrong, ma'am?'

Lucy held up the journal. 'I can't read it. Oh! What's this?' A photograph had slipped out from between the pages and landed on the bed.

Mary rushed over and picked it up. 'Cor! She's a handsome lass, ain't she?' She tilted the photograph so Lucy could look at it.

'May I?' Lucy asked. Mary handed over the image. The lady was indeed beautiful, her hair dark, and her eyes holding an enigmatic expression.

'Have you seen this lady before?' Mary asked.

Lucy shook her head. 'No. I wonder who she is. She must have been important for Moreau to carry her picture with him everywhere.'

Mary's eyes welled up. 'A long-lost love. Poor thing. How can we let her know what's happened if we don't know who she is?'

Lucy nodded and checked the back of the photograph but there was no inscription. 'I'm sure she will read about it in the newspapers.'

Mary sniffed. 'That's fierce sad, ma'am, to learn of it that way.'

A floorboard creaked just outside. Lucy gripped Mary's arm

in alarm. Too late. The door swung open and in the doorframe stood Inspector Vauquelin. Much to Lucy's surprise, he burst out laughing.

'I should have known!' he exclaimed, coming into the room. 'The redoubtable Madame Lawrence.'

A Police Station in Cairo

Lucy and Mary sat across from Inspector Vauquelin. Not surprisingly, he had insisted they accompany him back to the station. With some amusement, Lucy thought about the number of police stations she'd visited in the last year: it was becoming something of a habit. But as she'd suspected, Vauquelin's office was in sharp contrast to Chief Inspector McQuillan's pokey and chaotic office at Vine Street, or the dirty storeroom used by Sergeant Wilson in Harrogate. Here, all was neatness and order. She waited patiently while the inspector read some messages handed to him as they entered the station.

'Now, Madame Lawrence, would you like to explain what you were doing in M. Moreau's room,' he asked, finally sitting back in his chair. 'It is a serious matter to obstruct the police in their investigations.'

Mary gave a little squeak, and Lucy shot her a quelling glance. 'I was concerned that M. Moreau's property might be removed. I wanted to ensure his family received his effects.'

Vauquelin pulled at his moustache. 'A very altruistic notion, madame. Would you care to try for something a little more realistic?'

Lucy smarted. 'Very well, I was looking for clues.'

'Aha! And there it is!' The inspector sounded delighted. 'You're meddling in my investigation.'

'I'm sorry, Inspector. I realise, of course, I should not have, but don't you see? I'm ideally placed to help you solve this.'

Vauquelin snorted. 'Your reputation for meddling is well

earned. But, madame, you're in Egypt, not London, and this is my jurisdiction. I do not tolerate amateurs. Give me one good reason why I should not charge you both. For all I know you're the murderers, and you were trying to remove clues.'

Mary grabbed Lucy's arm in fright. 'That's nonsense, and you know it,' snapped Lucy, peeling Mary's fingers from her arm. 'I want to find Moreau's murderer as much as you do.'

Vauquelin pursed his lips and gave her a long hard stare. Lucy knew this was going to be a battle of wills. Her respect for the inspector soared. If only she could persuade him to let her help in a more meaningful way than just answering questions.

'If you know something that would be of use to my investigation, madame, I strongly urge you to impart it now.'

Lucy sat forward, placing both hands on his desk. 'Inspector, you said it yourself. I know the likely suspects and might be able to give you insights into their possible motivation to do Moreau harm. Could we perhaps discuss the case, share our thoughts?'

'I'll happily listen to whatever you have to say on the matter, but there will not be any sharing of police information.'

Lucy knew it was as good as she was going to get. 'I have thought much about the murder, Inspector. What I can't fathom is what possessed Moreau to go out to Giza at night. Such a bizarre thing to do.'

'We could speculate on that for days, madame. Let us start with the facts. There was a public argument between M. Moreau and M. Whitmore at a dinner, hosted by you, the night before last. Immediately after, M. Whitmore and his sister departed abruptly and, at about eleven, M. Moreau left your hotel and was not seen again until his body turned up in the Great Pyramid. Sometime between his departure from your dinner party and the middle of the night, someone lured him to Giza, and he was murdered.'

'How are you so sure he was murdered there? Perhaps he

was killed somewhere else and his body brought into the tomb afterwards?'

'No, that is impossible. Firstly, he was murdered in situ for there was a pool of blood under the body in the sarcophagus. Most likely he was taken by surprise, hit over the head—there is a gash at the back of his skull—and manoeuvred into the sarcophagus, where the dagger finished him off. I would guess the murderer did the deed alone and in the King's Chamber. Secondly, if he had been killed outside the pyramid, or in Cairo, it would be extremely difficult to carry a body all the way inside the pyramid and along those narrow passages. M. Moreau was a large man.'

Lucy recalled the limited space and having to crawl into the King's Chamber. 'Yes, it would be quite a job to manoeuvre a dead body. If it happened in the chamber, a man working alone would manage all of that fairly easily.'

Vauquelin nodded. 'Yes, most likely it was a man. The murderer's choice of location is intriguing, I must admit. Does it hold significance for the killer or for Moreau? All of which points to the killer making a statement. Why there and not a back alley in Cairo? That would have been considered an unfortunate case of being in the wrong place at the wrong time. This killer has an ego and wants us to marvel at his daring.'

Lucy shivered. 'Yes, I was wondering about that. Using that dagger... They were mocking him... Which sadly points to Mr Whitmore and his professional jealousy.'

'Unless, of course, someone very devious wishes us to think so, and he was killed for an entirely different reason. They were aware of the public argument and took advantage of it to encourage me to look at Whitmore as the prime suspect. Perhaps they'd been waiting for just such an opportunity.'

Lucy groaned in dismay. 'That would point to an aggrieved husband or lover or someone in the hotel dining room that night, or worse still, one of my guests.'

Vauquelin grunted and placed a file on the desk between them. With a sigh, he opened it. 'Then, madame, let's consider all the actors in our little drama.' His pen hovered over the page. 'You will agree anyone at your dinner party that night might be a suspect?'

'Yes, but you must not forget the American, Mr Hopkins,' she said.

The inspector quirked a brow. 'I have the distinct impression you do not like him. But dislike is not enough; there must be motive and opportunity as well.'

'You wanted a woman's perspective,' Lucy said, miffed. 'I think it is suspicious that he turned up in Cairo. We only have his word for it that Moreau summoned him.'

'In time it will be possible to verify the summons. Now let us apply judgement. We shall start with a list of suspects, then delve down into motive and opportunity,' he said. 'Would you like to start?'

'Thank you. The most obvious is Mr Whitmore.' Vauquelin looked across at Lucy expectantly, so she continued. 'His motive was professional jealousy – some kind of argument or situation which may have evolved over time, culminating in the problem at Sakkâra. Also, there are rumours of an argument last season over a woman, but I do not know who she is. I'm not sure about opportunity yet. But Whitmore displayed a deep-seated resentment on more than one occasion. Perhaps he lay in wait for Moreau to leave the hotel and followed him.'

'I agree with your analysis; M. Whitmore's behaviour warrants investigation.'

'I hope he doesn't abscond, Inspector.'

'Madame, I can assure you he will not. I have men at the hotel keeping watch on all the suspects. However, we must bear in mind the fact that the Whitmores are likely to give each other alibis, and it will be virtually impossible to disprove them, unless someone saw him leave the hotel or saw him out at Giza. My men continue to look for such a witness.'

'It is unlikely he was seen at Giza. I'm sure the site is deserted after dark,' Lucy said.

'Yes, it poses a difficulty,' he replied. 'Anyone out there at night can only be up to mischief, and therefore will remain silent.'

'I almost feel sorry for him. Mr Whitmore hasn't helped matters with his boorish behaviour,' Lucy said. 'In his milieu, Whitmore is an interesting and informative man, but in company he's little better than surly; though to be fair, that is not a crime. Miss DeLuca told me she was reluctant to work for him due to his reputation, but the money he offered her over-rode her misgivings.'

'He offered above the going rate?' Vauquelin asked, frowning. 'I thought he was short of funds like all these fellows.'

'So did I. He indicated to me he would welcome funding, but that could have been a deliberate attempt to hide the real state of his affairs. Maybe he's involved in the black market?' Lucy leaned forward. 'Perhaps he was the one who sent that threat to Moreau. If Moreau succeeded in curbing the trade, and Whitmore would suffer as a result, it gives him yet another motive.'

Vauquelin made a note on his page. 'That is an excellent point.'

Lucy was delighted: the inspector was taking her seriously. 'Is there anything to link Whitmore, or indeed any other suspect, to the burglary? The crimes must be connected. The dagger has to be significant.'

A mirthless laugh was the response. 'Madame, that particular robbery and every other theft from the dig sites are a constant drain on my manpower. Not even our usual contacts in Cairo's black market have heard so much as a whisper about the museum robbery.'

'But the dagger didn't leave Egypt,' Lucy pointed out. 'The other stolen items may turn up too.'

'As long as they don't turn up on another body!' Vauquelin exclaimed. 'However, getting back to our suspect; I'll have someone check Mr Whitmore's finances.'

'Excellent. But two thoughts give me pause. Firstly, half of Cairo society witnessed Whitmore's outburst at dinner that night. Why would anyone, and in particular M. Moreau, willingly meet Whitmore, late at night out at Giza, knowing Whitmore's state of mind? It seems unlikely when M. Moreau was aware of how volatile Whitmore is. Secondly, if you were planning to murder someone, you would avoid a public confrontation beforehand, surely?'

'Both good points. However, the fact is Moreau travelled to Giza, either because someone asked him or he received a message that brought him there. Did he give any indication he wasn't going back to his hotel?'

Lucy shook her head. 'Perhaps he just happened to meet his murderer on his way back to the Montgomery. His mood at the meal was jovial and mischievous. He didn't appear troubled to me. Obviously, his mood changed after the row at the table, but he refused to discuss it and left.'

'Either way, the fact he went willingly to Giza suggests he was not suspicious, and it was someone he knew reasonably well, not a stranger. As to your second point, perhaps the killer did not plan it. Perhaps the murder was an impulse borne out of rage.'

'Which points back to Whitmore,' Lucy said. 'But why would Whitmore entice him to Giza specifically?'

'Perhaps the location was important to them both. M. Joubert will tell us if they both worked at Giza at some point—assuming Whitmore is the guilty one, of course.'

'Whitmore definitely did work there,' Lucy said. 'Giza

would suit him perfectly. He knows the tunnels in the Great Pyramid better than most.'

'But let's not forget – there is a great difference between words spoken in anger and plunging a dagger into a man's heart.'

'Yes, you're right, and I do not wish to see any man hang based on speculation.'

'Who is next on your list, madame?'

'He has a weak motive, but we must include Moreau's assistant, Mr Hopkins.'

The inspector's lips twitched. 'Agreed. His presence in Cairo may be a coincidence, but it makes me suspicious. I'd like to find out exactly when he arrived here. He only checked in to the Montgomery last night.'

'Yes, but he may have stayed somewhere else since the night the deed was done,' Lucy reasoned. 'He's used to roughing it out in the desert. Or he might have friends in Cairo and stayed with them.'

'You may be right, but the site supervisor at Sakkâra should be able to confirm when he left, and the station staff at Bedrashên should remember him. There aren't many Americans here.'

'And Hopkins would be aware of that and would hardly lie about it.' She watched as the inspector wrote something on the page. 'He may have had opportunity, but I fail to see what his motive might be.'

'Something may come to light in due course. So, let's consider the others of your party,' Vauquelin said. 'At the very least, they must be questioned.'

'I doubt either M. Joubert, Miss DeLuca or Miss Whitmore wanted to kill Moreau. Joubert is one of Moreau's dearest friends, and neither lady would be strong enough to have overpowered Moreau. Again, I fail to see a motive.'

'We can't assume anything. We must use logic, not emotion. The fact is everyone at dinner witnessed the argument and may have decided to use it to their advantage. Goodness knows what troubles were bubbling away beneath the surface over past seasons. M. Joubert has indicated there were problems in relation to Whitmore's digs.' Vauquelin leaned back in his chair. 'Sometimes, it is the smallest of things that fester over time and result in this kind of tragedy. The answer often lies in the tiniest of details. Also, we must consider why Moreau was killed in the Great Pyramid, and why was that particular dagger stolen and used?'

'Joubert told me the dagger was one of Moreau's first significant finds, which strongly suggests the murderer is a fellow archaeologist,' Lucy said.

'Or very well informed,' the inspector replied. His words deflated her.

'Of course, there is another possibility, Inspector. Perhaps Moreau was too charming for his own good. He flirted with any woman who came into his sphere. I'll admit I was on the receiving end of his attention, but I'm a widow so it does not matter, except to the gossips. But husbands tend to find other men flirting with their wives unsettling, to say the least. Moreau may have unintentionally angered someone's husband or lover.'

'As to Moreau's intent, I'm not sure, but it would be a dangerous game to play,' the inspector commented.

'Bear with me. What if M. Moreau thought he was meeting a lover at Giza? Perhaps the killer overheard the arrangement being made, although it is a strange place to meet, I must admit. Could Moreau have been tricked into going there? Or, perhaps he or someone he knew had been threatened in some way if he didn't turn up?'

Vauquelin held up his hands. 'Or his lover was his killer? But who might she be, madame, this mysterious woman?'

'I can't tell you. He never singled anyone out in my presence. He flirted with every lady, young or old.'

'But if he were having an affair, it would be hardly something he would flaunt in public or discuss with you,' Vauquelin said. 'However, it's a possibility which can't be ignored.'

'Goodness! So many possible motives.'

'Time will tell, but it does complicate matters.' Vauquelin glanced at her. 'You aren't short of theories, but I think you are... what's the expression? Grasping the sticks?'

'Clutching at straws!'

'Ah yes,' he answered, his mouth twitching.

'But seriously, Inspector, if all of it was done in the heat of anger, anything is possible. Whatever the answer, one thing is for sure – Whitmore's life now hinges on whether he can establish an alibi or not.'

'Then I'll waste no time but go to your hotel and interview this M. Whitmore straight away,' Vauquelin said, reaching for his hat. 'Would you care for a lift?'

'Thank you, Inspector,' Lucy replied meekly.

He paused at the door. 'And, of course, madame, you will leave the investigation to the police. I'm not to find you meddling again.'

Mary nodded vigorously. Lucy smiled as best she could. As they followed Vauquelin out of the station Lucy realised she'd given away a wealth of information to the canny inspector, but had learnt very little in return.

EIGHTEEN

Firmly excluded by a brusque Vauquelin, Lucy retired to her suite in frustration while he questioned his suspects. But Mary, able to move freely through the hotel without arousing comment, kept Lucy informed of his progress. The inspector interviewed Isabella first but, not surprisingly, he spent the most time with the Whitmores. How Lucy would have loved to have been a fly on that wall!

When Mary rushed in and informed her the policeman was about to leave, Lucy raced down to the hotel reception area to intercept him. As she crossed the hallway, Vauquelin was heading for the front door.

Her sense of devilment rose to the surface, and she called out to him. 'Inspector?'

Vauquelin retraced his steps. 'Madame,' he sighed, his eyes wary.

'How did you fare? Have you learnt anything useful from your interviews?'

Amusement flickered briefly in the inspector's eyes. 'A great deal.'

'Anything you'd care to share? I'd be happy to discuss it with you – help you make sense of it.'

His gaze hardened. 'Do not test me, Madame Lawrence. Leave this to us. I'll bid you good day.' The inspector turned on his heel and left.

Hateful man! Well, he can't stop me chatting to the hotel guests, Lucy thought with a shake of her head. *There's more than one way to skin a cat.* Through the doorway of the small salon, she could see afternoon tea was being served. If she ingratiated herself with the other guests, she might glean some useful information about Moreau. As she entered the salon, she spotted Isabella and Rosemary Whitmore sitting apart from everyone else. They were in deep conversation. No doubt they were comparing notes after their respective interviews with Vauquelin. Lucy was pleased. She knew Rosemary wouldn't welcome her intrusion into their tête-à-tête, so she approached the Hamiltons at a far table. Lucy would bide her time and find out all from Isabella in due course.

'My dear Mrs Lawrence, I'm so glad to see you,' Mrs Hamilton greeted her, patting the place beside her on the sofa. 'Do join us.'

'Thank you,' Lucy replied, but took a seat with an unobstructed view of the other two ladies on the far side of the room. 'I was sorry to hear about the theft of your jewellery, Mrs Hamilton.'

'Yes, it is very distressing,' the lady answered, her fingers fidgeting at her neck. 'It was a wedding anniversary gift and of great sentimental value. But that pales into insignificance with what has happened to poor Mr Moreau. Such a dreadful crime. Robert and I were so shocked to hear about it.' Mrs Hamilton gave her a considered glance. 'How are you coping?'

'I'm trying to keep busy. It is awful, but the police are keen to solve it,' Lucy replied.

'Shocking business,' rumbled Mr Hamilton. 'Never heard the like in all my days.'

'I hope they'll make an arrest soon,' Lucy said.

'Why, one would hope so; they have been here these last two days. Most uncomfortable it is to have the police lurking around every corner.' Again, an arch glance. 'Did they interview you, my dear? Of course, you and poor Mr Moreau were *so* close.'

'Naturally, I'm doing all I can to help the police,' Lucy ground out, 'as M. Moreau's patron.'

The Hamiltons exchanged a look, and Lucy had to fight the urge to say something pithy. But that would achieve nothing. She stole a quick glance across the room. Rosemary was gesticulating at Isabella and shaking her head. Isabella appeared to be trying to placate her. So frustrating not to know what they were saying.

With a bland smile, Lucy turned back to her companions. 'You have been coming here to the Excelsior for years. Did you know M. Moreau well?'

Mrs Hamilton poured out some tea and handed Lucy a cup. 'Only by reputation. We were never formally introduced, but we knew him by sight, of course. All the archaeological people swan in and out of here. It's like an unofficial headquarters.'

'Was M. Moreau here with his assistant or was he visiting friends?'

'Well, I don't quite recall. Do you, dear?' Mrs Hamilton asked her spouse.

He shook his head. 'Any particular reason you ask, Mrs Lawrence?'

This was tricky. Lucy wanted to know if they'd seen him with one lady in particular in past seasons. The identity of the lady in the photograph in Moreau's bag was puzzling her. The woman had to be special to Moreau: why else would he have kept her picture with him at all times? Unfortunately, the picture was now in the inspector's possession. If only she had been quick enough to hide it when he had burst into the room, she could have shown it around the hotel now to see if anyone recognised the woman.

Lucy leaned forward and lowered her voice. 'As M. Moreau's patron, I wish to ensure that everyone who knew him is made aware of his unfortunate passing. The funeral will take place here in Cairo in a few days. As you know, I wasn't acquainted with M. Moreau for long, and I hoped you might be able to help me? I would hate for any *special* friends of his to be excluded.' Even as she said it, Lucy knew this sounded weak.

But Mrs Hamilton leaned over. 'Ah, my dear, how sweet of you.' She nodded slowly. 'I think I know what you mean by *special*. To be honest, I never saw any of his *lady friends*' – 'lady friends' was mouthed – 'but there were always rumours.' Robert Hamilton looked uncomfortable and sipped his tea, frowning at his wife above the rim of his cup. Mrs Hamilton continued. 'I wouldn't worry, dear Mrs Lawrence. The newspapers have been full of nothing but the terrible news. Anyone who matters in Egypt will know of it by now.'

Lucy had miscalculated. Either the Hamiltons hadn't noticed anything or Moreau had been careful to keep his paramour secret. The mystery lady would have to remain anonymous for now. Not even Hopkins knew her identity, if he was to be believed. Lucy had to let the conversation drift off onto other topics. However, Mrs Hamilton soon returned to the subject of her necklace.

'Can you believe it was stolen from my room the other evening while we were at dinner? So daring of the thief. Unfortunately, I didn't discover it was missing until the next morning.'

'That's unfortunate. I assume the police were called.'

'Yes, they arrived almost straight away, but it turns out that several robberies have been reported in the local hotels,' Mrs Hamilton said with a troubled frown. Lucy was on the point of telling them about her encounter but decided against it. It might only upset Mrs Hamilton even more.

'It's just outrageous; I told the manager here, it wasn't on, that kind of thing,' rumbled Mr Hamilton. 'Police seem to be useless. Not like back in the States.'

Lucy made sympathetic noises, but any hotel full of rich clientele was bound to be a target for professional thieves. When Mrs Hamilton had run out of chatter about the necklace, she turned to other gossip. Lucy did her best to remain attentive, but her antennae were twitching. She was keenly aware of Rosemary and Isabella still in deep conversation. What did they have to discuss for so long?

At last Rosemary Whitmore walked past, eyes downcast and her shoulders hunched. Lucy could, at last, take her leave of the Hamiltons.

Isabella greeted her with a knowing smile. 'You look rattled, my dear. Has Mrs Hamilton tired you out with her chatter? No doubt you heard all about the robbery. The woman talks of nothing else.'

Lucy sat down with a sigh. 'She's very upset about it.'

'Hamilton is so rich he can afford to go out and buy her another one, and the necklace was bound to have been insured. I don't know what all the fuss is about.'

Lucy was slightly taken aback at Isabella's insensitive remark. 'I would imagine it had sentimental value.'

'Then she should have taken better care of it. What have you been up to today? Did you start your investigation yet?'

Lucy briefly outlined what she had found in Moreau's room that morning and what she'd been trying to achieve by talking to the Hamiltons. 'Of course, the inspector confiscated the photograph, so I can't even show it to you. You might have recognised her.'

'But have you not considered, Lucy? The lady might be

back in France and not someone he was involved with here in
Egypt.'

'Oh Lord, I hadn't thought of that. Of course, she could be
from Nice.'

'Moreau's private affairs can't be your concern, Lucy. You
must leave it to the police.'

Lucy shrugged. There was little point in arguing about her
intentions: Isabella didn't understand. 'Did Vauquelin interrogate you?'

Isabella smiled. 'Yes, he's intimidating, is he not? Such a
stern gaze. Even if you were innocent, you would begin to doubt
yourself.'

'What did he ask you?'

'Mostly about the dinner party and what my impressions of
the people at the table were. He wanted to know what
happened directly afterwards, and if I had any romantic
connection to Moreau. Much as he asked you, I suspect.'

'Yes. We had a long chat this morning. Rosemary appeared
to be very agitated just now. How did the Whitmores fare with
Vauquelin?'

Isabella shook her head. 'I think Mr Whitmore is in serious
trouble.'

'Is that so? What did Rosemary tell you?'

'Ah, Lucy, can you not leave it be?'

'No! I can't. Please Isabella. You know Rosemary will not talk
to me about it.' Lucy reached across and gripped her friend's hand.

Isabella sighed. 'Very well, if you insist. The inspector questioned Whitmore at length about the incident at the tomb at
Sakkâra. Reginald told him he had been provoked by Moreau's
language and manner, and all attempts at civilised conversation
about the tomb fell on deaf ears. Moreau just laughed at him.'

Lucy recalled Moreau's mood that day. 'I didn't hear any of
their exchange but Moreau did act strangely, almost as if he

were goading Whitmore. By the time I tried to intervene, Whitmore was like a smouldering fuse. No doubt that was Moreau's intention; it's as if he wanted to bring about the collapse of relations.' Lucy was suddenly struck by an idea. 'If Moreau was certain that Joubert would find in his favour regarding the tomb, it was the perfect opportunity to humiliate Whitmore.'

'And that was likely, Lucy. What better way to destroy your rival than to rub his nose in your ability to manipulate the authorities? That would have been a huge blow to Whitmore and damage his career in the eyes of any possible patrons and the EAS.'

Lucy shook her head. 'Inspector Vauquelin suggested Moreau was ruthless, and I wouldn't believe him.'

'You only knew him a short time,' Isabella said. 'As I warned you at the beginning, Lucy, you stepped into the middle of a war.'

'So it would appear! And then at my dinner, Moreau behaved in exactly the same way. Provoking Whitmore yet again.'

'I think you are correct. Unfortunately for Moreau, he pushed too far, and Whitmore snapped.'

'Perhaps,' Lucy replied.

'The inspector asked the Whitmores about your dinner party. Rosemary told me Reginald became very agitated by Vauquelin's questions. Well, he would, wouldn't he, Lucy? He knows he must be the police's chief suspect. Poor Rosemary. She's adamant he's innocent.'

'But he has the strongest motive, even she must see that,' Lucy replied. 'She would defend him no matter what, I suppose. What happened after they left my dinner party? Did they go to their suite?'

'Yes, they did. Rosemary said Reginald had hoped your efforts to broker a resolution would be successful, but he realised early on in the evening that his hope was in vain. When they returned to their suite, he ranted that the EAS, by its nature, was pro-French and that Joubert would pretend to deliberate. But it would be all for show and, in due course, he would decide in Moreau's favour. Rosemary tried to calm him down, but he became ill. Rosemary informed me he's prone to migraines when he's upset. I think that is why he wears those awful glasses. Anyway, the valet administered some laudanum, and Reginald went to bed.'

'So, he has an alibi,' Lucy said. 'He hardly left the suite if he had taken something like that.'

'Miss Whitmore said she would have heard him leave as she's a light sleeper,' Isabella added. 'In fact, Rosemary said they'd difficulty wakening him the next morning.'

'And it will be easy to verify their alibis. I'm sure Vauquelin will question the servants.'

'They don't travel with their own servants but use the ones supplied by the hotel.'

Lucy frowned. 'And the servants will have no particular loyalty to the Whitmores – they'll tell the truth.'

'You almost sound disappointed, Lucy.'

'I just don't see who else could have done it, but part of me doesn't want it to be Whitmore,' Lucy replied. 'I know, I know, but I feel sorry for him. Moreau manipulated him so cunningly. This is so frustrating.'

'But there is one more thing.' Isabella's eyes were alight.

'Tell me!'

'The inspector confronted Reginald with a piece of evidence.'

'No! What was it?' Lucy asked, her heart pounding.

'A pair of grey-tinted spectacles, which were found in the King's Chamber close to the body.'

. . .

After dinner, Lucy retired to her suite, exhausted. It had been an interesting and yet frustrating day. She needed solitude in which to gather her thoughts. But she knew she was no nearer to discovering who the murderer was. Going through the possible suspects, Whitmore still stood out as the most likely. He had motives galore; the problem was he also had an alibi. But then there was the inspector's coup de grâce. How sneaky of Vauquelin not to tell her and to produce that vital piece of evidence. How astonished Reginald must have been. From what Isabella had told her, Whitmore had given the inspector a weak enough explanation. He claimed he had several pairs as he was constantly putting them down and losing them.

But there was something not quite right about those glasses being found at the scene of the murder; it was far too convenient. There was always the possibility that the killer had taken a pair of Whitmore's glasses and planted them at the scene to incriminate him. But Lucy also had to consider how damning it was when combined with all the other factors. Perhaps Whitmore had been careless. The glasses had come off during the struggle with Moreau, and he had forgotten to retrieve them before leaving the King's Chamber. But no! The day they explored the tomb, Whitmore had removed the glasses; he only used them in strong sunlight or brightly lit rooms. Unless, they were in his pocket and fell out...

Lucy tried to remember the night of the dinner. She was fairly certain Whitmore had been wearing his glasses early in the evening. But whether they were still on him when he left the dining room, she couldn't recall. So, anyone at the table could have picked them up and slipped them into a pocket to use later. Bother! She was going around in circles. And, of course, there was that damned alibi.

Mary came in from the bedroom. 'Are you ready to retire now, ma'am?'

'Yes, Mary, I think I will. We have work to do tomorrow.'

'But, ma'am, the inspector warned – '

'What he doesn't know, won't hurt him, Mary. First thing, I wish to visit poor M. Joubert, and in the afternoon the carpet bazaar. I want to pay a visit to my friend with the mummy's hand.'

Mary gave a shiver. 'If you're sure,' she replied in a failing voice.

'Don't worry; we'll take Rafiq along too.'

Mary smiled. 'That's a relief, ma'am.' Lucy headed for the bedroom and sat down at the dressing table while Mary unpinned her hair. As Mary brushed it out, she remarked, 'Well, ma'am, I thought you might be interested in something I learnt down in the servants' quarters.'

Lucy immediately straightened up. Mary had *that* look in her eye. 'Do tell!'

'The valet—the one those Whitmores used—he's only gone off!'

'Has he indeed! And where has he gone?'

'Nice cushy number, ma'am, looking after some gentlemen as has gone on a Nile cruise,' Mary replied with a triumphant grin.

'Thank you, Mary, that is useful information. It will be impossible to verify Mr Whitmore's alibi now.' Lucy briefly outlined to Mary what it was. 'I'd like to find out more about the circumstances, Mary. Do you think you could discover when the valet was chosen for this job? It may just be an unhappy coincidence.'

'Nothin' easier, ma'am. Leave it to me. Sure I can do a bit of sleuthing when I'm fetching your breakfast in the morning.'

'In particular, we need to know if Reginald was given laudanum and where it came from. And if you should overhear any other interesting gossip...'

''Nuff said, ma'am.'

· · ·

Early the next morning, Mary woke Lucy bearing her morning tea and more news.

'I found out who the maid was that night. She confirmed they called for her services about eleven. There was an almighty row going on when she answered the summons. Miss Whitmore was tryin' fierce hard to get Mr Whitmore to calm down. The maid said Mr Whitmore was ill. Ashen, she said he was, complaining of a terrible headache and ranting and raving.'

'About?'

'The maid said she didn't know what it was about, and chose not to listen, stupid girl,' Mary replied with disgust.

'You would never be so negligent, Mary. Any luck with the laudanum?'

'The maid didn't see the valet administer it, but she did see an open medicine case on the table, through the doorway.'

Lucy pondered this. 'Most likely it was their own supply. It could have been diluted, though. I hope the inspector has it tested.'

'But who's to say it would be the same bottle, ma'am; sure, they might have switched it with a proper one by now,' Mary said.

'True. Do you know what time these hotel servants left the Whitmores?'

'Shortly after both of them retired to their own bedrooms. She reckoned about eleven thirty.'

'So, as the servants sleep in their own quarters, they can't confirm the alibis.'

'Correct, ma'am, except for the laudanum and whether it was administered or not.'

'Yes, that is vital, and only the valet can confirm it. Though, if it had been tampered with, prior to the valet entering the room... Oh dear, this doesn't auger well for Mr Whitmore.'

'They are an odd pair to be sure, ma'am, them Whitmores. Fierce close for just a brother and sister, if you ask me,' Mary said darkly. 'I wouldn't put it past them to do the vile deed. However, if they'd snuck out during the night to do it, would the front door porter not have seen them?'

Much as she hated to admit it, Lucy had to agree, unless of course there was easy access to a rear door, just perfect for those with murder on their mind. Mary could check that out easily enough.

NINETEEN

The Egyptian Museum, Boulaq

The sunlight streaming in the window hit Joubert's face side-on, emphasising his pallor. Lucy felt sorry for him for Moreau's murder had affected him deeply. Joubert was surprised by her presence but appeared to accept it was a visit of condolence. As Lucy commiserated, Joubert laced his fingers on the desk before him and stared down, his mouth tight. But once the niceties were over, Lucy plunged in.

'I can't help but relive my dinner party, M. Joubert. It must have been the trigger for what transpired later. Did I miss something that might have prevented M. Moreau's death? What do you think?'

Joubert took a deep breath and slowly looked up as if coming out of a daydream. 'Of course, it was a disaster with neither man acting well, but who could have foreseen what would happen later.' Joubert shook his head. 'Your idea to bring the men together in a social setting was excellent and might have worked but, alas, the trouble ran too deep between Moreau and Whitmore. I, too, wish I'd not underestimated the seriousness of the situation. I might have persuaded them to see sense.'

'And I wish someone had warned me they hated each other,' Lucy said.

'I assumed it was common knowledge. It was one of the reasons I was taking my time making a decision on Sakkâra. Moreau and Whitmore needed time to work out their difficulties on their own, and I hoped my procrastination would force them to do just that. The finding of that tomb put me in an awkward position, for I knew whatever decision I would make, one of them would be very angry indeed. And that would have made matters worse, Madame Lawrence. Compromise between the men was my hope. Of course, now I realise it was a forlorn one.'

'It is unfortunate, but you couldn't have known. What I don't understand is M. Moreau's behaviour that evening at dinner,' Lucy remarked. 'I wonder why he was deliberately baiting Mr Whitmore.'

M. Joubert shrugged. 'Armand was in one of his tiresome moods. No doubt he was annoyed with me for delaying the decision; he couldn't take it out on me, so he took it out on his competitor instead. There was a cruel streak in Moreau sometimes. He would bait people purely for the fun of it. It was his way.'

'You had seen him act like that before?'

'Yes, many times. Mischief was never far from the surface with him.'

'Did he always view Mr Whitmore as a rival?' she asked.

'Not at first, for Moreau was far more experienced, but last year Whitmore made some interesting finds. Moreau was getting older; maybe he was worried young Whitmore would eclipse him. You must remember, Madame Lawrence, this profession is fraught with difficulties. Funding is the main one, and reputation is the key to it. As a result, the competition can be fierce.' Joubert sighed. 'Two ambitious men chasing the same dream. Unfortunately, the recent problem at Sakkâra had brought their enmity to a new level.'

'Could there have been another reason apart from the trouble at Sakkâra? I heard rumours of an argument last season.'

Joubert frowned over this. 'With M. Whitmore? If there was, I did not hear of it but it wouldn't surprise me.'

'Do you think Mr Whitmore is guilty?' she asked.

'We must leave such matters to Vauquelin, but I assume he's the chief suspect. A volatile young man, and I fear Moreau's teasing went too far.'

'I don't think the inspector has ruled anyone out at this stage.'

'Has he spoken to you about it?' Joubert asked, frowning heavily at her.

'No, but no arrest has been made as yet. As far as I know, his enquiries are continuing. Everyone who was at the dinner has been questioned. I assume he has visited you too?'

'Yes, we spoke yesterday evening,' Joubert replied. 'You know, I attempted to talk some sense into Moreau after Whitmore left the dining room, but to no avail. He was probably regretting his behaviour but was too proud to apologise to the company. I made it clear to him what I thought of his conduct, but that it was in everyone's interest that the difficulty at Sakkâra be resolved as quickly as possible. He gave me to understand he found this acceptable. We parted on reasonable terms. Then I too sought the comfort of my bed.'

'Do you live out here at Boulaq, M. Joubert?'

'No, no. I rent a house about ten minutes' walk from your hotel.'

'On your way home did you see M. Moreau?' she asked.

'*Mais non*. His hotel is in the opposite direction.'

'And what time did you reach your home?' Lucy asked.

'Madame, why do you ask all these questions of me? You are not the police. It is hardly appropriate.' Joubert glared at her.

Lucy had to rein in; she didn't want to alienate Joubert by being too enthusiastic, especially as he was so prejudiced. 'I'm merely trying to piece together what happened that evening. For my own peace of mind, monsieur, nothing more.'

Joubert grunted but eyed her suspiciously. 'Well, if you must know, I arrived home about eleven thirty. My servant, Louis, can confirm this.'

'And you didn't leave your home again that night?'

Joubert gave her a bewildered look. 'Why would I? No, I slept soundly and rose at my usual time the next morning.'

'Do *you* think there is any significance to the location of the murder? I can't help but feel there is.'

Joubert rubbed his chin. 'I can only assume it held importance for the murderer in some way. Moreau never worked there. Of course, he had visited it on many occasions. Few who visit Egypt fail to.'

'But the murderer must have been very familiar with the site.'

'*Mais oui.* I should think so, Madame Lawrence, and only one man comes to mind – Reginald Whitmore.'

Lucy climbed back into the hired carriage waiting outside the museum. Mary greeted her eagerly. 'How did it go, ma'am? Did the gentleman have anything useful to say?'

'M. Joubert has an alibi of sorts, but I must say, Mary, he seems an unlikely murderer to me. They were friends.'

Mary's brows drew together. 'Could they have argued over something in the past? Were they rivals at any point?'

'That's interesting, Mary. I hadn't considered that. But they always appeared to me to be on the best of terms. Both spoke highly of each other. No, I just don't see it. Anyway, M. Joubert says his servant can verify what he says.'

'But ma'am, it is in a servant's interest to lie for their master or mistress.'

'I suppose you might be right. It is a difficult position for a servant to be in. Would you lie for me?'

Mary smirked. 'That would depend on what you had been up to, ma'am.'

'Hmm. Well, getting back to M. Joubert. He has no obvious motive, and I would also doubt he would have the strength to overpower a man of Moreau's build. I wonder if there could be another motive besides the ones we have been considering. What if the motive for the murder—remember the death threat Moreau received—was to silence him because he was trying to stop the black market trade in antiquities? Those involved in the black market would have a lot to lose if he had succeeded.'

'But then any archaeologist in Egypt could be the murderer.'

'I know! But we can't ignore the possibility,' Lucy answered.

'Then, I take it, ma'am, we will be visiting the bazaar this afternoon?'

'Yes, Mary, most definitely. As soon as we get back to the hotel, send a message to Rafiq. I'd be happier going in there with him by my side.'

Mary sniffed. 'I agree, ma'am. Can't be too careful.'

'However, before we return to the hotel, I think we might pay a call to that poor unfortunate museum porter in the hospital. If he has regained consciousness, he might have something interesting to tell me.'

The European Hospital, Cairo

Before leaving the museum, Lucy had enquired of M. Japp, Joubert's assistant, which hospital the unfortunate porter was in. Japp looked surprised at her request but told her the hospital was further down the riverbank and gave her directions. On arrival, it took some time to find the ward Tarek was in, and Lucy wasn't too surprised to see a policeman sitting outside. Vauquelin was far too thorough for Lucy's liking.

She approached the door, but the officer gave her a warning look. Lucy contented herself by looking in the window into the ward. But the room was crowded, and as Lucy didn't know what Tarek looked like, it was futile, anyway. Waylaying a passing nurse, she requested a meeting with the ward sister.

After a frustrating half an hour wait, one of the Sisters of Mercy nursing staff arrived. Luckily, the nun's English was sufficient for Lucy to ask her about Tarek.

'You are good lady to visit him,' Sister Angelina said. 'But he sleeps, madame, all day. He is not good. No one see him but wife.'

'And what is his condition? Does the doctor think he will recover?'

The nun shook her head. 'Very sad. Bad poison, madame. Doctor not hopeful.'

Lucy handed her one of her visiting cards. 'If he should recover, could you send me a message at the Excelsior Hotel? I would like to visit him, and perhaps do something for him and his family.'

Sister Angelina agreed, tucking the card into a pocket in her habit. But Lucy left the hospital less than hopeful

Cairo Carpet Bazaar

Rafiq answered Lucy's request and appeared at the Excelsior just after lunch. They set off on foot, but it took Lucy and Mary half an hour to find the right shop again, for, despite Lucy's description, Rafiq didn't recognise it. Telling Rafiq to wait outside, they entered the gloom of the interior. The atmosphere was stale with a strong smell of cheap tobacco. A ladylike cough didn't summon the merchant from the shadows at the rear of the tiny shop. Lucy gave Rafiq the signal to act as lookout.

As methodically as possible with so little room to move about in, Lucy searched the piles of rugs while Mary stood by watching her closely. As Lucy reached the back of the shop, she took a furtive glance out to the front. No sign of anyone other than Rafiq who was leaning against the wall of the building across the alleyway. Catching her eye, Rafiq scanned the street and shook his head. Lucy began to search in the area where the owner had pulled out the horrible box on her last visit.

Behind the makeshift desk were many boxes and small drawstring bags.

'All clear, Mary?' Lucy asked.

Mary nodded and moved closer to the front of the shop, pretending to examine the rugs.

Lucy hunkered down and snooped around. Some boxes were empty, others contained artefacts, but whether they were genuine or fake, she couldn't tell. As Lucy's eyes adjusted to the gloom, she noticed a leather bag tucked behind an adjacent pile of rugs. Pulling it out, she reached inside. It felt like several small statues were resting at the bottom. She extracted one but then frowned. It was remarkably similar to the ones Moreau had found in the tomb in Sakkâra. Lucy rolled back on her heels, staring at the little figure. Turning it over, she saw the notch left by the maker.

'I don't believe it!' Lucy exclaimed.

'What is it, ma'am?' Mary asked rushing towards her.

'Look! Do you recognise this?'

'Well, ma'am, I can't say I do,' Mary replied, squinting down at the statue.

'It's a shabti from Sakkâra and from my dig! How on earth did it end up here in Cairo?' Mary shrugged. A rush of anger almost made Lucy topple. Deftly, she pushed the little figure into her bag. Then she closed over the merchant's leather bag, pushing it back into its original position.

A sudden fit of coughing from Rafiq was the warning signal. Lucy managed to stand up and step away before the owner came rushing into the shop.

'Lady see something she like?' he asked, coming up to her. When she turned to him, he blinked as if he suddenly recognised her.

'No,' Lucy said. 'I'm not interested in rugs today. Something *special...*'

The owner glanced at Mary, then out at Rafiq. He looked undecided. Lucy smiled. It did the trick. He motioned for Lucy to come further into the shop.

'I want turquoise and gold jewellery. I want a bracelet.' Lucy mimed pushing one up from her wrist. 'Can you get one? It must be old. From a tomb. Do you understand?' she asked in a whisper, hoping she had described the stolen bracelet from the museum, accurately.

'Yes, yes, understand, but not have today. Must find. Lady come back tomorrow,' he said.

Lucy nodded, suppressing a frustrated sigh. 'Is there another dealer who might have such an item?'

A cunning glint came into his eyes. 'No, no. Lady trust me only. Lady like other things? Have fine mummy. You look?'

'No, thank you. Just the jewellery, please.'

The man smirked and bowed as she and Mary swept out of the shop.

Rafiq fell into step with Lucy, one eyebrow raised. 'Was your visit satisfactory?'

'Interesting, Rafiq; in fact, more than interesting. Our friend has shabti from *our* site,' she said.

Rafiq shook his head. 'Ali will not like this.'

'*I* don't like it much, either,' Lucy muttered under her breath. It begged the question: was that tiny figurine and the others pilfered from Moreau's site, the reason for his murder? And, if so, that brought Hopkins neatly into the frame, in her opinion.

Suddenly, Mary gripped her arm and pointed down an alleyway. 'Ma'am, I could have sworn I saw Miss DeLuca just now. Had you arranged to meet her?'

'No.' Lucy strained to see, but the light was too poor; however, she caught a glimpse of pink skirt as the lady disappeared around another corner. Isabella was wearing a dark pink dress today, but wasn't she supposed to be working out at Boulaq all day? When Lucy had left after her chat that morning with Joubert, Isabella had been hard at work in one of the anterooms.

But most curious of all, who had been the tall gentleman in Isabella's company just now?

TWENTY

The Next Day

The funeral was ghastly. Even with Isabella by her side in the small Catholic church and again at the graveside, the whole experience was surreal. As the priest's voice droned on, his Latin incomprehensible to her, Lucy studied the other mourners closely. None of Moreau's family had come, not even his parents, as they were too elderly to travel. At the grave, all Lucy thought about was Moreau's last moments. Who had been the last person he had seen in that tomb? Was that person standing here now, pretending to grieve? The idea made Lucy angry, and her body tensed. Isabella squeezed her arm in concern, but Lucy shook her head and focused her gaze on the casket as it was lowered into the earth. Isabella gave a tiny sob, clutching her lace handkerchief to her mouth. Lucy's grief, however, was spent. The night before the tears had flowed freely in the privacy of her room. Now, her only wish was to find the man responsible.

When the prayers finished, Lucy lifted her gaze and locked eyes with Joubert across the grave. The man looked dreadful.

Even though it was a warm day, he was huddled in his coat, as if his grief had shrunken his already frail frame. He must feel Moreau's loss more than most of the people gathered in the cemetery. They'd been good friends. Despite the inspector's insistence that anyone at the dinner that night might be a suspect, Lucy struggled to come up with a motive for Joubert. Physically, she doubted he would have managed it either, and she'd never witnessed any real animosity between the men. Granted, they'd fallen out over the tomb at Sakkâra, but they'd made up quickly afterwards.

Hopkins also stood pale and solemn, his eyes downcast. No doubt contemplating what his future might hold now his mentor was gone. Behind him stood Ali, Rafiq and a group of fellâheen. Moreau would have appreciated their presence, probably more than the attendance of some of the other men who stood around, dressed in black. They were his fellow Egyptologists and his competitors, she realised now. How naïve she'd been when people had warned her about the animosity between these men. Moreau had paid the ultimate price for it. But perhaps one of *them* was the killer for a reason they weren't aware of.

No. It had to be Whitmore. And there he was. Standing a little back with Rosemary at his side, inscrutable behind those grey glasses of his. How she wanted to rip them away from his smug face and denounce him before the entire congregation. Her only consolation was Vauquelin's steady gaze on his chief suspect.

A cat playing with his mouse.

But what was he waiting for? The evidence was, admittedly, circumstantial but there was enough of it.

At last the burial was over, and the crowd began to disperse. Isabella clung to her arm, her veil masking her face. 'Poor Armand,' she whispered. A lament which echoed in Lucy's mind, too. *I'll not rest until your killer is found, Armand.* Lucy made the silent promise before turning to thank the cleric. They were the last to leave the graveside.

Near the entrance, Lucy noticed Joubert again, standing and staring at a headstone. His shoulders were hunched almost as if he were in pain. The poor man – that must be his wife's grave. Lucy's instinct was to go over to him, but she feared it would be too intrusive. It was so sad but also romantic; no wonder he couldn't bear to leave Cairo. Lucy moved on through the gate to the roadside where the carriages were lined up waiting. Isabella climbed in. Just as Lucy put her foot on the step, there was a cry. Swinging around, Lucy saw Vauquelin and his men surrounding Whitmore and Rosemary at their carriage, a little further down the pavement. As one of the deputies handcuffed Whitmore, Rosemary became hysterical, clutching her brother's arm. Vauquelin said something to her which Lucy didn't hear, and Rosemary stood back. They marched Whitmore away to a police carriage, and all the while he protested his innocence. Rosemary stood staring after them, her hands tightly clenched by her sides.

'We can't leave her like this,' Lucy said to Isabella, now seated inside the carriage. 'Look how distressed she is.'

Lucy covered the short distance in a matter of seconds. Rosemary had her back to her, so Lucy reached out and gently touched her arm. 'Miss Whitmore, may we be of assistance?'

Rosemary swung around, her face a mask of hatred. 'This is all your fault,' she hissed.

Back at the Excelsior, Lucy handed Rosemary a glass of brandy and sat down opposite her. Rosemary was still upset, her eyes red from weeping. For the entire journey back into Cairo, she'd swung between lamentation and anger, setting Lucy's nerves on edge. As soon as they reached the hotel, Isabella had hastily made her excuses, leaving the two women alone.

'I do sympathise. This is a horrible situation for you, Miss Whitmore.'

Rosemary narrowed her eyes before taking another sip. 'It is!'

'You must be very worried about your brother,' Lucy said, in the hope of gaining some sort of common ground.

'Why, Reginald wouldn't hurt a fly,' Rosemary said, her voice breaking. 'How stupid the police are. Why couldn't *you* have left well enough alone? Matters might have calmed down in due course. Your dinner party caused all this trouble.'

'Somehow, I doubt it, Miss Whitmore. It was unfortunate, but someone took advantage of the public row to carry out a vicious murder,' Lucy answered, just about holding on to her temper.

'Huh! And as for Reg's glasses being found in that awful chamber, it is a ridiculous piece of mischief, and I would like to know who is responsible for it. As if Reg would do anything so stupid.'

'I agree, Miss Whitmore, it is suspicious, but the police will not give it more weight than it deserves.'

'But they have arrested him!'

'But not based entirely on finding his glasses. After so many people witnessing the words exchanged at dinner that night, you can understand why they might suspect your brother.'

'Idiots!' Rosemary snapped. 'They should be looking at someone else in my opinion.'

'Indeed? Who do you suggest, Miss Whitmore?'

Rosemary huffed. 'That DeLuca woman for instance. Someone should be asking questions about her.'

Isabella? 'Would you care to expand on that?' Lucy's heart sank.

Rosemary shrugged and a sour expression settled on her features. 'She was chasing after Moreau and always flirting with him. Every season she has been involved with someone. I wasn't happy about Reg engaging her this year, I can tell you. She's bad for morale.' Her words dripped like venom.

Lucy wracked her brains but, although they'd all dined in company on several occasions, she'd never noticed anything between Moreau and Isabella other than common courtesy and being at ease with each other. If Isabella had flirted with him, it had been done in private.

'I'm as anxious as you, Miss Whitmore, to discover the identity of M. Moreau's killer, so if you can remember anything which might help? Perhaps you would be good enough to tell me what happened after you left the dining room?'

Rosemary's eyes lit up, and she leaned towards her. 'You have doubts my brother is guilty?' Lucy gave a non-committal shrug. Rosemary settled back in her chair and regarded her mournfully for several moments. 'As for the night in question, there is nothing to tell. We retired for the evening, after I managed to calm Reg down. We only learnt of Moreau's murder later the following day, like everyone else.'

'Might your brother have left the hotel for any reason after you had gone to bed?'

'That would have been impossible.'

'Your brother being upset about the situation at Sakkâra is understandable, but I was wondering if there might be another reason for their animosity. Were there previous problems on other sites? I believe there were digs at Sakkâra last year and some kind of trouble...?'

'That is nonsense,' Rosemary said. 'Although Reg had to dismiss the photographer last year. Would that be what you're referring to? The man's work was sub-standard. The fool went running to Joubert to complain.' She put down her now empty glass. 'I don't take kindly to everyone thinking ill of my brother. Reg was provoked. That exchange of words in the dining room was ill-timed, but Reg is under considerable pressure from the British Museum. They have only partly funded him this year. If he can't make a significant find this season, there will be no hope of future funding. The issue at Sakkâra is stressful for him as a result. But you must understand my brother is an academic, and he certainly wouldn't have killed a man over such a matter. Reg cares deeply about Egypt; his only focus is on his work. Moreau's posturing was merely an annoyance, and we were used to it,' Rosemary snapped. 'Now, if that is all, I must see about engaging a solicitor for Reg.'

But it is very convenient Moreau is out of the way, Lucy thought as she watched Rosemary leave. And what on earth had happened to make Miss Whitmore such a bitter and angry young woman?

TWENTY-ONE

Two days later, Lucy was only back in her room after an early breakfast with Isabella, when Mary came to her with a card on a small silver tray.

Mary stood by while she read it. When Lucy looked up, the maid's demeanour was dour. 'Is anything the matter, Mary?'

The maid regarded the card in Lucy's hand, biting her bottom lip. 'It's that Mr Hopkins, ma'am, turning up here again. Does it mean we are going back to that awful desert?'

'My plans are uncertain at the moment, Mary. M. Joubert hasn't made a decision regarding the site at Sakkâra since poor M. Moreau's death. For now, we shall stay in Cairo.'

'Very good, ma'am,' Mary replied with a grin.

'But show Mr Hopkins in. I'll call if I need anything.' Mary bobbed and left muttering under her breath; Lucy was sure she heard *snake* mentioned.

A minute later, Hopkins was advancing across the room. He was smartly dressed, and his smile was friendly. So much so, it put Lucy on edge.

'Good morning, ma'am.'

'Do take a seat,' she said. 'Would you care for some refreshment?'

'No, ma'am, thank you kindly. I'm here purely on business.'

'Indeed?' Lucy was instantly on the alert.

'As I see it, we have all suffered a great shock, and I have lost a good friend, however...'

Lucy smiled her encouragement despite a prickle of annoyance. 'However?'

'Well, ma'am, poor Moreau is buried now, and I was wondering if it would be possible for the excavation to be reopened?'

Lucy sat back. *How brash!* And Moreau barely cold in the ground.

'With that Whitmore fellow behind bars, I don't see why M. Joubert would object. Naturally, I would be more than happy to continue Moreau's great work. There is so much work to be done, and the season is short.'

Lucy's mind began to whirr. But she could understand his motivation. He wished to grab this opportunity to prove himself, both to her and Joubert. But perhaps there was a more sinister reason?

'Have you considered it might be too soon to approach M. Joubert about it? Moreau was a great friend, and he's grieving.'

'Yes, ma'am, that is true. However, the men are restless with nothing to do; we can't hold on to them much longer. If they leave, the site will have to be closed down until next season. If they find employment on other digs, we will never convince them to come back.'

'I understand,' she said. And she did: Hopkins assumed she would continue to fund the dig. But the glamour and excitement she'd felt on first starting out on this adventure had dimmed for Lucy. With Moreau not there, it would be so odd to go back. And yet... Moreau had wanted so desperately for the excavation to be a success. Did she owe it to his memory to continue? And if her suspicions about Hopkins were correct, what better place to keep him under surveillance then at Sakkâra?

'Let me consider your proposal, Mr Hopkins,' she said at last.

'Thank you, ma'am. Most kind of you. I'm sure M. Joubert could be persuaded if you were to ask him in person.'

After Hopkins left, Lucy sat for some time mulling things over. If only she had someone to talk it through with. If she persuaded Joubert to let them return, might she be walking into danger? Should she go back? But it was a golden opportunity to observe Hopkins and investigate who might be stealing from the site. Her growing suspicion was that Hopkins had some involvement. There was nothing she could do in Cairo. Besides, was she not an independent woman? Was this not her venture at Sakkâra and her money? Yet, she needed to tease out Hopkins' request and its possible consequences with someone. It would be interesting to see how Miss DeLuca would react to the proposal.

Lucy found Isabella getting ready to go out, resplendent in a green visiting outfit and fixing a matching bonnet with a pearl hat pin. She was always beautifully turned out, but had she made a particular effort today? Lucy's curiosity was stoked. For all Isabella's talk of being carefree, wasn't it somewhat odd that Isabella was unattached? And Lucy still hadn't discovered who the mysterious stranger was that day when they'd seen Isabella in the carpet bazaar, although Lucy did have her suspicions. However, when Lucy had broached the subject, Isabella had laughed it off and flatly denied being there.

'Isabella, you look very well this morning. Are you off somewhere nice?'

Isabella flushed a deep pink but shook her head. 'Is it

urgent, Lucy? I promised M. Joubert I would work for him today.' Isabella pulled out her watch and consulted it. 'A carriage is waiting to take me out to Boulaq. I must hurry. If I do not work, I do not eat! And with Whitmore now in prison, I must take whatever assignments I can find.'

'It will only take a few minutes. I wanted some advice,' Lucy said. 'Perhaps I'll come with you, as I wish to consult M. Joubert.'

Isabella blinked rapidly, her expression unreadable. 'Certainly. If you don't mind sharing a carriage with all of my equipment.' If Lucy didn't know better, she might think Isabella was trying to put her off. It only made her more determined to go.

Once settled and on the road to Boulaq, Lucy explained about Hopkins' visit. 'What do you think of his request?'

'Mr Hopkins is eager,' Isabella said. 'I understand it is a well-known trait in Americans.'

'Yes, but is it too soon? I doubt M. Joubert will agree to it.'

Isabella shrugged. 'It can't hurt anyone. The work is important. Moreau had every faith in David Hopkins. And with Reginald Whitmore in prison, I can't see why Joubert wouldn't consent. Why Moreau told me at dinner the other evening he was impressed with Mr Hopkins' work of late and hoped to sponsor him next season. He intended to speak to Joubert on his behalf.'

'Moreau told me none of this,' Lucy said with a frown. Had Moreau and Isabella been closer than she believed? Why had he not said anything to her? Or was there another reason for Isabella to champion Hopkins?

'I'm sure Moreau would have, in due course. I didn't know M. Moreau that well, but longer than you, Lucy. Also, I'm familiar with how the system works out here. It is all about who you know.'

· · ·

Lucy and M. Joubert walked slowly through the museum gardens. While pointing out various monuments and artefacts in a half-hearted manner, Joubert spoke quietly of his dear friend Moreau. Lucy was dismayed to discover the director so listless and down.

'Let us sit here a while,' he said, leading her to a stone bench in the shade of some gnarled trees. Mariette's tomb was straight across, and he nodded towards it.

'Thank goodness he is not alive to experience all of this,' he said. 'I begin to wonder if there is a curse on Sakkâra. Why else all of this... trouble.'

'Oh, M. Joubert! You aren't serious.'

'No? Do you see those four sphinxes at the front of the tomb? They come from the sacred avenue leading to the Serapeum. Mariette found them half-buried in the sand. Perhaps we should not have brought them here. It was bad luck.'

'You must not dwell on these things.'

'Dear Mrs Lawrence, forgive me. You're a welcome sight, I can assure you. Since poor Moreau's death I can't concentrate. Such a terrible thing to happen,' he said. 'I can't bear to think about it; yet it is all I *can* think about. I shall never be able to visit Giza again.'

'His murder was vile, but he wouldn't have wanted you to be so distressed.'

Joubert patted her hand. 'You are kind, but this coming so soon after the robbery makes me feel my age. I'm seriously considering retiring.' The director took a deep breath and pointed to Mariette's tomb. 'It was his dearest wish to be interred here in Egypt, no more than Moreau, but I realise now how much I miss my family back in Deauville. I do not want to die here, be buried here and be forgotten.'

This struck Lucy as odd, remembering he had said he didn't want to leave Cairo as his wife was buried here: the vision of

him standing over her grave crystal clear. Lucy put it down to
being momentarily depressed.

'That wouldn't happen, I'm sure, and you would be a great
loss to the Service, monsieur, if you left Egypt,' she said,
suddenly finding a lump in her throat.

'The plain fact is I'm an old man. Plenty of young blood
about. Probably make a better job of this old place, too. I look
around now and all I see are my failures.'

Lucy made some comforting comments. The poor man was
really taking it all to heart.

After a few minutes, Joubert turned to her. 'I don't suppose
there is any progress on Moreau's murder or the robbery?'

'I have heard nothing new,' Lucy replied. 'The dagger
turning up as the murder weapon suggests Reginald Whitmore
must have had something to do with its theft. I imagine
Inspector Vauquelin is pursuing that line of investigation. I, too,
have been making enquiries.'

Joubert treated her to a sharp glance. 'Why? It is hardly a
fitting pastime for a young woman of good birth. I object most
strongly.' His face took on an alarming hue.

'Please don't distress yourself, M. Joubert. As I told you
before, I have some experience in investigating wrongdoing.'

'I recall, yes,' he said, still frowning. 'Most odd! Well, I must
rely on the local police. Will Vauquelin find the murderer, do
you think? I do hope so; the weight of responsibility lies heavily
upon me.'

'You should not feel that way. It's not your fault the robbery
took place at your museum, and the knife subsequently used to
kill M. Moreau. It is my belief the thief and the murderer were
in league.'

'Does Vauquelin agree?'

'I believe so,' she replied. Or at least; she assumed he did.

Joubert grunted and stared out across the garden.

This was as good a time as any. Lucy plunged in. 'Strange

you should speak of young blood... Mr Hopkins has approached me about the tomb at Sakkâra.' Anxiously, she watched for Joubert's reaction, as she was still not quite comfortable with the idea.

His expression became stern. 'What of it? I never did get to visit the site or make a decision on it.'

'Well, now that Mr Whitmore has been arrested, he can hardly contest the right to the tomb Moreau found.'

Joubert scoffed. 'And I suppose the young buck is willing and eager to take over?'

Lucy smiled. 'Yes, though it is a little soon, but it would be a shame for the tomb to be closed up until next year.'

'But is he experienced enough, Mrs Lawrence? I can't afford any more mistakes on digs.'

'Moreau thought highly of him,' she answered, remembering Isabella's comment. 'He was going to sponsor him.'

Joubert's brows shot up. 'I must admit I'm surprised to hear that.' With a sigh, he took off his glasses and drew a handkerchief from his pocket. 'Would you be willing to continue to fund the dig?' Lucy nodded, and he continued: 'I would have to be sure someone was keeping an eye on him.' He ran the cloth back and forth over the lenses almost absentmindedly.

'Who do you suggest?'

Joubert placed the glasses back on his nose and turned to her. 'Why you, Madame Lawrence. You enjoyed being at the dig, did you not? I'm sure I can trust you to ensure he does everything properly. And that you ensure all finds are properly recorded and sent straight here to the museum. Would you be willing to do that?'

Lucy beamed back at him. 'Absolutely!'

TWENTY-TWO

To Lucy's surprise, she received a visit from a grim-faced Inspector Vauquelin the next day. 'To what do I owe the pleasure, Inspector? Have you come to arrest me?' From the look on his face, it was no joking matter. 'Please, sit down,' Lucy continued sheepishly.

With a frown, Vauquelin shook his head. 'Thank you, but I won't. I do not intend to stay long.' He exhaled slowly as if to calm himself. 'I probably *should* arrest you. I'd hoped I'd made myself clear about interference in my case. However, that is not why I'm here. Unfortunately, I'm the bearer of bad news, yet again, Madame Lawrence. Tarek, the museum porter is dead.'

'Dead!' Lucy exclaimed, staring up at Vauquelin. 'The poor man! Was it definitely poisoning?'

'Yes, he died in agony yesterday evening. He never regained full consciousness,' the inspector said, taking up position in front of the fireplace. 'There will be a post-mortem this afternoon, but there can be no doubt.'

'I'm grateful to you, Inspector, for coming to tell me, but I'm not sure—'

'You attempted to visit the man a few days ago,' Vauquelin replied.

'Ah, yes... Well, I—'

'Wanted to interrogate him,' Vauquelin drawled. Lucy blushed. 'Madame, I already warned you to keep out of this. Do you think your enquiries go unnoticed?'

'Obviously not.'

'If I'm aware of what you're up to, the murderer probably is too. Whoever he is, he's ruthless. You risk your life by disobeying my orders.'

'I promise I'll be more careful from now on,' Lucy said.

'You will promise not to do it anymore,' snapped the inspector.

'Of course.' Lucy did her best to look contrite. 'And now we have two murders,' she continued, anxious to change the subject. 'How cruel! Did the museum porter have a large family?'

'A wife and three young children. M. Joubert has indicated he will do something for them. The man worked at the museum for many years.'

'So shall I, Inspector. Before I leave, I'll arrange for some money to be sent to M. Joubert. It is probably best it comes from him. Thank you for coming to tell me.'

If Lucy didn't know better, she could swear a flicker of hope ignited in the inspector's eyes. 'You are leaving Egypt, madame?'

'Well, no. Cairo. M. Joubert has given his permission to re-open the dig at Sakkâra. Mr Hopkins and I return there tomorrow to resume the excavation.'

Vauquelin stared down at her. 'I do not like this, Madame Lawrence. I do not like this at all.'

Lucy tensed. Would he try to stop her? 'But the murderer is in custody. Look, Inspector, it is best we are honest with each other. I mentioned to you before that Moreau was concerned about the black market. I have reason to believe someone is stealing from the dig at Sakkâra. I came across an artefact from our site in the carpet bazaar here in Cairo. If the excavation is re-opened, the culprit may be tempted to do it again. If I'm on hand, I'll catch them in the act.'

Vauquelin stared at her for a second as if she were mad. 'Why did you not come to me with this information? How long have you known about the theft from Moreau's dig?'

Lucy huffed. 'I only discovered it a day or two ago. Besides, you haven't been sharing information with me.' Too late, she regretted her words.

'I'm the police, madame, *I* do not have to.' The inspector was turning an alarming shade of red.

'Of course. But you see, I have promised M. Joubert that I'll manage things for him there. What possible objection can there be? You won't let me help you here, and there is no point in kicking my heels in Cairo, especially with Mr Whitmore in jail. My time would be much better utilised trying to find out how artefacts from my site ended up in Cairo.'

'Hopkins is still a suspect in M. Moreau's murder,' Vauquelin ground out. 'Indeed, anyone on the dig might be involved. Have you not considered the danger? You will be stuck out in the desert with them.'

'Inspector, it is unlikely the thefts from the site have anything to do with Moreau's murder. Besides, I'll have my dragoman with me for protection and will be perfectly safe.'

'You can't assume you will be safe, madame. We still do not know the motivation for Moreau's murder.'

'But you have Mr Whitmore in custody, and he has a strong motive. The way I see it, Inspector, I owe it to Moreau's memory to put a stop to the stealing. Moreau's murder is your enquiry; I wouldn't dream of interfering in that.'

'Only because I have made it very clear what will happen if you do!' Vauquelin's expression was one of incredulity.

Lucy didn't like deceiving him, but she was determined. 'Come, Inspector; Hopkins' only possible motive is too weak. He wouldn't risk his neck on a mere chance of taking over the dig. M. Joubert might just as easily close the site permanently or give it over to someone else to excavate.'

'And yet Mr Hopkins is now in exactly that position thanks to your intervention with M. Joubert. You see, Madame Lawrence, I know you went to M. Joubert to plead Hopkins' case.'

So that was why Vauquelin was really visiting her, Lucy realised. He suspected what her plan was and wanted to thwart her. 'How do you know that?'

'M. Joubert sent me a message yesterday evening apprising me of it. He, unlike you, likes to keep me informed.'

Lucy smarted. Why had Joubert done that?

The inspector began to pace the carpet. 'You forget Hopkins may have been in Cairo on the night of the murder. We have had no success in verifying his movements as yet. And even if he didn't burgle the museum, an accomplice might have carried it out for him. I implore you, Madame Lawrence, think this through. Moreau's killer was likely a big man. Hopkins could easily have tackled Moreau – he is at least six inches taller. And don't forget, he may have had an opportunity any time over the last two years to take a pair of Whitmore's glasses for the very purpose of incriminating him. Both teams were at Sakkâra last season.'

'Possibly, but is that realistic, Inspector? Would someone plan something like this for that long? I just don't see Mr Hopkins as a murderer, no matter how much I dislike him. Moreau was Hopkins' mentor; there was no sign of animosity – quite the opposite. Moreau treated him like a son. Whoever killed Moreau hated him. Why else would he go to such lengths to mock him and to use such a symbolic weapon?'

'There may have been something in Moreau and Hopkins' past we are not aware of,' Vauquelin replied. 'A camp is a small world with people stuck together in the heat for months on end. Issues of little importance, tiny grievances, fester and grow out of proportion. You were only on site for two days with both men.'

'You're forgetting I travelled with them for many days on the way here to Egypt, and had time to observe them together. I saw nothing to indicate there was a problem. Whitmore is your man.'

Vauquelin grunted and came to a stop before her chair. 'But is he? Even you have expressed some doubt, and I'm not completely comfortable about all the circumstantial evidence. Hopkins is still a suspect in my mind.'

Lucy shook her head. 'Mr Whitmore looks far more likely to be the guilty party. There is no real evidence against anyone else.' The inspector gave her a doubtful glance. She returned a steady gaze. Lucy was determined to find out who was stealing the shabti and hoped it would lead her to Moreau's murderer too. 'Mr Whitmore could have carried out either crime. He was in Cairo on the two nights in question. Do not worry, you have the right man.'

'But as it happens, I may have to release him,' he replied. 'His solicitor and his sister have been haunting my office. With his alibi still unsubstantiated, it leaves me in a difficult position. I can't assume he is guilty and must continue to investigate other possible suspects and motives.'

Lucy smiled her most winning smile. 'Inspector, I implore you, do not release him. At least, not just yet.' If Whitmore was released Joubert might rescind his permission to re-open the site, and the whole argument would be re-opened.

Vauquelin's eyes narrowed. 'My only concern, madame, is

justice. I care nothing for the vagaries of these Egyptologists and their squabbles. Or your own desire for fame.'

Lucy gasped. 'That is ridiculous!'

The inspector shook his head. 'Is it? Are you being honest with yourself? If the tomb turns out to be intact, you and Hopkins will be famous.'

'I don't care for anything like that; only that Moreau's work is recognised as it should be.'

'Don't you realise you're being manipulated by Hopkins?' Vauquelin sounded incredulous.

Lucy smarted. 'On the contrary, it is the other way around.'

The inspector raised his brows and looked as if he wanted to throttle her. 'You're playing with fire. Reconsider. If Whitmore did not do it, Hopkins is probably our man.'

'And as I said before, Hopkins wouldn't risk his neck without being certain the dig would be handed over to him. It is mere luck Joubert has agreed to this now.'

'I do not trust you, Madame Lawrence. Despite my warnings, I'm well aware that you continue to investigate. I can't stop you going to Sakkâra, but I urge you to stay here in Cairo where I can provide some protection.'

'I'm only trying to be useful,' Lucy grumbled.

Vauquelin rolled his eyes. 'Then stay *here*.'

Lucy realised it was time for a different tack. 'But Inspector, just think; if I return to Sakkâra I can verify when Hopkins left Sakkâra before turning up in Cairo. If I discover he has been up to no good, I'll send a message to you. Let us not fall out over it. Mr Hopkins and I plan to leave tomorrow. M. Joubert has entrusted me with this, and I'm determined not to let him down.'

'Even if it means risking your life?' Vauquelin snapped.

'It will not come to that,' Lucy said, more to convince herself than the inspector.

TWENTY-THREE

Sakkâra

Lucy knew Mary was afraid to comment and give offence by the wariness in her eyes. Lucy was disappointed, for she'd spent ages in the bazaar with Isabella trying to find something appropriate to wear for scrambling around in the desert and down in the tomb. Catching a glimpse of herself in the mirror which was leaning against the side of the tent, Lucy smiled, then twirled round once more. In fact, she thought, I look quite smart. The blue-grey of the jacket and trousers were set off beautifully by the crisp whiteness of her blouse. The little waistcoat was a dashing addition Isabella had begged her to buy.

'Come, Mary, we are acquainted long enough; what do you think?' Lucy asked. Mary continued to stare at the offending clothes. 'Are you shocked to see me in trousers?'

Mary swallowed and nodded.

'But surely it is far more practical than a petticoat and skirts?'

'Aye, but is it... ladylike?'

'Miss DeLuca assures me this kind of attire is acceptable for women out here in the desert. Obviously, I wouldn't wear it in Cairo or London. I hoped you would approve, for it will save my good clothes from being ruined. And see, the trouser legs are so wide it almost looks like a skirt.' Lucy held out one foot. 'And these boots are sturdy and much easier to walk in.' Lucy nodded towards her heeled boots now abandoned beside the makeshift bed.

Mary sniffed and looked askance at Lucy's new boots before coming forward and fingering the fabric of the trousers. 'That's a nice bit of linen, ma'am,' she conceded at last, 'for a *gentleman's* suit.'

Lucy closed her eyes, and prayed for deliverance.

If Hopkins was surprised by Lucy's attire, his expression didn't change as she entered the main tent. He appeared to be in a good mood. Lucy was relieved as she knew what she was about to tell him might not go down well.

'Settled in, ma'am?' he asked as he straightened up. The table before him was covered in shabti figurines and shards of pottery.

'Yes, indeed. Thank you for giving me the bigger tent,' she said. 'With two of us, it is much more comfortable.'

'Moreau would have wanted you to have it, ma'am.'

'I've asked Mary to pack up the last of Moreau's property. We can send it back to M. Joubert; I'm sure he would be willing to forward it on to his family for us.'

'Yes... sorry, I didn't get to it,' Hopkins replied, waving at the items spread out before him.

'I understand.' Lucy nodded towards the table. 'Did you find a name for our tomb owner yet?'

'No, and at this stage I have given up hope. Moreau's theory was the person died unexpectedly as the shabti were hastily made; possibly destined for someone else's tomb. There was no time to inscribe the name.'

'Might there be a clue to the tomb's owner in the burial chamber if we find it?'

'There usually is. If we find a sarcophagus, it may give us a name.'

'Then we must be patient, Mr Hopkins,' Lucy said. 'Are you about to take a break? I'd like to talk to you about the dig.'

He frowned. 'Was there something in particular?'

Lucy sat down on the bench beside the table. 'Two things, actually.' Hopkins nodded his encouragement. 'Firstly, I wondered how you would feel if I were to hire Miss DeLuca. The poor dear was dependent on Mr Whitmore to employ her this season and, of course, now that job will not materialise.'

And, if there was something going on between Isabella and Hopkins, it would be hard for them to disguise it working in close proximity.

'But do we need her? I thought you were enjoying sketching?' he said, frowning down at the figurine in his hand.

'Yes, but your camera hasn't been repaired yet. It would be much more efficient if we use a photographer as opposed to my amateur efforts. Also, there is the matter of the terms imposed on us by M. Joubert.'

Hopkins frowned again. 'I don't understand; what *terms*?'

'The director was explicit about one thing in particular. But I assure you I have every confidence in you and your work. However, M. Joubert was concerned that everything should be done correctly with regard to recording and shipping of artefacts. It was one of the conditions for allowing us to re-open the site that I personally look after it. Hiring Miss DeLuca would help facilitate this as it would free me up to do just that.'

Hopkins glared at her. 'Does he not trust me to do my job? I have worked for four years on digs. I know what I'm doing and what's expected of me.'

'Of course you do. I don't doubt it for an instant. But I'm afraid M. Joubert was adamant.'

Two spots of high colour appeared on Hopkins' face. 'I see.'

Lucy gave him her most winning smile. 'I rather hoped you would show me what to do?'

Hopkins' mouth twitched, but he managed a smile. 'Of course, it will be my pleasure.'

Lucy sensed he was rattled, but it was the only way she could ensure nothing would go astray. Since Hopkins' request to re-open the site, she'd become convinced he had an ulterior motive. Lucy hoped she wouldn't live to regret it: poking a nest of vipers wasn't a particularly clever thing to do. *No,* Lucy replied to her phantom Phineas, *but sometimes it is the only way to discover the truth.*

A week later, Lucy was an expert at logging finds and, with Mary's help, packing them for shipment to Boulaq. The days were long and the heat in the tent was unpleasant, so she often walked out to the dig site for a break in the monotony. But she also wanted Hopkins to be aware she was keeping an eye on things. He always greeted her in a friendly fashion, but she guessed he would prefer she remain at the camp. Each evening he made his excuses and ate alone in his tent. Lucy found his company irksome at best so didn't mind. She enjoyed sitting with Rafiq and Ali and listening to their stories.

Isabella accepted Lucy's offer to join them, and she promised to travel as soon as she finished her work for M. Joubert. Hopkins had merely grunted when Lucy informed him. Lucy hoped they'd find it impossible to feign indifference once the pair were in close proximity. Lucy's plan was falling neatly into place.

A growing mound of debris, rocks and broken pottery was building up a little distance from the entrance to the tomb.

Hopkins had several of the men down on their hunkers going through it meticulously. Lucy felt sorry for them, for the heat during the day was unbearable, but when she voiced this concern to Hopkins, he merely shrugged and said they were well used to it. Lucy watched as the separated material was laid out in rows: pottery shards, pieces of shabti and what looked disconcertingly like human bones. Hopkins would then inspect the items, and if he felt they were of value, they were packed in boxes and sent back by donkey to the work tent at the camp for Lucy to work on.

Down in the tomb, the heat and dust were almost sickening, but Lucy forced herself to go down. Watching the men removing the stones from the collapsed roof, she sensed Hopkins' impatience. The blockage was proving a challenge. When the fallen rocks were removed, the roof had to be shored up with timber. And there was still no sign of an end to it.

'Perhaps Miss DeLuca will bring us some luck. I expect her this afternoon,' Lucy remarked to Hopkins who was leaning against the passage wall, arms folded as the men worked just ahead of them.

He grunted. 'Little enough for her to do when she gets here.'

'There is plenty of material for her to work on back at the tent.'

'Most of it is worthless, ma'am. We have yet to find anything of great interest or value.'

'Then we must hope your work down here is successful.'

Hopkins shrugged. 'So far it is not particularly promising, but it's your money, ma'am.'

'Yes, it is,' she replied. There was a slight tensing of his shoulders, but he didn't respond. Lucy resented the implied criticism but was determined not to rise to it.

A shout came from one of the men working on the blocked

passageway. Hopkins started forward. The man was pointing into the rubble and speaking rapidly in Arabic.

'What is it, Hopkins?' Lucy asked.

'If I'm not mistaken, it is the entrance to another chamber,' he replied, peering into the gap.

Within half an hour, they'd cleared enough of the fallen rocks for Lucy to see through the opening. Hopkins climbed through first, holding up a lantern. Lucy followed close behind.

Hopkins gasped and turned to her. 'There is a body in here!'

'A mummy?' Lucy asked, trying to see around him.

'No! I'd say it was a tomb robber, trapped by the roof collapse,' he said.

'The poor man; what a horrible way to die.'

Hopkins moved aside and held up the lantern. In the corner of the small room, a skeleton sat hunched beside a large square box, the only object in the room. 'Hazard of the trade,' Hopkins said. 'They appear to have cleared the room of most of its contents.' He nodded towards the box. 'The roof collapse must have occurred when he returned for this last one.'

'What should we do with him?' Lucy asked. 'We can't leave him here.'

'I'll order the men to bury him.' But Hopkins was paying little attention to the unfortunate robber. He was scrutinising the texts on the walls, before turning to the large box.

It was square and inlaid with ebony. With reluctance, Lucy came closer, all too conscious of the body beside it. 'What is it?'

'Treasure, hopefully,' Hopkins said, placing the lantern on the floor. He manoeuvred the lid to get a grip on its smooth surface. With a grinding noise, it moved slowly, a cloud of dust rising up making Lucy cough. A huge grin spread over Hopkins' face as he peered inside. Lucy held her breath as he rummaged around before withdrawing his hand. Nestled in his open palm was a scarab ring and a gold anklet. He looked up at Lucy. 'It's

full of jewellery, ma'am. It appears Miss DeLuca will have
something of interest to photograph after all.'

Isabella settled into camp quickly, taking up residence in the
tent beside Lucy's. It was past midnight when they finally
retired, having exhausted all the Cairo gossip. Moreau's murder
was still the main topic on everyone's lips. The news of Whitmore's continued incarceration didn't surprise Lucy, but she did
wonder how Vauquelin's investigation was proceeding. Keeping
her informed of progress was definitely not on his list of
priorities.

Next morning, Lucy observed Isabella at work with her
camera, fascinated by the whole process. The box from the
tomb, along with its contents, was now safely at the camp. Each
piece of jewellery was placed on a sheet of white paper and a
ruler was placed beside it to show its scale. Then Isabella
photographed the object from several angles. As Isabella
finished, Lucy and Mary took over, logging the find, assigning it
a number and writing up a description, using the textbooks
Hopkins had left out for them. Each piece was then carefully
wrapped, boxed and numbered.

After a couple of hours, Lucy insisted they take a break.
Mary retired to their tent to rest. Isabella and Lucy settled
down just inside the tent entrance, the vast expanse of desert
shimmering away into the distance before them in the early
afternoon sun. They sipped their tea in silence for a few
minutes. Lucy's thoughts turned to Hopkins and one of her
reasons for inviting Isabella to the camp. Although they spent a
lot of time together, she hadn't detected anything suspicious
between Isabella and Hopkins. They treated each other with
politeness, and sometimes spoke of mutual acquaintances in the
archaeological community. Perhaps Lucy had been mistaken
that day in the bazaar. It may not have been Hopkins she'd

spotted with Isabella. After all, the alleyway had been quite dark. She was fairly certain it had been Isabella, for that outfit she'd worn that day was distinctive. But if Isabella had a secret assignation with someone, and it wasn't Hopkins, why had she not spoken of it to Lucy? They'd become friends, and had shared many personal revelations. Lucy saw no reason for Isabella to keep it from her unless she was seeing a married man. And could the warm and vivacious Isabella really be involved with Hopkins? He was such a taciturn individual.

However, the more time Lucy spent with David Hopkins, the more convinced she was he was up to something, but what? If he was siphoning off finds, how was he doing it? He couldn't manage it alone; someone had to be working with him and taking the artefacts to Cairo to sell off. Those men she'd seen him arguing with on the first day they'd arrived in Sakkâra had not been seen since. So who was he using? Lucy decided to share her concerns about the site thefts to gauge Isabella's reaction.

'What do you make of Hopkins?' Lucy asked airily.

'I hardly know him,' Isabella replied, continuing to stare out across the desert. But Lucy noticed Isabella's hard grip on the armrest of her chair. This was interesting; why was she uncomfortable talking about him?

'But you've met him several times at different sites. I'm trying to figure him out and was hoping you might give me some insight. He is difficult to get on with, being so prickly.'

'Perhaps he does not handle pressure well. I can't comment, Lucy, for I barely know him, and I've never worked for him. I'm sure that blockage in the passageway in the tomb is very frustrating. Days of work and so little progress in clearing it. You must consider he may be finding it hard to be here without Moreau. He knows M. Joubert will be keeping a close eye on his work, and judging him.' Isabella clasped her hands in her lap.

'Through me, unfortunately! Hopkins resents my presence,'

Lucy said with a little laugh. 'He doesn't object to my money funding his exploits, however.'

'Most men would resent working for a woman; I wouldn't take it personally.'

Lucy lowered her voice. 'The problem is, I suspect he is up to something underhand.'

Isabella swung around, her expression one of deep concern. 'Whatever do you mean?'

'I have no proof as yet, but he may be siphoning off finds and selling them on the black market. You've worked on many sites. How easy would it be to do it?'

Isabella stared at her. 'No! I don't believe you. Moreau would never have tolerated it. Mr Hopkins might be odd, but that is hardly reason to accuse him of stealing.'

'But you have to admit his behaviour is strange.'

'I don't agree and, besides, M. Moreau trusted him.'

'Yes, which baffles me as Moreau was such an intelligent and insightful man. He did know finds were going missing but seems to have assumed it was some of the fellâheen that were to blame. Moreau told me he quizzed the men here, and Hopkins helped him do it.'

'There you are! Moreau didn't have reason to suspect him,' Isabella pointed out, her face flushed.

'Or was blinded by their friendship. If he had suspected Hopkins, he would have reported him to the police, I'm sure. Perhaps Moreau assumed the items were going missing after they left the dig. Maybe he thought the boat crews were pilfering the finds en route to the museum.' Lucy sighed. 'Please don't say anything—it's only a hunch.'

'But you must have some evidence before you can say such a thing, even to me.' Isabella sounded annoyed with her.

Lucy was intrigued by her reaction. 'As I say, it is only a suspicion. I saw him with some unsavoury characters the first day I arrived, and the day I went to the carpet bazaar to bait the carpet merchant, I found one of the shabti from this very site in his shop.'

Isabella glanced away. 'How can you be sure it was from here? You're not an expert, Lucy. Shabti tend to be similar. It must be a coincidence. You are reading far more into it than necessary. Besides, if Mr Hopkins was up to something like that, I'm sure M. Moreau would have found out.'

'Perhaps,' Lucy said, but she had to wonder why Isabella defended Hopkins so vigorously.

TWENTY-FOUR

Later, as Lucy changed for dinner, she noticed a battered trunk by the flap of the tent and asked Mary if it was Moreau's.

'Yes, ma'am. Mr Hopkins gave me the key, and I sorted through it as you asked. The last of M. Moreau's papers and letters were in it, ma'am. I thought it could go back to Cairo with the rest of the boxes tomorrow.'

'What kind of papers?'

'Journals, ma'am,' answered Mary.

'And the letters?'

'I didn't read them, ma'am. They looked very personal, like,' Mary said. 'Didn't seem right to go a-looking at 'em.'

Lucy nodded, but as soon as Mary left the tent, she went straight to the trunk, her curiosity raging. Leather-bound journals made up the bulk of the contents. She flicked through them. They contained detailed accounts of the various digs he had been on in the last couple of years: facts, figures and locations with descriptions of artefacts found. M. Joubert would love these journals for the museum, Lucy thought.

However, at the bottom of the trunk were letters, tied

together in bundles. Lucy took them out and brought them over to the bed. The first batch were letters from Moreau's mother in Nice. She couldn't bear to read them, re-tied the ribbon and moved on to the next set. Odd. There were no envelopes, just a bundle of letters. It was immediately obvious by the faint perfume, that they were written by a female hand. Lucy had no right to read them. She sat for several minutes mulling it over. But what if they had something to do with his murder? Would Vauquelin or Phineas Stone ignore them? She was certain they would not.

Lucy unfolded the first letter. It was dated two years' previously but, puzzlingly, it was not on headed paper, and there was no address. Subterfuge, Lucy concluded with a smile and dived in.

Dearest Armand,

We set sail for Alexandria next week. How the months drag by! I can't wait to see you again. Letters, lovely as they are, are no substitute for being with you. All I have are our stolen moments to think about when we are apart. I keep busy, but you are constantly in my thoughts and prayers. My family ask what ails me, my love, but I know I must keep our secret safe.

Stay true to me, my dearest, as I have to you.

It was more a note than a letter, and obviously written in haste. The next three missives were much the same with an illegible scribble of a signature. The letters were in English, not French or Italian. Who was the lady? Was it the mysterious woman in Moreau's treasured photograph? Obviously, she came to Egypt for the winter season but from where? Lucy scanned each one, desperate to identify the letter writer, but

there was no clue. Why was their relationship a secret? Was the
lady married? The next letter was dated December 1886, a
year ago.

Armand,

*Darling, I do not understand. I thought you would be pleased by
my news. Why did my last letter come back unopened? You're so
near, and yet so far from me. If only we could meet. You said you
loved me – that we would be together soon. I have given up so
much. Don't take away hope. Please answer this letter for I fear
I'll go mad. What am I to do?*

Another, dated two weeks later.

Armand,

*Please, I beg you. You are breaking my heart. How can you deny
your own child? I forgive you for I know you are afraid of any
hint of scandal, but I love you. Soon, I'll not be able to hide that
I'm increasing. How can I keep this hidden from Reginald, out
here in the desert?*

Rosemary! Lucy stared at the letter in her hand, her heart
thumping. How extraordinary! She would never have guessed it
based on how they'd acted in each other's presence but, of
course, their relationship happened, and no doubt ended, before
Lucy was in Egypt. If Rosemary had a child, and Moreau
wouldn't admit it was his, no wonder Rosemary hated him. But
what happened to the child? Was it back in Scotland? Then she
remembered Isabella telling her Rosemary had been ill and had
left Egypt after Christmas the previous year. She'd gone home
to give birth to her child. Lucy felt a chill down her spine. My

God! How could Moreau have been so cruel? And then there had been those snide remarks from Moreau about Rosemary. Lucy felt ill.

She flew through the other letters, but there were no more from Rosemary. Why had Moreau kept the letters if he had not acknowledged his child? Had he enjoyed Rosemary's distress? Was it some kind of perverted pleasure he got from watching her anguish? My God, Lucy thought, he was incredibly cruel if that were the case. No wonder Rosemary had turned into a bitter young woman.

But had that bitterness turned to murder? Lucy remembered Rosemary's reactions to Moreau on the various occasions they'd been in company. Lucy had thought it was jealousy when Rosemary had glared at her that night at the dinner, when she and Moreau had laughed and mildly flirted. And that malevolent look Rosemary had given to Moreau as the Whitmores had quit the table. Had that been the look of a murderer sizing up her victim? Lucy shivered at the thought. Vauquelin had concentrated on establishing Reginald's alibi, but what if Reginald was Rosemary's alibi? If he had been in a deep sleep due to laudanum, he wouldn't have known if Rosemary had left their suite.

There was one problem, though. Rosemary might have had a motive, but Lucy didn't believe she was strong enough to overpower a man of Moreau's build; nor had she the opportunity to go out to Giza alone at night without someone at the hotel having noticed her leaving, her absence or her return. And would she kill the father of her child? Again, Lucy recalled the look of hatred Rosemary had given Moreau at the dinner table that night. She wasn't convinced either way.

As Lucy worked in the tent the next day, she mulled over Rosemary and her circumstances. Watching Isabella work, she was on the point several times of sharing the information with her, but something held her back. It was a pitiful secret Rosemary kept, and she had no right to ruin the woman's reputation.

Hopkins suddenly appeared in the doorway, his face red and his voice shaking in anger. 'You will not believe it!'

'Whatever is the matter?' Lucy asked. Isabella stared at him. 'Whitmore!'

'I don't understand,' Lucy said. 'What about him?'

'I just saw him outside. His entire entourage passed by, with him at the head of it, as smug as you please, on his way back to his dig site. Those stupid police have let him go. You must contact Joubert at once and have him stopped.'

'I shall certainly inform him, but I can't imagine Whitmore has come back without Joubert's permission or knowledge,' Lucy said. 'Was his sister with him?' He nodded. 'Calm yourself, Hopkins. And please, no confrontations. Unless we hear otherwise, we will continue our work.'

Hopkins smarted and looked angrily to Isabella as if he was going to say something. 'That sounds like good advice, Mr Hopkins,' Isabella said calmly. A knowing glance passed between them. Lucy dropped her gaze, her heart racing. That glance had spoken volumes. Hopkins stomped out.

'I wonder why Whitmore has been released,' Isabella said turning back to her work. 'This can only cause trouble.'

'Yes, but Vauquelin wouldn't release him unless he has been able to validate his alibi. The missing valet must have turned up and confirmed it.'

Hopkins appeared at breakfast the next morning, his expression sullen. After several attempts at conversation, Lucy gave up and left him and Isabella to finish their meal. She had little doubt the pair had lots to talk about. However, as much as she wanted to, hanging around outside the tent in broad daylight was out of the question.

Lucy loved the early morning when the air was still fresh and relatively cool. She waved off Rafiq and strode out into the desert towards the Step Pyramid. She wanted to be alone to mull over the latest developments. Most of all, she needed to figure out how to flush those two out. There could be only one reason for them to keep their relationship secret. If she were lucky, they might give themselves away; let their guard down. A few provocative remarks here and there might just do it.

About fifteen minutes out from the camp she spotted a small party approach on donkeys. To her amazement as it got nearer, she discerned M. Joubert at the head of the group. Lucy waved and continued on towards them.

Soon M. Joubert was dismounting and greeting Lucy with a wide smile. 'Madame Lawrence, you're surprised to meet me here.' He shook her hand.

'Yes, sir, but pleased all the same. How are you, and what brings you to Sakkâra?'

'A colleague suggested it would be a good idea to get away from Cairo, and when Vauquelin informed me Mr Whitmore was free, I suspected Mr Whitmore might come straight here. Within an hour of his release, I did receive a note from him informing me that was his very plan. Under the circumstances, I thought it best to be on hand if any problems arise.' Joubert looked about and turned back to her with a smile. 'It is just like old times being here. I feel the better for it already.'

Lucy frowned. 'I'm glad for you, sir. As it happens Whitmore arrived yesterday afternoon. Are you here to stop him?'

'On the contrary, my good lady, I have come to encourage him.'

Lucy stopped in her tracks. 'Both teams can't work on the same tomb.'

'And why not? Whitmore will excavate from his side.'
Joubert chuckled. 'A race if you will.' Appalled, Lucy could
only stare at him as he chatted away. 'Now, I'm making my way
to Mariette's house where I shall set up camp. Once I'm settled,
I shall pay a visit to your sites, and I look forward to seeing how
much progress has been made. *Au revoir, madame.*' Joubert
bowed over her hand and rejoined his entourage.

Later that evening, Lucy broke the news to her dinner
companions. If Hopkins had reacted badly to the sight of Whitmore the previous day, his expression on hearing of Joubert and
his scheme frightened Lucy. He couldn't speak a word for
several minutes. Isabella insisted he sit down and poured him a
drink. With shaking hands, he took a sip. Slowly, the colour
came back into his cheeks.

'This is madness!' Hopkins said at last.

'I agree,' Lucy said. 'Joubert's behaviour is strange. Moreau's
murder has disturbed him greatly.'

Hopkins glared at her. 'An understatement, ma'am. Joubert
must be deranged. I have never heard of such a thing. Two
different teams excavating the same tomb? Why it is
outrageous!'

Isabella handed Lucy a glass and sat down beside Hopkins.
'What can we do about it?'

Hopkins shrugged, then frowned. 'I have no idea. I'm still
trying to take this in.'

'Does Whitmore have any chance of finding the other end
of the tomb?' Lucy asked him.

'Unfortunately, it is very likely. Don't forget he has already
been down into our shaft. Remember the day of the confrontation with Moreau?' Lucy nodded. 'Whitmore had ample time to
go down that morning before we arrived. I'm certain he knows

which direction the passageway heads. Tombs tend to follow a layout pattern; it would be relatively easy to map.'

'That could mean he will find the burial chamber before us,' Lucy said, surprised at how disappointed she felt. 'I don't want him to.'

Hopkins' answering smile was without humour. 'Neither do I!'

TWENTY-FIVE

The Next Morning

Lucy stood, shielding her eyes with her hand. 'I can just about make it out. Are they on the right track?' she asked Hopkins. He grunted then signalled to Ali to start lowering him down into the shaft. Lucy remained at the top, staring in the direction of Whitmore and his men, a dark blur against the golden cliffs in the distance.

Lucy turned to Rafiq. 'Come with me, please. I wish to pay a visit to our neighbours.'

Rafiq nodded and smiled before saying something hurriedly to Ali in Arabic.

'What did you say to him?' she asked as they set off.

'I told him not to say anything to Mr Hopkins. He is a volatile man.'

'Hopkins?'

'Yes, madame. I have seen him lose his temper more than once. M. Moreau was not happy with him. Ali does not like him or the way he talks to the men. M. Moreau treated everyone well.'

'It is a pity I was not aware of some of this before,' Lucy remarked. And what was she doing traipsing across the hot sand to talk to a man who must blame her in some part for his incarceration? What kind of welcome would she receive? Lucy didn't really have a plan; she was acting on impulse by going to the Whitmore camp. Perhaps the sun was getting to her. But she had to do something.

As it transpired, it was Rosemary who saw her and stepped forward to acknowledge her. 'What excellent timing, Mrs Lawrence, I was just to take tea. Won't you join me?' she said, for all the world as if Lucy were making a morning call in Mayfair.

'Thank you,' Lucy answered. Whitmore, who was several feet away, leaning over some of his men who were down in a trench, looked up and touched the brim of his hat. He didn't seem to be put out; in fact, it was almost as if he had expected her. With a nod back, she turned and followed Rosemary to a tent a little away from the trench. Rafiq followed at a distance and took up position outside, giving Lucy some comfort. Was she about to take tea with a killer? It was a difficult notion to dispel.

When the servant had left, Rosemary picked up the teapot. 'Shall I be mother?'

Lucy gulped at the unfortunate reference, but recovered enough to nod.

'I suspect you're surprised to see us here?' Rosemary asked, handing her a cup. There was no polite answer so Lucy smiled. 'That stupid police inspector had to let Reg go. The hotel valet who served us in the hotel saw a newspaper article about Reg's arrest. Luckily, he is a man of honour and sent a telegram to the police which confirmed Reg's alibi.'

'That was lucky indeed,' Lucy said. 'And so you came back here.'

'Yes, why shouldn't we? Joubert continues to procrastinate.

In the end, Reg sent him a note to say we were coming back, more out of courtesy than anything else.'

'But this situation is highly unusual. Joubert has just arrived but not to intervene as I thought. He has decided to let both teams work on the tomb. Now, he has set up camp at Mariette's old house near the Serapeum and plans to visit both our sites.'

Rosemary shrugged. 'What of it? Is it not a fair solution to the problem? Mind you, I shall send him to the rout if he comes here and tries to stop us. Joubert is not fit for the job anymore. Reg intends to make a formal complaint.'

'Isn't that harsh, Miss Whitmore. The man is grieving.'

'Yes, indeed he is, but for whom?' Rosemary gave an odd little laugh. 'Anyway, as I said, this is the fairest way to settle things. May the best team win.'

It was almost as if Rosemary were gloating. Lucy felt uncomfortable, but had to admit a race to open the tomb added an element of excitement. But she wasn't going to indulge Miss Whitmore's mood. 'That is all well and good, but I understand it is highly irregular. However, I'm glad your brother was released. I had my doubts.' Rosemary raised a brow and sipped her tea. 'His glasses being found in the tomb was far too convenient.'

'They were left there on purpose to make Reg appear guilty,' Rosemary said with a sneer. 'Well, it's backfired on whoever was mean enough to do it. With Reg cleared, the police must be closer to finding the real murderer.'

'I hope so too,' Lucy replied.

Rosemary shook her head and started to laugh. 'Oh Mrs Lawrence, you do not fool me. You're suspicious of everyone, including me. You're wrong, however. I had nothing to do with Moreau's murder.'

Lucy put down her cup and took a steadying breath. It was a gamble as she had no way of knowing how Rosemary would react. 'I have seen your letters to Moreau, Rosemary. He had kept them. I came across them while preparing his things to be returned to his family. If I have interpreted them correctly, you had every reason to hate him.'

Rosemary's face twisted in memory. 'He kept my letters? Typical of the man!' Rosemary spat the words at her. 'Yes, I hated him, but I didn't hurt him, and nor did Reg. What Armand put me through no woman should have to bear. You know, I wasn't surprised he was murdered. He liked nothing better than to goad people. It was probably only a matter of time before someone decided to take revenge. I suppose you thought he was all charm?'

'I regret to say I did, at first. I was at a crossroads in my life when I met him. I saw only what I wanted to see. And, of course, I didn't know him well, Miss Whitmore.'

'Lucky you!'

'And the child?' Lucy asked gently.

'I lost it.'

Lucy sucked in a breath. 'I'm so sorry.'

Rosemary's eyes welled up. 'It was on the voyage home. I was ill from the very beginning; I couldn't work I was so sick. The heat affected me, and I couldn't bear the smells of the camp cooking. Reginald insisted I go back to England to an elderly cousin of ours. I couldn't go home to Scotland in disgrace. Cousin Ruth was happy to take me in until my confinement. Don't think I blame Reg for making me go home – it was the right decision. Unfortunately, the crossing was dreadfully rough. Perhaps I would have lost the child anyway, but it was horrible, Mrs Lawrence. Luckily, a kindly lady helped me. She believed my tale of being a widow returning home from India. I hated the deception, but I was desperate for help. Afterwards, when I reached Scotland, I was so taken down by it. What was worse was having to keep it from my mother, but the knowledge of my having a child out of wedlock would have killed her.'

'So you went home, unable to share your pain or grieving with anyone. How awful for you.'

Rosemary drew herself up. 'It was for the best in the end. Moreau would have been a terrible father. Reg said he would never marry me, more particularly because I'm a Protestant and Moreau was Catholic. And he was right. Moreau flung my religion in my face; can you believe it? He even had the audacity to question my morals and my fitness to be a mother! This from a notorious womaniser. Now, I realise what a lucky escape I had, but I'm ashamed to say I begged him at the time, fool that I was. I don't know what I would have done if the child had lived. The shame—' Rosemary's voice broke.

Lucy reached across and squeezed her hand. 'I'll not tell anyone. I'll have the letters returned to you.'

Rosemary bit her lower lip, then her chin rose. 'Thank you – more for Reg's sake than my own. I was foolish beyond belief to let that man seduce me.'

'No! Moreau must take all the blame.' Lucy said, suddenly angry with her dead friend. She remembered how preoccupied he had been when they'd arrived in Cairo. Lucy had assumed he was caught up in his work, then disturbed by the horrible note, but now she realised it was more likely he was afraid of what Rosemary might do or say. Did he fear she would make their affair public knowledge? It also begged the question of how many other women had been victims of his charm.

Rosemary sat perfectly still, staring into her cup. 'Moreau never asked what happened to the child when we arrived last autumn. He ignored me. How did I fall for such a cruel man, Mrs Lawrence?' Slowly she raised her eyes. The devastation in her expression brought a lump to Lucy's throat, but Rosemary's next words chilled her to her core. 'Moreau had a heart of stone. I'm glad he's dead.'

TWENTY-SIX

Lucy lay awake. Rosemary's troubles at Moreau's hands lay heavily upon her. Vauquelin had read his character perfectly, and to think she'd defended the Frenchman. Lucy groaned. Had she been that bored and frustrated that she'd let herself be fooled by Moreau's outward charm? With the benefit of hindsight, going to Nice had been a great misfortune, meeting Moreau a disaster. And now, here she was trying to solve his murder and investigating who had been stealing from him. Lucy could almost see McQuillan and Phineas shaking their heads in disbelief.

She turned over and caught a flash of light through the canvas. It was well past midnight so there shouldn't be anyone about. To the music of Mary's snores, Lucy grabbed her shawl and crept out of bed. Carefully, she moved the door flap to peep out. The full moon cast an eerie glow, and it was bright enough for her to see the campsite clearly. Across from her tent, two figures stood by the side of Hopkins' tent, one holding a lantern. Both figures appeared to be agitated, one gesticulating, the other bent forward and whispering furiously. Suddenly, the second and taller figure grabbed the other by the upper arms, swung them around and marched them across the sand. In Lucy's direction. She ducked back. The two figures walked past, close to Lucy's tent. Lucy waited for a minute before peeping out again. They'd stopped at the next tent. Lucy had a clear view: it was Hopkins and Isabella.

'Don't do it!' Isabella whispered hoarsely. 'It's far too dangerous.'

'I have to, Bell; I can't let Whitmore get to it first,' Hopkins said. 'You just concentrate on getting those shabti to Cairo. Have you a good enough excuse ready for her?'

'Yes, I was going to tell her I needed to go back to fetch a part for the camera. It will be easy to fool her; she knows next to nothing about the equipment. But she's getting suspicious, David. I told you what she said about you. Maybe we should leave her a warning note, like the one we sent to Moreau? If we scare her sufficiently, she might high-tail it back to Cairo and out of our way.'

'No, she's far too clever; she'd realise it was from us. Every attempt we have made to throw her off the scent has failed.'

Isabella stamped her foot. 'I know! I've never encountered such a meddlesome woman.'

'And that is why I must act tonight, before she finds out. Bell, you must go to bed. We can talk further tomorrow at the tomb. She'll be busy back here.'

Lucy scowled. *Oh no she won't!*

Isabella threw her hands up in the air in a helpless gesture. Hopkins stepped forward and took her in his arms. As Lucy watched, Isabella's arms snaked around his neck, and they became locked in a passionate embrace. Lucy sat back on her hunkers. Her suspicions were now fully confirmed. And what was it about the shabti? Were Hopkins and Isabella—her *friend* Isabella—robbing her? A sense of betrayal was quickly followed by white-hot anger.

As Lucy watched, Hopkins broke free of his lover and

strode past the opening of her tent. Lucy shrank back just in time. When she peeked out again, he was walking away to where the servants slept. Unsure what to do, Lucy kept watch. Minutes later, he returned with one of the men. They spoke quietly, then Hopkins turned on his heel. If Lucy wasn't mistaken, he was heading out in the direction of the tomb. What the devil was he up to? She would have to follow him.

Waking Rafiq was not easy; waking him without disturbing his brother was impossible. Both men sat up and stared at her, blinking in the light of her lantern. With haste, she explained that Hopkins had set off for the dig, and she needed to go after him to find out what he was up to. The men exchanged meaningful looks.

'What do you know?' Lucy demanded angrily. Could she trust anyone?

Rafiq looked at his brother who nodded. 'Ali suspects Mr Hopkins has been removing artefacts.'

'Yes, I figured that out! I knew someone here at the dig had to be involved when I discovered one of our shabti in a Cairo shop.' Lucy turned to Ali. 'But why didn't you tell anyone, Ali?'

'He say I lose job if I tell,' Ali said with a look of pure misery.

'When did you suspect?'

'Two days ago he send me to tent for journal. When I look I find bag of shabti under bed. He came in and find me with bag. He threaten me. Said he would tell police I steal.'

'Did Moreau know about it?' Lucy asked, dreading the answer.

'No, madame, M. Moreau think it was someone at museum,' Ali said.

'What a mess! Right, gentlemen, you will come with me. We are going to sort this out tonight.'

'Is this wise, madame?' Rafiq asked. 'Police would be better to deal with this.'

'I'll go on my own, then. Give me your rifle,' Lucy demanded, her hand outstretched.

Rafiq pulled himself up to his full height. 'No!' He glanced at his brother. 'We will come.'

Lucy let out a slow breath of relief.

Twenty minutes later, the three of them were crouched down behind some rocks near the entrance of the tomb. A shadowy figure stood at the top of the shaft. One of the fellâheen. Lucy cursed under her breath. Of course, Hopkins would have needed someone to man the hoist.

'I can take him by surprise,' Rafiq whispered. He made a cudgelling action with his hand.

'You are too big. He will see you,' Ali hissed.

'I do not wish you to harm him, Rafiq. He's only doing what Hopkins told him,' Lucy whispered.

'How do we get past?' Rafiq asked with a bewildered expression.

'I shall walk up to him and tell him to go back to camp,' Lucy replied.

'Madness! What if he has a gun or a knife?'

'The men know me, Rafiq. He may be surprised, but I'm sure he will obey me.'

Rafiq shook his head. 'You are stubborn lady.'

'Soon be dead lady,' Ali muttered.

'Pooh!' she said. As Lucy began to rise, Ali tugged at her arm and pulled her back down. Lucy looked across to the tomb entrance. Someone was coming up from the shaft. The man was heaving the rope, his straining face illuminated by the lantern of the person being hoisted up. As Hopkins was swung onto firm ground Lucy saw all he held was a lantern. There was no bag.

No artefacts. So why had he gone down there? Had he found another chamber and not told her about it so that he could spirit away its treasures? She had expected to see him with something. Puzzled, Lucy watched Hopkins and his helper set off back towards the camp.

'Waste of time,' Ali mumbled.

Lucy shook her head. 'No, he must be up to something. I'll have to go down and investigate. You two stay up here and keep watch.'

As Lucy's boots touched the shaft floor, a shiver went through her body. The silence was unnerving and this was the first time she'd been down here alone. Holding up her lantern, Lucy started off down the passageway. During the last couple of days, the men had made steady progress. Another ten feet of the corridor had been cleared.

A sudden scuttling sound almost made her drop her lantern. Heart pounding, she halted as she caught sight of a scorpion as it scurried off into the darkness. *Calm down!* she told herself, *just be on your guard*. She looked about. But there was no sign of a hidden room. Putting the lantern down on the ground, she checked first for more wildlife and once satisfied there was none, she felt along the walls with both hands. She knew from the descriptions of opened tombs in Moreau's books, there were often hidden chambers, cleverly concealed. And goodness knows, Hopkins would be clever enough to conceal one, too. Perhaps the secret room was off one of the already opened chambers?

The room where they'd found the jewellery proved unfruitful. Beginning to feel a little foolish, Lucy trudged out into the corridor and into the first chamber. There was Osiris, all green and forbidding. Lucy tried to ignore the figure, and set about searching along the walls. Nothing. With a frustrated sigh, she leaned back against the wall and tried to figure out why Hopkins had come out here so late at night, if not for some nefarious purpose. If he was stowing artefacts down here to smuggle out at a later time, she was baffled as to where he was hiding them. Remembering the overheard conversation between him and Isabella, she recalled his words: *I can't let Whitmore get to it first.* What did he mean? The burial chamber? Something precious hidden down here?

'I don't suppose *you* know what he's up to?' she asked Osiris. But the Lord of Silence kept his secrets. Disgruntled at being so easily defeated, she decided it was time to go back to the camp. She could tackle Hopkins and Isabella in the morning. Just then a prickle of fear coursed through her. She could have sworn the image of Osiris moved! Frozen to the spot, all she could do was stare. Her mouth went dry and her heart pounded. This was ridiculous. It must be the heat of the tomb or lack of sleep. It was as if the ancient god was pointing out towards the passageway...

She needed to leave. Now!

But just as Lucy reached the doorway, there was a loud bang and a blast of heat.

The world turned pitch black.

There was a pain, and it was a bad one, too: a throbbing sensation throughout her body. Lucy heard a groan and realised it was hers.

'She's waking up!' she heard Mary say, before the blackness swallowed her up again.

Then there were dreams and a green-faced man stalked through them. Everywhere she looked she saw vivid images of pharaohs and their queens, and two-dimensional scenes of chaos on tomb walls. And in the corner sat Moreau, a ceremonial dagger sticking out from his chest. He was laughing at her.

The next time Lucy woke up she was looking up into the concerned eyes of her maid. Lucy tried to speak, but her throat was dry and sore.

'Oh, ma'am! I thought you were dead!' Mary said, her lower lip trembling. 'But the doctor said you were incredibly lucky. Not that you'll agree when you see your poor face and hair, and I'm sure you're awful sore.' Mary was babbling. Lucy closed her eyes again, then opened them. Thankfully, Mary was still there; she hadn't imagined her.

Lucy glanced beyond Mary. To her surprise she was in a room not a tent or a tomb.

'Rafiq brought you here, ma'am,' Mary said. ''Tis a house of sorts. Well, not a house exactly, more like a ruin with a few home comforts. Would you like some water?'

Lucy nodded and instantly regretted it, as pain seared through her head. Her sharp intake of breath brought Mary running back to her side. 'Oh, you poor dear! Here, let me help you sit up a bit.'

Lucy gritted her teeth as Mary manoeuvred her into a sitting position, plumping pillows and fussing. 'There now, that's better,' Mary said, holding the glass to her lips.

After several swallows, Lucy croaked. 'Cairo?'

'No, ma'am. We are still in the desert. The doctor said not to move you,' Mary replied. 'M. Joubert has been awful kind.'

Lucy realised she was in Mariette's house at Joubert's camp. 'What happened? I don't remember anything.'

Mary sat down on the edge of the bed. 'Well, ma'am. I don't know where to start. Sure it was pandemonium, it was. In the middle of the night, that Ali fellow runs into the camp yelling and shouting for help. Mr Hopkins tells him off, but Ali insisted he needed all the men as quickly as possible. When he said you were trapped down in the tomb, I nearly died. Mr Hopkins, he went as white as a sheet and dashed off to fetch Miss DeLuca. I didn't wait for her, I can tell you. I dressed as quick as a flash and ran out to the tomb with the men. We didn't know if you were alive or dead, ma'am. I offered up a few decades of the rosary for your safe deliverance. And thanks be to God, didn't they find you unconscious in some room and not under a pile of rubble which some of them had expected. And you were still alive. I wept, I did. And so did Rafiq. But I wouldn't mention it, ma'am. He was fierce embarrassed about it after.'

Lucy smiled, but her face hurt. She wouldn't do that again for a while.

'Then,' Mary continued, 'there was this big discussion about what to do. Rafiq sent a messenger off to M. Joubert. For some reason he didn't want to bring you back to our camp, which I wanted him to do. After all, your things were there. But he was insistent. So they made up a stretcher and brought you here. A message was sent out, and a doctor appeared this afternoon, all the way from Cairo.'

'How bad is it?' Lucy croaked.

'Ah, now, don't you be worrying. The doctor said it looks a lot worse than it is.'

'I hurt everywhere.'

'You've a lot of bruising and some nasty scrapes and scratches, but aren't you lucky to be alive, at all? So you remember nothing?'

'Not a thing.'

'Just as well, ma'am. Now, I've to give you some laudanum – doctor's orders. It will help with the pain, and you can get some sleep.'

Lucy watched Mary mix up the medicine and gagged at the smell of it. 'Come along now, ma'am, it doesn't taste the best, but sure doesn't it work wonders. That's it, down the hatch!'

TWENTY-SEVEN

Mary guarded her with a zeal Lucy found endearing. No visitors were allowed past the door, bar Rafiq and Ali, who Lucy desperately wished to thank. The brothers were clearly upset and begged her forgiveness for not preventing her accident. Lucy scolded them for being so foolish and, as both of them looked exhausted, she ordered them back to camp to get some rest.

But after three days, Lucy was sufficiently recovered to venture out of bed. The image which stared back at her from the mirror was shocking. There was some interesting yellow and purple bruising to her face and neck, and one side of her hair was scorched. What would Phineas say if he could see her? No doubt he would scold her severely for being so foolish and getting herself into a dangerous situation. At that moment, she would have welcomed even a rebuke from a friend, for it seemed everyone she had considered her ally and trusted here in Egypt, had betrayed her.

Tentatively, she touched the bruises and grimaced. Mary fussed about, suggesting this dress or that but, in the end, Lucy sent her off on the pretext of making her tea. Sitting before the mirror, she desperately tried to remember what had happened. But it was all a very frustrating blank.

Mary reappeared bearing the tea tray and a message from M. Joubert requesting she join him for lunch on the terrace in an hour, if she was well enough.

'Ma'am, you must put yourself first,' Mary said, hands on hips. 'I'll not have you worn down by his mithering.' At that moment, Lucy swelled with affection for her maid. She didn't deserve such unflinching devotion. Hadn't she dragged the poor girl into nothing but trouble since Charlie's demise?

With a gulp to disguise the lump in her throat, Lucy took up the powder puff and did her best to hide the worst of the discolouration. 'No, it's fine. And I'll wear the light silk with the blue ribbons—they'll go well with my bruises.'

'Oh, ma'am!' Mary admonished.

'I must face people at some stage, Mary. I only hope I don't put M. Joubert off his meal.'

Mary glared at her. 'I'll have something to say about it—'

'Mary, I'm joking.' Lucy stood up gingerly. 'Once I'm decent, you might escort me, my dear, for I'm still unsteady on my feet.'

Joubert rose to greet her, his expression full of concern. 'Madame, I'm delighted to see you up. You gave us all such a fright.' The director took her hand and squeezed it, then drew out a chair for her at the table. Above, a white linen awning fluttered in a gentle breeze. Lucy sighed. It was good to be out in the fresh air.

'Thank you for your hospitality, and I'm sorry my servants imposed upon you by bringing me here,' she said.

'Not at all. They were perfectly right to come here, and it was my pleasure to be of help.' The director sat down opposite her. 'The facilities at your camp were not suitable for someone with your injuries, and it was decided you were too badly hurt to risk the journey back to Bedrashên. I would have insisted on your being brought here even if your men had not come to me first.'

'I appreciate it, monsieur,' Lucy said. She gazed out from the coolness of the stone terrace, across the shimmering landscape of bleached white and gold. In the far distance, purple peaks formed smudges of colour on the horizon. 'There is something utterly beautiful about this place, for all its bleakness.'

Joubert smiled. 'Your soul is that of an archaeologist, my dear Madame Lawrence, despite all that has transpired. No one else views this desolate place in such a way. Sand and secrets, and the promise of unknown wonders.'

'Moreau said something similar to me once,' Lucy said with a pang. 'It is hard not to be drawn to the mysteries of the desert.'

'It can drive a man to madness, if he lets it,' Joubert said. 'However, I'm certain madness is a prerequisite for hunting artefacts.'

What a strange thing to say, Lucy thought. She wondered what was on his mind, but something held her back. Instead, she tried to draw him out on his favourite subject. 'What brought the ancients here to such a desolate place?'

The director looked up. 'Ah! It was a different landscape then. I doubt it was always this dry, inhospitable place. The Nile gave life to this place, or at least to Memphis. Sakkâra was convenient and to the west. They were certain the soul journeyed into the west to the afterlife, and so built their tombs out here.'

Lucy glanced back at the house. 'Why did Mariette build this house here and not at Bedrashên?'

'It made perfect sense rather than setting up camp every year, for he knew as soon as he uncovered the first tantalising glimpse that it would take many years to excavate the

Serapeum.' Joubert pointed to the north past the two sphinxes standing guard on the terrace. 'The entrance to the Serapeum lies in the sandy hollow just beyond here. Mariette didn't want to waste time travelling back and forth to a local village, or indeed Cairo. Even when the excavation was complete, he continued to live in this house. Nothing gave him greater pleasure than to bring travellers here and to show them the wonders of the Apis vaults. I was lucky enough to have him as my guide on my very first visit.'

'How wonderful!'

'Yes, I was privileged,' Joubert said. 'Mariette may be gone, but the house now stands welcoming anyone who travels to this place – a tiny island of civilisation and one of his many gifts to this country. The buildings at the back still house some broken statues and stelae. Most of his discoveries, however, were sent to the Louvre.' Joubert rubbed his chin. 'In those days, finds left Egypt far too quickly. Now, can I tempt you with some wine?'

'Thank you, monsieur, that would be lovely,' Lucy replied as he poured and handed her a glass. 'When I'm a little steadier on my feet, I would like to explore the Serapeum. Would that be possible?'

'It would be my honour to show it to you,' Joubert responded.

As the servants laid out the dishes for lunch, Lucy and Joubert sat in silence. Once they were alone, Joubert turned to her. 'I'm afraid I have some bad news. David Hopkins and Miss DeLuca have disappeared. Your dragoman told me you suspected them of stealing from the site, and that was why you followed Hopkins that night.'

'Yes. But I found no evidence in the tomb.'

'And then the dynamite exploded,' Joubert said, shaking his head. 'You were extremely lucky not to have been out in the corridor. The full force of that blast would have killed you instantly.'

Lucy nodded as a niggling memory momentarily teased her, frustratingly close, but it vanished just as quickly. 'Dynamite?'

'Yes, indeed. Frustrated by Whitmore's return and the possibility he would find the burial chamber first, Hopkins decided to use explosives to remove the blockage in the passage-way. Crude but effective,' Joubert remarked. 'There was a time when such methods were common, I'm afraid.'

'But frowned upon now,' Lucy said.

'Yes, of course, the risk of damaging valuable artefacts, inscriptions... it does not bear contemplating.'

'He might have destroyed the entire tomb, stupid man!' All her hopes and dreams of being the patron to a great find were dead. Lucy would gladly wring the man's neck. It was just as well he had made a run for it.

'Hopkins was willing to take the gamble. When your servants came back to the camp and informed him you were trapped, he realised you had followed him out to the dig, and you were on to him. Panic made him run.'

'Yes. You see, I knew for certain they were involved in the black market as I overheard them discussing it. Miss DeLuca was Hopkins' accomplice and involved in the thefts. Has Vauquelin been informed?'

'Yes, indeed, as soon as we knew they'd taken off. I'm afraid in the furore at your camp, Hopkins also managed to take what-ever artefacts were still there and light enough to carry.'

'You would nearly admire his sangfroid!' Lucy exclaimed. 'Except for the fact he almost killed me, of course. I do hope Vauquelin catches them in Cairo and, better still, finds the missing items on them.'

'Of course, it is obvious Hopkins must be the murderer, don't you think, Mrs Lawrence?'

Lucy frowned. 'I'm not sure. Without doubt, he's a thief and getting Moreau out of the picture was to his advantage, but I'm just not convinced he is capable of murder. Did he hate Moreau enough? I don't believe so. I never detected anything of that nature in their relationship.'

'I disagree, madame. It's likely he and Miss DeLuca lured poor Moreau to his death, fully intending to take advantage of his absence on the dig. Did the man not come to you and beg you to intercede with me to re-open the site?'

Lucy nodded. 'He did, and Moreau only buried a few days. And Isabella led me to believe that Moreau had been willing to sponsor Hopkins the very day I went to you to ask about re-opening the dig.'

'You see! If you think about it, it had to be Hopkins' plan. And Miss DeLuca must have carried out the robbery at the museum.'

Much as Lucy didn't want to admit it, Joubert was probably right. 'Yes, she must have, because we know Hopkins was here in Sakkâra,' she said.

'Exactly!'

'I wonder which one of them took a pair of Whitmore's glasses. It must have been Isabella, that night at the hotel.' Lucy frowned.

'Indeed, it had to be. A cunning pair!'

'Luckily, Inspector Vauquelin treated the presence of the glasses in the King's Chamber with suspicion. We must hope he will find more solid proof that Hopkins was the murderer. So far it is all circumstantial, as it was with Whitmore.'

'I'm sure the proof will surface, Madame Lawrence. They'll hang for what they did to my poor friend.'

Lucy shuddered. 'I still can't believe Isabella was involved in murder. How devious she was, and all along she was feeding information back to Hopkins. I did wonder about them as a couple and watched them closely, but they hid their relation-ship well. It was only the night of the explosion that I saw them together and could no longer doubt they were romantically entangled. But why did she become embroiled in the black market? She comes from a wealthy family and has no need of the money.'

'Are you sure she's wealthy? Perhaps she was living off the proceeds of their thefts from previous seasons. Both she and Hopkins have been coming to Egypt for many years. Do not underestimate how lucrative the trade in black market artefacts is.'

'Yes, I suppose you could be right. From her clothes and her ability to stay at the Excelsior, I never questioned Isabella's financial status. And, of course, when Moreau became angry about the upsurge in thefts and started to make enquiries, they must have panicked. The threatening note he received was from them – they admitted it. But murder? I can't fathom why she would risk so much.'

'Some individuals thrive on danger and excitement, or maybe Hopkins talked her into it,' Joubert said in a bleak voice. 'People do strange things in the name of love.'

'All too true, M. Joubert.' Suddenly, Lucy was overcome with despondency. 'One thing is certain – my detection skills aren't as good as I supposed. Though, I inadvertently revealed Hopkins was up to no good at the dig. Mind you, I would have preferred to catch him in the act. I do hope Vauquelin is not too late; if they flee Egypt, they'll never be found.'

Joubert smiled down at his plate but, when he raised his eyes, there was no humour to be seen. 'Vauquelin will do his job, you can be certain of that. However, now you must agree this investigating business is far too dangerous. You must give it up at once, dear lady. When you're recovered sufficiently, I hope you will go home and let your family look after you.'

Her family! If only he knew. 'Admit defeat and leave? I do not think so.' Joubert frowned at her but she continued. 'How ironic it is that matters have transpired in such a way.'

'Forgive me; I do not follow.'

'Why Whitmore has free rein now. I assume you will let

him continue at the site? Poor Moreau; how he would have hated that.'

'It is true you must give up the concession. You aren't qualified to continue the work alone. But I would have thought, in the circumstances, you would be happy to leave. You were lucky to escape with your life from the tomb. The ancient gods of Egypt must be looking out for you. It does no good to tempt fate.'

'On the contrary, I believe it *is* fate. My plans here at Sakkâra may be in tatters, but I'll talk to Reginald Whitmore. I would like to see the excavation of Moreau's find completed. I'm sure Whitmore wouldn't object to my being involved if I offer him funding. What do you think?'

Joubert stared at her open-mouthed before shaking his head. 'I... He would hardly accept.'

Lucy shrugged. 'Why would he not? Would you object?'

Joubert shook his head, frowning heavily. 'The British Museum will step in, I'm sure. There is no need for you to be involved. You have already diced with danger far too often.'

'But the explosion in the tomb was an unlucky accident! Hopkins didn't know I was going down there after he left. No, the more I think about it, it would be the perfect solution. Until Moreau's murder is solved, I refuse to leave Egypt. My instinct is screaming out to me – I'm missing some vital clue or connection. If Whitmore accepts, it will give me a good reason to be around his camp. Perhaps I can glean some new clues. It is still possible he *was* the murderer. What if that hotel servant was paid off to give that alibi, or the laudanum had been tampered with, diluted or replaced by something innocuous? Then it is possible he did leave the hotel during the night, unseen.'

'Really, I do not think...' Joubert appeared to be struggling to keep up.

'Rosemary may be involved too. She certainly had reason to hate Moreau. No, I must stay. I'm sure Vauquelin would agree.'

'And if Whitmore refuses your offer?' Joubert asked.

'I can but try. Some would say I'm very persuasive, you know,' Lucy said. 'Besides, he will hardly refuse the money. Don't worry, monsieur, I won't outstay my welcome.'

'Trust me, madame, that would be impossible.'

TWENTY-EIGHT

A week later, Lucy was reading out on the terrace when she spotted two figures approaching on donkeys. Rafiq and Ali soon materialised and greeted her warmly. She bade them sit down and, eventually, after some protest, both men did so.

'Is everything in order?' she asked Ali.

'Yes, madame. Men are paid and told to go home. Camp is gone,' Ali said. 'I take last of boxes to Cairo this evening.'

'I'm sorry, but I had no choice, Ali. M. Joubert insists, in the circumstances, we must cease to work the site.'

'Yes, I understand. Men understand too, and happy with money you give,' Ali said. 'Very generous.'

'No, not at all. They have families to feed and may not find other work this season. It wasn't their fault the site had to close.' Ali nodded.

'Some have gone to the Whitmore camp, madame,' Rafiq said. 'Is this a problem?'

'I have no right to dictate who they work for, Rafiq. Do you think he will have work for them?' she asked.

'Mr Whitmore will take the most experienced and those

who are most familiar with the tomb,' Rafiq answered. 'Will help him find rest of tomb faster.'

'I can't blame him; I'm sure I would do the same in the circumstances. But I'll thank him when I meet him all the same. If I'm feeling better tomorrow, I'll visit his camp,' she said. 'Despite all that has happened, I'm so glad I met you both. I wish you luck, Ali, as you return to your family.' Ali's eyes shone as he nodded vigorously.

Lucy turned to Rafiq. 'My plans are uncertain, but if Mr Whitmore is agreeable, I hope to remain in Sakkâra as his patron. I wish to see the tomb completely opened up. It is what Moreau would have wanted, and I must admit, my curiosity is boundless; I desperately want to discover what lies hidden there. In light of this, I was hoping you would agree to stay on with me for now?'

Rafiq smiled and turned to his brother. 'I told you she's bravest woman in Egypt and not run away.' Ali grinned back at her.

Rafiq suddenly grew serious and frowned at her. 'M. Moreau entrusted you to my care. I'll not leave your side until you depart Egypt.'

That Evening

Thirty years of blazing sun and encroaching sand had taken their toll on Mariette's desert house. Yet, Joubert's servants managed to present the small room, which served as a sitting room and dining room, with a homely atmosphere. The walls were roughly hewn local rock, the floor slabs of the same. But with a fire lit and the lanterns flickering from the tables dotted around the room, it might have been a room in a ramshackle Scottish castle and not a near-ruin in danger of being swallowed by the greedy desert. However, the ubiquitous sand was a constant reminder that outside the door were the tombs of the

ancient dead, barely covered by a wind-carved sea of sand
stretching out towards the Libyan hills.

Lucy looked up from Mariette's *The Monuments of Upper
Egypt*. Somewhere in the house a window was banging. Since
her solitary dinner an hour earlier, she'd been aware of the wind
starting to rise. The house being exposed on a rocky plateau, the
gusts sang their way around the building. Consulting her watch,
she was surprised Joubert had not returned. He had set off mid-
afternoon for Whitmore's camp at her behest. She hoped Whitmore would be more amenable to her offer if it came through
Joubert. Perhaps M. Joubert had stayed for dinner. Picking up
the tome once more, she soon found her eyes were drooping.
With a snap, she shut the book and replaced it in the bookcase.
Time for bed.

As she passed the table beside Joubert's favourite armchair,
she paused. Half-hidden behind the pile of books she spotted
some photographs. It felt intrusive to look at them, but her
curiosity won out. The first was a group of men standing before
a tomb, a much younger Joubert, easily recognisable, peering out
at the camera. The next was a family group, posing stiffly. She
assumed it was his parents and siblings. As she placed it back
down, Lucy realised there was another frame, partially
obscured. It was of a lady in profile. There was something
familiar about her expression and her dark eyes, but Lucy
wasn't sure. Since the accident in the tomb, she'd found it difficult at times to recall names and faces without a struggle. The
doctor had assured her this would pass in time. Lucy glanced at
the woman again. She flipped the photograph over. 'Rebecca,
1880' was inscribed on the backplate. It must be his dead wife,
she thought, placing it carefully back in its original position.

Mary was waiting for her with a smile, as ever, ushering her
to take a seat at the makeshift dressing table. 'Ma'am, your
bruises are healing nicely. Why, the ones on your face are
nearly gone entirely.'

Lucy grimaced at her reflection in the mirror. 'I don't know, Mary. I still look as if I went several rounds with a prize-fighter, and I ache everywhere.'

Mary chuckled, unpinning her hair and taking up the comb. 'The things you say, ma'am.' A gentle knock on the door stopped her mid-stroke. 'Now, whoever can that be at this hour?'

'Best answer it, Mary,' Lucy said, taking the comb from her.

Through the mirror Lucy saw Mary open the door and was surprised to see her slip outside. The murmur of voices continued for a minute before Mary reappeared.

'Ma'am, that was M. Joubert's manservant, Louis.' Mary hesitated as if trying to come to a decision.

'Well, what is it? Is something wrong?'

'He's not sure, ma'am. M. Joubert arrived about ten minutes ago, and Louis gave him a telegram which had arrived earlier.'

'And?' Lucy asked.

'Well, that's just it, ma'am. Seemingly, M. Joubert took whatever was in it very badly, frightening Louis. M. Joubert has left the house in quite a state, and Louis is concerned and doesn't know what to do. I told him not to be mithering you with it and sent him off. You need your rest. I'm sure M. Joubert will be back when he has calmed down. Let him have his tantrum in peace. These Frenchies are fierce temperamental, if you ask me!'

An hour later, Lucy was still awake, her ears straining for the sound of Joubert's return. It was no good; she couldn't sleep. Something might have happened to him. Dressing quickly, Lucy tied back her hair with a ribbon. Once she was reasonably decent, she headed off in search of one of Joubert's servants. She found Louis in the sitting room, a worried frown on his face as he tidied.

'Has he not returned? Do you know where your master has gone?' Lucy asked him.

Louis straightened up. 'Sometimes he goes to the Serapeum if he has one of his turns. The quiet helps him think, he says.'

What an odd thing to do, Lucy thought, I wonder why he has gone there. 'Turns? Does this happen often?'

'Lately, yes, madame,' Louis said with a miserable expression.

'Has he gone alone? Did he take one of the servants with him?'

'No. He expressly forbade it, and before he left, he ordered the men to board up the outhouses against the wind. We haven't been here in two years, and some of the shuttering has come loose. M. Joubert would be terribly angry if any of the artefacts were damaged.'

'Yes, of course. But why are you so concerned about M. Joubert this evening?'

'There is a sandstorm blowing up, and if M. Joubert loses his way... I'm sorry, madame, but if I go, he will be very angry with me. He likes you; he wouldn't mind if you go to his aid... You see, sometimes, he frightens me.'

Frightened of Joubert; this was silly, Lucy thought. Besides, she was curious as to why the old man would find solace in such a strange place as the Serapeum. 'Fetch me a lantern, Louis, quickly please. He's old and upset; I can't ignore this. If I were in trouble, he would come to my aid.' Lucy sent the manservant out the door with an impatient wave of her hand.

She crossed to the fire to warm her hands. A piece of white paper caught Lucy's attention. The scorched and crumpled remains of Joubert's telegram were at the edge of the grate. Perhaps she should look; it would help her understand what had upset the poor man so badly. She grabbed the poker and flipped the piece of paper out onto the hearth. But she was too late. The only part of the charred telegram she could read, when she managed to flatten it out, revealed part of one word: – *uquelin*.

Hearing Louis's returning footsteps, Lucy shoved the telegram back into the grate and threw a log on top of it. As he drew closer, she made a show of poking the fire, all the while her mind buzzing. Why had Vauquelin sent a telegram to Joubert? Was it an update on the investigation? More importantly why had Joubert thrown it on the fire? Its contents must have really upset him. The poor man. He had been through so much lately.

'It is a trifle chilly, is it not?' Lucy said as Louis approached.

The servant regarded her gravely, his eyes straying to the grate. 'It is always thus at night in the desert, madame.'

'Yes, indeed. I wonder if I'll ever get used to it.'

'Most do, eventually,' he replied, about to hand her the lantern.

'Best you stay here, Louis, in case your master returns and has need of you, but I'll need you to point out the way. I must fetch my coat. I'll meet you on the terrace in a few minutes.'

Once in her room, Lucy pulled on her coat. How unfortunate Rafiq wasn't around, but he had gone to see Ali off at the train station at Bedrashên and would stay there for the night. Her only other option was Mary. Lucy crept up to the door of Mary's room. A succession of snores told her Mary was dead to the world. Lucy smiled; Mary wouldn't take kindly to be pulled from her bed and out into a storm. She was being silly; she didn't need a bodyguard anyway. The worst that could happen was that she would lose her way in the sandstorm.

Lucy returned to her own room and, as she stood at the end of the bed, her eyes fell on her carpet bag tucked under the footboard. Rummaging in the bottom of the bag, she found what she was looking for. Carefully, she pulled it out and checked it was loaded. In case of snakes, she said to herself. But her hand was shaking as she shoved the pearl-handled pistol into the pocket of her coat. Phineas would understand, would laud her caution.

But it was ridiculous! Joubert was an old man; what harm could he pose? With an impatient sigh, Lucy placed the pistol back into the bag. Exhaling slowly, she decided to play it safe, nevertheless. She scribbled a note saying where she was going and left it on the table beside the bed.

TWENTY-NINE

As soon as Lucy left the shelter of the house, swirls of sand were whipped up into her face. She had to pull her scarf over her hair, mouth and nose. It was not a night for venturing out into a storm. The thought of her warm bed popped into her head, but she had to shake off the treacherous longing: her host was in distress and needed her. In the distance, Lucy heard hammering. The men must still be working on the outbuildings.

She found Louis waiting at the edge of the terrace, muffled up against the gritty onslaught of the high wind. He had the lit lantern in one hand and a large key in the other. 'In case he has locked the door,' he shouted above the wind. 'It is only a short distance down to the hollow.' He pointed to a rocky outcrop silhouetted to the north. 'Be careful, madame, for it can be difficult to keep your footing. The sand moves so under one's feet.'

'Do you have any idea where he might be?'

Louis shrugged. 'I'm not even sure he's there at all, madame. But he's fond of the place and finds comfort in it when he's low.'

'If I do not find him in the Serapeum, I'll come back, and we will have to set up a search party as soon as there is daylight,' Lucy said. Louis nodded in agreement.

Lucy stepped down from the terrace, her boots meeting resistance from the soft sand. She'd read about the Serapeum only a few hours ago and wracked her brain trying to remember the map of its layout. It wouldn't be easy to find him if he didn't wish it, for the complex was large with many corridors and vaults.

'This must be where the sphinxes from Mariette's tomb once formed an avenue,' Lucy murmured as she descended the steps, walls rising up on either side. At the bottom of the incline was a stout wooden door. Taking a deep breath, Lucy gently pushed against it. The door swung open noiselessly, and a wave of heat hit her face. Joubert must be inside; why else would the door be unlocked? Placing the key in her coat pocket, Lucy held up the lantern. Some granite steps disappeared down into the darkness. She continued on into the oppressive atmosphere. Suddenly, the door shut behind her with a dull clang which echoed back from the walls making her jump. Immediately, she felt perspiration forming on her skin, along with a prickle of anxiety. Her mouth was so dry her tongue stuck to the roof of her mouth.

This is silly! I shouldn't be so jumpy.

There was total silence within. It was hard to believe just outside the wind was raging. What if the weather worsened? If it turned into a sandstorm, how would she find her way back to the house? Rafiq had told her how bad they were, and it would be infinitely worse in the dark. Lucy took a deep breath. There was no point in worrying about that now. It wasn't every day one entered an ancient tomb complex for sacred Apis bulls. However, it would be preferable to explore it with a guide and not to be wandering around in search of a man who might not wish to be found. Gnawing at her lower lip, Lucy was determined not to give in to regret. This is an adventure she told herself; something to tell Lady Sarah about in her next letter.

Lifting up the lantern, Lucy saw she was in a huge space

carved out from the rock with a vaulted ceiling and roughly hewn walls. 'Monsieur Joubert?' she called out. Her voice resonated around the chamber, then silence. A shiver went through her.

Lucy blinked, trying to adjust her eyes to the gloom. Where could he be? There was only one passageway ahead, black as night, and she set off to find out where it might lead.

As Lucy moved forward, the only sound was the crunch of sand underfoot. And then, suddenly, she came across the first of the burial chambers: a vaulted recess with a sunken floor about six feet down from where she stood, in the middle of which stood a huge granite sarcophagus. The enormous lid had been pushed back a few feet. Awestruck, Lucy stooped and stared inside. It was vast. The polished granite shone: its surface perfectly smooth. The interior was large enough to host a tea party for three or four of your friends quite comfortably, if one were inclined to take tea in a coffin. Lucy's smile quickly faded. There was no mummified bull or living man to be seen. Could Joubert have fallen and be unconscious somewhere? Now, she'd have to check all the vaults. She sighed in frustration. Lucy's sympathy for the elderly man began to wane. Could he not have indulged his megrim under a palm tree instead and preferably in daylight?

Several more identical vaults lined the corridor, each as empty of any living thing as the next. Just as Lucy was contemplating a return to the house, she heard a scraping sound: metal on stone, if she wasn't mistaken. Tilting her head, Lucy stood perfectly still and listened. Yes, it was coming from up ahead. Could it be Joubert? The passageway turned and split in two. But the corridor to the left showed a trace of light. It was faint, but her eyes were accustomed enough now to make it out. Hopefully, she'd found him.

An extraordinary sight greeted Lucy. Joubert was sitting cross-legged in his shirt sleeves, his back against a sarcophagus.

A dagger, clasped in his right hand, was being scraped up and down on the stone floor. He didn't appear to notice her as she approached. With caution.

Lucy stopped a few feet away, confused. 'Monsieur! Are you unwell?'

Slowly, he raised his eyes, squinting at her. 'What are *you* doing here?'

'I was looking for you. Your servants were concerned for you, M. Joubert. Louis said you were upset, so I offered to come and find you and offer my assistance.'

'Can the world not leave me in peace!' he roared at her.

Lucy took a step back. His lips were twisted as if he had tasted something sour, and his eyes had a strange glow. Then she realised his pupils were dilated. There was a bottle by his side on the floor. The name on the label was unfamiliar, and she had no idea what it might contain. Had he taken something? What was making him act so strangely?

'Perhaps you should come back to the house, and let your servants take care of you?' she said, keeping her voice gentle.

Joubert began to laugh; it echoed off the walls, making her skin crawl. He leaned his head back and said so quietly she almost didn't hear him. 'No! We are staying here.'

'It is getting late, monsieur. Why do you want to stay here?'

'Is it not a fitting place to commune with the old gods? Is this not a fitting place to die, madame?'

Lucy concluded he *was* acting under the influence of something. 'But M. Joubert, why would you want to die?'

Joubert pulled off his glasses and rubbed at his eyes. 'I wish to choose the manner of my passing. There will be no rope for me. I prefer a more honourable death.'

Why was he talking about hanging? Lucy backed up another couple of steps, her blood running cold. 'I don't understand. No one must die, monsieur.' Just then a horrible realisation clicked into place. The photograph in Mariette's house.

Now she knew why the woman was familiar. It was the same lady in the picture in Moreau's travel bag. Moreau's long-lost love was... Joubert's wife?

'It was your wife Moreau loved,' Lucy exclaimed. '*You* murdered Moreau!'

'Bravo! At last you stupid woman. Of course it was me,' he scoffed.

Lucy as aghast. 'But why? I don't understand. Moreau was your friend.'

'Friend? Non! He was a *fiend*. The great seducer! Did you know he particularly liked married women because they were such a challenge? He couldn't help himself, but the day he stole my wife he was doomed. They thought they were very clever. Sneaking around behind my back, but a camp is a very small world, and I began to suspect. Her blushes, his smiles, and then one night I returned early from Cairo and saw them together.'

Lucy almost groaned. 'I'm sorry if he did that to you, I truly am, but this isn't making sense,' Lucy said. 'You still worked together for years. You were his mentor.'

Joubert flipped the dagger and caught it, his face twisted in a humourless grin. 'I fooled them. They didn't realise I'd found out. I decided to bide my time to take my revenge. A year later, my opportunity arose. It was a simple matter of pushing her down the shaft when no one was around. The expression on her face as she fell – surprise, I suppose. But I saw no regret. Rebecca was a harlot, and she'd betrayed me.'

The image of Joubert standing at his wife's grave, and his words of sorrow and grief in the garden at Boulaq came back to Lucy – all false! 'And Moreau?'

'I was beginning to despair I would ever get a chance to rid the world of him, it is true, but I'd already determined this was the season I would do it. I'd let him live too long. And then, some weeks ago my doctor confirmed that I'm dying, Madame Lawrence. I'll not see another winter. So, it had to be this season. And then fortune smiled upon me. Whitmore's jealous outburst at the hotel that night gave me the perfect opportunity. The police would suspect him, not me. I could still do the deed while I had some strength left. At least my last few weeks would be free of the torment of having to see and hear Moreau.'

'You were happy for someone else to take the blame?'

'Pah! It was all working beautifully, but Vauquelin didn't have the stomach for it. He let him go!'

'Whitmore's alibi was confirmed.'

Joubert sniffed. 'That was unfortunate. And now, the great inspector asks more questions of me that, of course, I can't answer.'

'The telegram in the fireplace?'

'Don't you ever stop, woman! Always you ask too many questions. Prying into everyone's business. Why do you think I sent you back here to Sakkâra with Hopkins? I wanted you out of the way. And now, all your probing has brought you here to me tonight. I knew you'd follow me. Louis is a coward, and I made sure he was scared of me this evening. Then, I knew, he would go running to you. Curiosity is your besetting sin. It was an easy trap to bait.'

Her blood ran cold. She didn't want to dwell on what his words meant. How could she have been so stupid? Her only chance was to play for time. 'How did you kill Armand?'

Joubert wiped his hand across his glistening forehead. 'Moreau left the hotel before me, if you recall, but I knew he wouldn't go back to his hotel, when he was in such a dark mood. I went home and, once my servants were in bed, I crept out. Moreau was easy enough to find in one of the seedy bars he favoured. Several whiskies later, and he was happy to accompany me out to Giza.'

'But why would he? On what pretext?'

Joubert leaned back against the sarcophagus. 'I may be old, but I'm clever,' he said, stabbing a finger into his temple. 'Only too well was I aware of that man's weaknesses. It was simple. I played to his vanity. I told him of a secret passage in the Great Pyramid, and I wanted him to excavate it. But it was highly secret and I could only show him at night, when no one would be around. It was laughable, his reaction. He was so grateful. I don't know how I wasn't ill. He was fawning over me, as he must have done to my wife. Of course, Moreau's ego couldn't resist such an opportunity.'

'Why Giza?'

'My dear madame, so it would look like Whitmore was the murderer. And luck was running in my favour. That oaf Whitmore left his glasses on the table in his hurry to make his dramatic exit from your dinner party. It was a simple matter to scoop them up.'

'So you led Moreau into the King's Chamber...'

Joubert jerked the dagger down, then laughed. 'It was *too* easy. Revenge *is* sweet, I assure you. I imagine the irony of killing him with his most famous find does not escape you?'

'No, monsieur, it does not,' she replied in disgust. 'And you would have let Whitmore hang for it?'

He shrugged. 'Happily! He would have been a small loss to the world of archaeology – or humanity, for that matter. It was the perfect solution until you and Vauquelin made a mess of it. Then I offered you up Hopkins, and still you couldn't do as I wished. Two perfectly acceptable suspects, but you and your *investigations*. Pah! How ridiculous you are. You know *nothing*.'

Lucy swallowed hard. 'What was in the telegram, monsieur?'

'The sealing of your fate and mine, madame.'

'But how has Vauquelin discovered you were the murderer?' Lucy asked. If she could keep him talking an idea of how to get out of this sticky mess might materialise. Unfortunately, in her panicked state, few ideas were emerging.

'I have no idea. His telegram merely stated he was on his

way.' Joubert struggled to his feet. 'Your friend Vauquelin will explain it all... *Mais non*! Of course; he will not have a chance, for you will be dead by the time he gets here.' Joubert laughed and shook his head. 'Now, I have enough of talking. Don't worry; I shall make this as quick as possible for both of us.'

Scared as she was, Lucy's temper flared up. 'But I do not wish to die.'

'But you must!' Joubert suddenly lunged towards her, the dagger raised, but Lucy had anticipated it. With all her strength, she threw her storm lantern at his face, and heard him howl in pain as she escaped into the darkness of the tunnels, running for her life.

THIRTY

Lucy ran blind for several minutes with her hands outstretched from her sides, praying hard the layout in her head would lead her back to the entrance. But Joubert wouldn't be stalled for long. The sound of her footsteps ringing out on the stone floors would give her away. Reluctantly, Lucy stopped and felt her way along the wall until she came to an opening. Her injured body was aching and her lungs screaming for air. Hiding was her best option for now. Gingerly, Lucy felt for the edge and, with a silent prayer, manoeuvred herself and dropped down into the vault. The fall into space was terrifying but brief. Her boots hit the floor with an unfortunate thud, leaving her cursing under her breath.

The stone was cold to the touch as she moved along as quietly as possible down the side of the sarcophagus to the rear of the vault. Lucy crouched down with her back to the coffin.

And waited. The minutes crawled and her fear grew.

Which was worse: the charged silence or the thump of her heart against her ribcage? Despite the heat, she began to shiver. *Stupid girl! Why did you put the pistol back in the bag?* If she got out of this alive, she would never undertake an adventure ever again. She would live quietly in some leafy suburb and take up — No! It was no good. She was doomed to always give in to her curiosity. Lemmings came to mind.

There! Footsteps, she was certain. Moments later, Lucy heard them more distinctly. She held her breath and watched in horror as a shadow formed on the wall, moving slowly across the back of the vault. Lucy could visualise him standing at the entrance, lantern raised. Joubert was searching for her. A scrape of a heel, and it sounded as if it were at the entrance of the chamber. A grunt broke the silence. Was he looking inside the sarcophagus? When she thought she couldn't stand it any longer, the shadow moved off. Shaking, Lucy exhaled slowly, willing her racing heart to slow.

'Come now, Madame Lawrence, you can't hide forever. I know this place far better than you. I'll find you,' Joubert said, as he moved away down the corridor.

Damn, she thought, he's now between me and the exit. I'm trapped. Should she risk moving up to the next chamber? How many chambers were there between here and the entrance hall? She hadn't counted them. One false move, one sound, and he would hear it, because every noise was amplified by the stone.

But waiting was worse. She'd risk it.

Just as Lucy gained the safety of the next chamber, she heard him. Joubert was coming back down the passageway, this time running the dagger along the stone wall. The hairs on the back of her neck prickled and her heart pounded. She squeezed her eyes shut, trying to work out where he was. The sound of the dragging blade passed by, then suddenly stopped. Lucy's eyes flew open, and she found herself in pitch blackness. He had put out his lantern.

Joubert was lying in wait.

Anger bubbled up inside her. She didn't deserve to be trapped in catacombs with a mad murderous Frenchman.

Damn you, Moreau! This is all your blasted fault. But what to do? Joubert had said Vauquelin was on his way, but he was unlikely to arrive until tomorrow at the earliest. Her only hope was Rafiq or Mary discovering she was missing from the house, but they wouldn't notice till morning. The note, at least, would tell them where to find her cold, dead body.

Or perhaps Louis would intervene before then? However, Lucy suspected the servant had gone to bed as soon as she'd left, secure in the knowledge Lucy had taken on the task of finding his master. An all-round coward that man was. But that didn't help her situation. Lucy wasn't even sure what time it was. Midnight? Later? It was going to be a long night, and she dared not close her eyes and sleep. Joubert might be waiting right outside the vault. Charlie had always joked about her snoring. Well, one snore tonight and she would be dead. Digging her nails into her palms, Lucy began to recite multiplication tables in her head. If Joubert could stay awake, so could she.

Lucy woke with a jolt, a quiver running through her body. Aghast, she strained, listening for the slightest sound. How long had she been asleep? Terrified to move, in case the mere rustle of her coat or skirts should give her away, Lucy's mind raced. Where *was* he? Was it night or had the day dawned? She had no way of knowing as she was in total darkness. *At least I'm still alive.* But there was little reassurance in the thought.

Time dragged, and Lucy's body grew stiff. She longed to stretch but dared not risk it. And it was then she heard faint muttering, as if someone was talking in their sleep. It was indistinct, though. Dare she move and investigate? If he was further down the corridor, she might be able to make a run for it. Anything was better than the interminable waiting for the trap to spring.

As slowly as possible, Lucy moved to the front of the chamber, stopping every few seconds to listen. The muttering continued, but she was unable to judge how far away he was. Lucy took a few deep breaths. Hoisting herself out of the chamber took several seconds, as her hands were slick with sweat, and the stone's polished surface offered no grip.

But no sooner had Lucy gotten to her feet, when a light flared. Joubert was about twenty feet away and struggling to his feet with a growl. Lucy took off down the corridor, hoping her sense of direction was taking her the right way. Joubert was gaining on her. With a spurt of adrenalin, Lucy burst into the entrance hall.

To her astonishment, the door opened, and two figures were silhouetted against the light of day. With a cry of delight, Lucy flung herself forward, aware of how close Joubert was. But she missed her footing, and her own momentum brought her crashing to the ground. Joubert roared with rage. Lucy felt a whoosh of air as a dagger passed within inches of her face. A rifle shot reverberated around the chamber, followed by a howl of pain. Then a ghastly silence fell.

Time was suspended. Lucy lay panting, wondering if she'd been hit. No, there was no pain or, at least, no new pain. As she opened her eyes, the two figures advanced towards her from the doorway. As they took on recognisable forms, Lucy began to weep with relief. It was Vauquelin and Rafiq.

Vauquelin helped her to her feet, as a loud groan emanated from Joubert on the other side of the room. Joubert had dragged himself to a sitting position with his back to the wall, clutching his arm, the blood seeping through his fingers. The light from the open doorway fell upon him. He shied from it.

'Perfect! You have winged him. An excellent shot,' Vauquelin said turning to Rafiq. 'I want this man to face the noose.'

Joubert looked up at him, malice etched on his features. 'And you a Frenchman!' he wheezed.

A pained expression crossed Vauquelin's face. 'As was M. Moreau, I'd remind you... sir.' Vauquelin's gaze returned to Lucy. 'Are you unhurt, Madame Lawrence?'

'Yes. Nothing some sleep won't cure,' Lucy replied somewhat shakily, as she watched Rafiq haul Joubert to his feet and out the door. All the while Joubert cursed him, but he was no match for the dragoman.

'We must get you back to the house,' Vauquelin said, looking at her with concern.

'Yes, but please. I must know. How did you find out it was M. Joubert? I never suspected him.'

'Why my superior detecting skills, madame!' Vauquelin grinned back at her.

'I have no doubt... But do tell.'

Vauquelin offered his arm, which Lucy gratefully accepted. They made their way out, blinking, into the morning sunshine.

'Yesterday morning, I had an unexpected visitor to my office. It was Joubert's young assistant from the museum at Boulaq, M. Japp. While searching for some papers in Joubert's office, he made a startling discovery. Luckily, he's a clever young man and realised what he had to do.'

'What did he find?'

'The missing bracelet from the robbery. It was hidden at the back of a drawer, rolled up in a piece of muslin.'

'Good gracious! How foolish of Joubert to hide it there.'

'On the contrary, it was quite clever of him. We took the robbery at face value and assumed the items had either left Egypt or were for sale on the black market. No one thought to search the director's office,' the inspector said.

'But why did he keep those things?'

'I imagine he was waiting for an opportunity to ensure they'd be found at the Whitmore camp.'

'Good Lord! He went there yesterday,' exclaimed Lucy.

'Then I have little doubt but that Rosemary Whitmore is

now in possession of the other missing items: a fabulous ring and a gold necklace.'

'Yes! The one with the golden cats. So that was why he was so eager to go there yesterday – not to discuss my offer of funding, but to plant evidence.' Lucy was shocked at the callousness of the man. 'What a lucky escape Reginald and Rosemary have had. If those pieces of jewellery were found at their camp, you would have had no option but to assume they were the burglars *and* the murderers.'

'I like to think, Madame Lawrence, I would have been sceptical even then. Remember, Whitmore and his sister had confirmed alibis. I would view any evidence in that light.'

'They had plenty of motives, although professional jealousy seemed the most likely. However, there was another possible motive, and to protect the lady's reputation, I didn't share it with you when I discovered it.'

'What?' Vauquelin's tone was icy.

'Last season Moreau seduced Rosemary. She... Well, there was a child, but Moreau would have nothing to do with her or the baby. The child was lost early on, and I hate to tell you, but Moreau's treatment of Miss Whitmore was scandalous.'

'Enough to make a brother want to kill him?'

'Yes, but luckily, Miss Whitmore persuaded her brother that Moreau wasn't worth it,' Lucy said.

'*Mon dieu*! What a man Moreau was.'

'Indeed, Moreau was no saint and, in the end, his sins came back to visit him tenfold. Tell me, what was in your telegram to trigger Joubert's episode?'

'Yes, I'm sorry for the consequences for you, Madame Lawrence. But there was very little in it, as I did not wish him to bolt. I merely indicated there had been a new development in the case, and I wished to discuss it with him.'

'And his guilty conscience must have filled in the rest,' she said.

'Perhaps.'

'What will happen now, Inspector?'

'Once we patch him up, we will take him back to Cairo.'

'Did you notice his dilated pupils, Inspector? I think he has been taking some kind of drug. There was a bottle on the floor beside him when I found him. He told me he's ill and dying.'

'Did you see what it was?'

'Bromocarpine. Are you familiar with it?'

'Yes, it is a nerve tonic and very popular in France.'

'I don't think the drug made him a killer, Inspector,' she said.

'No, but it may have warped an already sick mind.'

'Sick or evil, I'm still not sure,' Lucy said. She was suddenly struck by an awful thought. 'Inspector! You don't know the worst of it!' Vauquelin stopped and looked at her expectantly. 'Joubert admitted to me he murdered his wife. He pushed her down a shaft at his dig. It was considered an unfortunate accident at the time.'

The inspector's eyes widened. 'Why did he do that?'

'Rebecca Joubert had an affair with Moreau,' she said.

'Ah, so that is why he killed Moreau. I admit I was scrambling for a motive.'

'Once he knew of the affair, his hatred grew but he was cold-blooded enough to wait for the right opportunity to kill Moreau. I assume the inevitable awaits him?'

'Indeed. As soon as we reach Cairo, he will be charged and will stand trial eventually.'

'And he will hang,' Lucy said with a sigh.

'Undoubtedly, but do not waste your sympathy, madame. He dispatched his wife, and don't forget he poisoned the porter at the museum as well, and that was a particularly cruel and prolonged death.'

'And then he butchered Moreau in such a dreadful way, and each crime was worse than the other. But what good will come of hanging him? It can't bring any of them back. What comfort can it bring their respective families?'

Vauquelin gazed at Lucy as if she were mad. 'I do not make the law, Madame Lawrence, I enforce it.'

THIRTY-ONE

Vauquelin and his officers left in the afternoon, a silent and brooding Joubert in their custody. He wouldn't respond when Lucy attempted to speak to him, and his baleful gaze did nothing for her equilibrium. Saddened, Lucy stood on the terrace and watched their departure until they were mere specks in the distance. Joubert had had such an illustrious career, but none of his work to preserve Egypt's heritage would be remembered now, only his infamy. Lucy shuddered as she imagined the headlines. With a heavy heart she turned to Rafiq beside her. 'Thank goodness it is over,' she said.

Rafiq pursed his lips and looked down at her. 'Yes, but what now? Will you leave Egypt?' Lucy inhaled deeply and shook her head. Rafiq raised a brow. 'You have plans, Mrs Lawrence?'

'Always, Rafiq! First, some sleep, and then I need to write to Mr Whitmore to make arrangements for him to take over the entire dig before the French impose a new director on us.'

'I'll gladly deliver your message to him,' he said.

'Thank you. Once I have explained my plans to Mary, I'll have a very important job for you to undertake.'

'Yes?'

'Come back in the morning, and I'll explain it all,' she said.

As soon as Rafiq had departed, Lucy headed back into Mariette's house and made straight for her bedroom. Mary was fussing about, making a show of dusting, but Lucy knew well she was watching her keenly. Lucy sat down on the bed as a wave of exhaustion hit her.

Mary glanced at her. 'Well, ma'am, will that be enough adventure for this year? You had me worried sick, and no mistake.'

'I'm sorry, Mary. What I did was incredibly foolish; I see that now. I shall have to curb my enthusiasm for helping those in distress in future.'

Mary sniffed. 'I'll believe it when I see it! Now, you must be droppin' on your feet. To bed with you, ma'am.'

Lucy gave her a grateful smile. Scolding or not, Mary was the queen of maids. 'I will, I promise, in a little while. My head is buzzing with all that has happened. I'd like to just sit quietly for a few minutes.'

'Very well, ma'am, I'll fetch some water. Call out, if you need anything. I'll be back shortly.' Mary threw her a concerned look before departing.

Lucy remained still, but her mind was churning. What a debacle, and worst of all, how had she read all the players in this drama so incorrectly? Joubert had seemed the quintessential college professor-type, mild and innocuous; Moreau, the darling of Egyptology, had turned out to be nothing but a philanderer whose darkest secrets had hurt so many. And to think she had considered a liaison with him. Even worse, she had compared him favourably to Phineas. The thought made her squirm.

Lucy reached down and pulled out her carpet bag from under the bed. She removed the small canvas and took off its protective linen cloth just as Mary came back into the room.

Lucy stared down at the picture of Ramesses II and began to smile. Phineas's gift, although well-intentioned, had been the catalyst for a disaster which she'd mistaken for a good omen.

Mary cleared her throat. Lucy turned the picture around for Mary to see. The maid's eyes narrowed. 'Don't tell me; you wish to go to that place?'

'Yes, I do. When I met M. Moreau in Nice, and we hatched our plan to travel together to this great country, it was as if fate had drawn us together. It would be a great pity not to go there, for I may never have another opportunity. It was always my intention to see it at some stage this winter. So, yes, we are going to Abu Simbel, Karnak and all the other wonderful sites along the Nile. Rafiq will make all the arrangements.'

Mary's face dropped.

'Don't worry, my dear, it will be by boat up the river. No camels, I promise.'

Mary blew out her cheeks. 'Thank Gawd for that!'

THIRTY-TWO

Lucy woke to bright sunshine and a smiling Mary hovering near her bed with a breakfast tray.

'Morning, ma'am.'

Lucy stretched, and then snuggled back down into the pillows after glancing out of the window. 'And a sunny one, too.'

'No shortage of them here. Would you like this now?' the maid asked, flicking a glance at the tray.

'Yes, sorry.' Lucy sat up and savoured the delightful smell coming from the covered dish. 'As much as I enjoyed our trip up the Nile, Mary, I'm looking forward to going home. I find the weather too monotonous here.' Lucy laughed. 'Isn't it dreadful to complain about too much sunshine?'

'No, I know exactly what you mean, ma'am. There are many things I won't miss, if I'm honest. Particularly the wildlife. London might be wet and grey, but at least there are no scorpions in your bed.'

'He wasn't that big, Mary, and Rafiq dealt with it very quickly.'

'Aye, and 'tis a pity we can't take the man back to London with us,' Mary sighed. 'Fierce handy he is to have around.'

'Rafiq's married, and his life is here, but I agree; I'll miss him. However, I don't think Ned would like it, Mary.'

'Perhaps not, but it'd stop the man making assumptions, now wouldn't it. Thinks he can click 'is fingers and old Mary here, will come a runnin'.'

Lucy wagged her finger. 'That's a dangerous game, Mary. Look what happened to M. Joubert when he let jealousy take over.'

Mary pulled a face. 'Yes, you're right, ma'am. Best not to tempt fate.'

Lucy laughed. 'The sooner we get home the better.'

'Haven't I been saying that since the day we arrived? I knew Egypt would be trouble.' Mary spoke with relish. 'Oh, ma'am, before I forget. The manager dropped by earlier with some post for you. Seemingly it has built up while we were away. Would you like to see it now?' Lucy nodded. Mary left a large pile of envelopes on the counterpane before going back out to the sitting room.

Lucy sifted through the letters. The first was from her brother, but the news was good. His solicitor was advising him that he might have grounds for an appeal of his sentence. To her astonishment, Richard informed her that Phineas Stone had agreed to speak on his behalf. *What?* Lucy re-read the letter. Was Phineas back in London? Frustrated, Lucy turned to the balance of the post. Several were from Judith, her friend in Yorkshire, but *she* wouldn't have news about Phineas, and there was nothing from Lady Sarah, the most likely correspondent who could shed light on the situation. But if she sent a telegram to Lady Sarah, she would be showing her hand and would never hear the end of it. *What to do!*

An envelope addressed in an unfamiliar hand caught her attention. Lucy tore it open to find it was a short and precise

note from Inspector Vauquelin, informing her that Hopkins and
Isabella had turned up in New York and were promptly
arrested. Not with a suitcase full of shabti as expected, but a
rather splendid collection of expensive items of jewellery, in
particular, a fabulous pearl necklace. Won't Mrs Hamilton be
pleased, Lucy thought, crumpling up the note. Who would ever
have suspected the glamorous photographer was a jewel thief?
Isabella had probably been working the hotels for years, the
inspector reckoned. Isabella would have had plenty of contacts
in the Cairo underworld for selling on her booty and Hopkins'
pilfered items. What a pair! With a smile, Lucy recalled the
night the mysterious thief had stood at the end of her bed. My,
but Isabella had been daring.

All of a sudden restless, Lucy wanted nothing more than to
be back in London. How frustrating that it would take several
weeks before she would set foot on English soil. Now, all she
wanted to do was make plans for the future. She'd find a small
but elegant house in town to call home, then see what adventures fate would throw her way. Certainly, her old life was dead
and gone. Lucy had relished her independence while in Egypt,
and she was determined nothing was going to take that away
from her. Deep down, she knew she wasn't the same woman
who had left England the previous summer. Her confidence
had grown and although luck had been on her side, everything
that had occurred had made her stronger. Eagerly, Lucy threw
back the bedclothes. With a bit of luck, they'd be on their way
to Alexandria the following day.

Mary entered the room, her expression sheepish. 'Sorry,
ma'am, I had dropped one of your letters,' she said, glancing
down at an envelope in her hand, 'It's from London.'

Even upside-down, Lucy recognised Phineas's writing.
Momentarily she froze, then, with a twisting stomach, she took
the letter from the maid's outstretched hand. Mary bobbed and

turned, but when she reached the door, she cleared her throat and grinned. 'I hope it's good news, ma'am.'

Lucy took the letter out onto her balcony and sat down, placing it carefully on the table. She stared at the letter, half dreading, half hoping. It had been forwarded many times, from Nice to Brindisi and finally Cairo. What if he had written to tell her about his affair with Mrs Vaughan? She gulped. She *definitely* didn't want to hear about that.

Don't be such a coward, Lucy Lawrence! To have come through so much and now to be fazed by a mere letter? Daft.

With unsteady hands she slowly extracted the letter from the envelope. It ran to several pages. Was that a good or bad sign? She dived in.

Westbourne Grove,
Kensington.

Dear Lucy,

Firstly, I must apologise for the delay in replying to your letter of last August. It was waiting for me on my return to London, yesterday morning. However, as I had the pleasure of meeting Lady Sarah yesterday evening at Covent Garden, I have learnt that events have overtaken you, and you no longer require recommendations on places of interest to visit in France!

As I feared from the outset, you have once again proven yourself a magnet for trouble, instead of safely playing the tourist. Lady Sarah's recounting of your exploits left me shaken, to say the least. I despair of you, Lucy. Did you learn nothing from your escapade last spring? Would it be so very difficult to leave the activities of criminals to the police? Instead, I learn you have been involved in robbery and murder and are, in fact, lucky to be alive. This was bad enough until

I learnt of what happened next. To confront a deranged murderer in
the Apis vaults defies logic. I can only conclude the injuries you
suffered in the explosion had left you temporarily insane!

I'm still struggling to understand your decision to go to Egypt.
Was the Continent too dull and safe for you? Why would you set
off for Egypt in the company of complete strangers, hand over
money to this archaeologist chap who then gets himself murdered
and then, instead of doing the sensible thing of removing yourself
from the situation, embark on a foolhardy investigation? From
what I hear, you're now funding half the digs in Egypt as well.

There, my rebukes are at an end, though I reserve the right to
drag this up and scold you again, when we meet in London.
(Assuming you intend to return home at some point, or is your
plan to indulge in new adventures? The East is certainly full of
mystery and intrigue, if you're looking for ideas.) –

Lucy dropped the letter down on the table in disgust. How
dare he criticise her! What was worse was the implication she
was unfit to investigate anything. Had he learnt nothing during
their short but eventful acquaintance? It took Lucy several
minutes to calm down, but then curiosity drove her back to
Phin's letter.

– Lady Sarah berated me last night. It would appear my sudden
departure from London in the summer resulted in conjecture of
the unpleasant variety. No doubt, she troubled you with that
particular news. However, despite the more salacious rumours,
my trip was entirely innocent.

I received a telegram from my father, informing me that my
younger brother, Sebastian, was extremely ill. Seb is a captain in
the Cheshire Regiment and has been stationed out in India for

the last five years. As my father is too frail to travel, he wished me to visit Seb to ensure he was receiving the appropriate care. The art theft case I was working on was not urgent, and I set off immediately.

On arrival in India, I discovered my brother had almost completely recovered from the malaria which had brought him so low. Having travelled so far, and desirous of exploring something of the country, I decided to stay for a few weeks. However, I was soon caught up in a case, courtesy of Seb's colonel. The investigation necessitated my journeying up country and took over a month to conclude. To my dismay, on returning to take my leave of Seb, I discovered that he had relapsed and was again severely ill. It was my opinion that the climate and conditions of the camp were not conducive to Seb's recovery. The colonel owed me a favour for sorting out his little problem up north, so I was able to persuade him the best solution for Seb was to come back to England with me to recuperate. As soon as Seb was fit to travel, I whisked him off before his commanding officer had a chance to change his mind.

Seb and I plan to travel to Kent tomorrow. My father has arranged for a nurse to attend Seb. He will hate the fuss, of course, but if anything, the mollycoddling will speed up his recovery for he will wish to escape it as quickly as possible.

I plan to stay in Kent until such time as Seb's recovery is well underway. Unfortunately, the next few weeks are likely to be challenging, with all of us back once more under the same roof. But I have no need to tell you about family jealousies and how corrosive they can be. I think you will like Seb when you meet him. On hearing of your Egyptian adventures, he's more than eager to meet you.

Stay well and try to stay out of trouble, dear Lucy. I'll not rest easy until you're back in England, and I can see for myself that you're hale and hearty.

Yours,
Phin

'Well! What nerve!' Lucy exclaimed, upsetting a sparrow perched on an adjacent tree. However, it wasn't long before her nose was buried in the letter again, her heart racing. Despite his opening harsh words, she detected warmth and concern for her safety. In fact, the letter gave her hope.

THIRTY-THREE

Lucy had just returned to her suite after lunch, to find a note awaiting her from Reginald Whitmore. He was at the hotel and wished to see her immediately as he had some good news. Lucy almost skipped down the corridor to the Whitmore suite. She found Reginald poring over some maps at the desk. On seeing her approach, a tentative smile appeared. Clearly, he was nervous about meeting his new patron.

'Mrs Lawrence, I'm delighted to welcome you back. Indeed, Rosemary and I had intended to visit you at Sakkâra but, before we knew it, you had left on a trip.'

'Thank you; you are most kind, Reginald. Do you mind if I call you by your Christian name?'

'No! No, not at all. Please, won't you take a seat? I'll ask for Rosemary to be fetched immediately.' He called out to the servant then turned his attention back to her. 'I'm sure she will be delighted to see you recovered so well from your ordeal, as indeed am I. How was your Nile adventure?'

'It was wonderful, thank you. Karnak was incredible and Abu Simbel was a joy. I'll never forget waking up at dawn and

looking out the window of my cabin to see the sun slowly illumi-
nate those figures of Ramesses. Breathtaking! It was just what I
needed. Rafiq was a fabulous guide, and surely a dahabeeyah is
the only way to travel up the Nile. Thankfully, the journey was
uneventful, otherwise I fear my maid would have given me
notice.'

'I'm glad you enjoyed it. But dear Mrs Lawrence, we were
horrified to hear about M. Joubert and what happened in the
Serapeum from Inspector Vauquelin. Is it really true Joubert
killed his wife?'

'He admitted it to me, I'm afraid.'

Whitmore shook his head as he took the seat opposite. 'I
never for a moment suspected Joubert capable of such vile
acts.'

'Unfortunately, none of us did. M. Moreau was no saint,
but he didn't deserve to die as he did. At least the right culprit
was caught in the end. We must put it all behind us.'

'Yes, we must. Although we frequently fell out, Moreau was
one of the best archaeologists working in Egypt. I must give him
credit for that.'

'That is generous of you, Reginald.'

Rosemary burst into the room. 'Mrs Lawrence! How
wonderful you're back. Reg, did you tell her?'

'No! Mrs Lawrence has only just arrived,' Whitmore said,
frowning at his sister. 'I haven't had a chance yet, Rosie.'

'Hello, Rosemary,' Lucy said. 'What is it you need to
tell me?'

The brother and sister shared a smile. 'It is best we show
you,' Whitmore said, rising and removing a large envelope from
the desk drawer.

Reginald handed it to Lucy with a smile. Lucy dove into the
envelope and pulled out some photographs. She examined them
closely. 'You broke through!'

Whitmore grinned. 'About a month after you left. The first

photographs are of the antechamber where the deceased's goods were left for the afterlife.'

Lucy examined the photographs closely. The ancient treasures lay in dust covered glory throughout the chamber. Behind the pieces of furniture and stacked pots were glimpses of wonderful figures and hieroglyphs.

But the next photograph made her gasp. 'Are those what I think they are?' she asked, as she gazed down at two skeletons, pictured just inside the entrance.

'Yes, I'm afraid. We knew from Moreau's side of the excavation the roof had collapsed. Those poor souls, most likely grave robbers, were trapped for eternity.'

'An unfortunate way to end your days.'

'Yes, but I wouldn't waste your sympathy. They knew the risks,' Rosemary said. 'So much of the ancient world has been lost through the actions of such men. Now, all of this can be preserved for generations to come.'

'We have been incredibly lucky. The robbers had reached the antechamber but no further,' Whitmore said. 'Keep going; the best is yet to be seen.'

Lucy picked up the next photograph which showed a solitary granite sarcophagus in the middle of a room. Lucy caught her breath. 'The burial chamber?' Whitmore nodded. Detailed paintings adorned the walls: some scenes depicted daily life while others showed gods and figures in ceremonial stances. Overcome with emotion, Lucy could only stare. If only she could see them in person. Surely, black and white photographs could not do them justice. Eventually, she found her voice. 'Whose tomb is it?'

'His name was Huya. He was a scribe to the pharaoh. The richness of the tomb and what we found in the antechamber suggests he was a very important man.'

'Which dynasty?'

'Eighteenth.'

'Ah! It is a New Kingdom tomb,' Lucy said with a lump in her throat. Just what poor Moreau had so desperately wanted to find.

'Yes. Lepsius had found a reference to Huya in another tomb. We always suspected he was buried in this part of Sakkâra.'

'Did you open the sarcophagus?'

'Yes, the mummy was intact,' Rosemary said with a smile.

'Since Joubert's arrest there has been no direction from Boulaq. The French are still trying to decide who should succeed him. I was reluctant to send the mummy, or indeed any of the artefacts, back to Cairo under such circumstances,' Whitmore said. 'I left the site heavily guarded in my absence.'

'A wise decision, Reginald. I trust you will document every find and forward them to Boulaq when the right time comes?'

'Absolutely! I give you my word,' he said.

Lucy took up the photographs again. The next one showed the interior of the sarcophagus. A thrill of excitement ran through her. This is what Moreau had meant that rainy afternoon in Nice when he had joined her for tea. No experience in her life so far could compare with this. It was beautiful, and not what she'd expected. Inside lay a wooden coffin, beautifully painted; the stylised face of Huya staring up at her from the centuries.

'Have you opened it?' she asked Whitmore, rather breathlessly.

'No. I dare not risk it. When it reaches Boulaq, the new director will organise it.'

Lucy felt a pang of regret for she wouldn't be in Egypt to experience it. 'You will document it; photograph it for me?'

'It would be my pleasure,' Whitmore said. 'It is a pity you will not witness it in person, but I thought you might like this.' From his pocket, Whitmore pulled a small object wrapped in a handkerchief. 'I'd like you to accept this as a memento. Thanks to you and Moreau, I have made the greatest discovery of my career. Unfortunately, nothing from this dig can be removed without the Board of Antiquities' permission. This is from my personal collection.'

'Oh, no! I couldn't,' Lucy protested, trying to hand it back. Whitmore just smiled and pushed it back towards her. Almost overwhelmed, with her throat tight, she removed the linen. Nestled in her palm was a glossy green scarab amulet, about three inches long.

'This is a heart scarab. Usually found in the dressings of the mummy just above the heart,' he explained. He nodded towards the photograph of the coffin. 'I have no doubt there is something very similar in there.'

'What was its purpose?' Lucy asked, enthralled by the beauty of the amulet. Its surface glowed in the afternoon light streaming in from the window.

'Heart scarabs were placed in the mummy's wrappings above the heart to protect it. They also act as a stand-in should the real heart be damaged. You see, in the Hall of Judgement, it was the heart which was weighed against the feather of Ma'at. If a person failed this test, they'd be devoured by Ammit, but if they passed, they'd go on to enjoy a blissful afterlife. It is not surprising the Egyptians were keen to protect their hearts.'

'How wonderful!' Lucy said at last, the tears streaming down her face. 'You must think me a very foolish woman!'

Whitmore chuckled. 'On the contrary, I think you have fallen under Egypt's spell. This country will haunt you for the rest of your life.'

Rosemary smiled. 'He is right. The magic never leaves you.'

Lucy looked at each of her companions in turn. 'Thank you. I begin my journey home to England tomorrow, but I would be happy to continue as your patron. I know M. Moreau did not prove to be a friend to either of you, but he lit a fire in me the day we met. Despite everything that has occurred, you're right;

this country will always be close to my heart. I'll treasure this amulet. It will have pride of place in my home.' Rosemary's lower lip trembled, and Reginald appeared to be having trouble swallowing. 'Now, my dears, despite the earliness of the hour, let's adjourn to the salon downstairs. I do believe there is a bottle of champagne waiting to be ordered!'

A LETTER FROM THE AUTHOR

Dear reader,

Many thanks for reading *Footprints in the Sand*, Book 2 in The Lucy Lawrence Mystery series. I hope you enjoyed Lucy's Egyptian adventure. If you would like to hear more about my books, you can sign up here for my newsletter:

www.stormpublishing.co/pam-lecky

If you enjoyed this book and could spare a few moments to leave a review that would be hugely appreciated. Even a short review can make all the difference in encouraging a reader to discover my books for the first time. Thank you so much!

Not unlike my heroine, Lucy Lawrence, I have been fascinated by the world of the ancient Egyptians since I was a child. Inspired by visits to the British Museum in London and reading the fascinating book written by Amelia Edwards, *A Thousand Miles up the Nile*, it was inevitable that one of Lucy's adventures would take place in Victorian Egypt.

However, initially, I was rather overwhelmed. Where should I set my tale? Unfortunately, it would not be possible to include every ancient site, so I had to choose just one or two. Giza, with its magnificent pyramids, just had to be included, and my research pinpointed Sakkâra, easily accessible from Cairo, as a wonderful site full of opportunities for mischief!

My next problem was place names. My Victorian texts and modern spellings often differ. In the end, I decided to use the spellings found in *Baedeker's Guide* (which was published in 1885, two years prior to my story). Also, my descriptions of places and monuments use the same contemporary source.

I reference several archaeologists in this novel, namely Mariette, Petrie, Perring and Vyse and, of course, Lepsius, but M. Moreau, Mr Whitmore and M. Joubert, although influenced by those men, are entirely fictional. It is important to note that Auguste Mariette was, in fact, succeeded by the very successful director, M. Gaston Maspero, and not my fictional director, Victor Joubert. The tomb discovered in Sakkâra by M. Moreau is unfortunately, fictional, although Lepsius did find traces of New Kingdom tombs at Sakkâra during the 1840s. Mariette's house in Sakkâra did exist and is described using the scarce sources I could find. As far as I can ascertain, it no longer stands.

The original Egyptian Museum was established in 1858 at Boulaq, on the banks of the Nile, in an old warehouse. Flooding issues prompted the building of a new museum in Tahrir Square, and the collection was moved there in 1902. The new Grand Egyptian Museum at Giza partially opened in February 2023. It is my dearest wish to visit it someday.

The earthquake referenced in the first chapter occurred on 23rd February 1887 and is known as the Imperia earthquake. The epicentre was just off the Italian coast, causing substantial damage and the death of over 600 people. The resulting tsunami damaged buildings along the Italian and French Riviera, including Menton and Nice.

Finally, I must apologise to Queen Ahhotep, a formidable warrior queen, for borrowing her funerary goods for my story. Her ceremonial dagger was just too good and distinctive a weapon to ignore!

Thanks again for being part of my writing journey.

Pam Lecky

KEEP IN TOUCH WITH THE AUTHOR

X x.com/pamlecky

○ instagram.com/pamleckybooks

in linkedin.com/in/pam-lecky-b0b646109

GLOSSARY

Abu Simbel: The twin temples of Abu Simbel are located in southern Egypt close to the border with Sudan. They were originally carved out of the mountainside in the 13th century BC, during the 19th Dynasty reign of the Pharaoh Ramesses II. They serve as a lasting monument to the king and his queen Nefertari and commemorate his victory at the Battle of Kadesh.

Ammit: An ancient Egyptian goddess, known as the devourer of the dead.

Apis bulls: These were sacred animals to the ancient Egyptians. They were believed to be the manifestation of the god Ptah.

Baedeker's Guide: A travel guide from the German firm belonging to Karl Baedeker. Comprehensive in nature, they include maps, local tourism guides, local customs, buildings of note, etc.

Bakhshîsh: Money given to someone who begs.

Battle of the Nile: A major naval battle fought between the British Royal Navy and the Navy of the French Republic at Aboukir Bay on the Mediterranean coast off the Nile Delta of Egypt, from the 1st to the 3rd of August 1798.

Bedouins: Nomadic Arab people who have historically inhabited the desert regions in North Africa, the Arabian Peninsula, Iraq and the Levant.

Boulaq: A riverside suburb of Cairo. The original Egyptian Museum was located there on the banks of the Nile.

Cartouche: A cartouche is an oval or oblong enclosing a set of hieroglyphs with a horizontal line at one end which indicates that the text enclosed is a royal name.

Coffin Texts: The Coffin Texts (c. 2134–2040 BC) are a collection of 1,185 funerary spells, incantations and other forms of religious writing inscribed on ancient Egyptian coffins to help the deceased navigate the afterlife.

Dahabeeyah: A traditional shallow-bottomed, barge-like River Nile vessel with two or more sails.

Dashûr: A royal necropolis located in the desert on the west bank of the Nile, south of Cairo. It is famous for several pyramids which are among the oldest, largest and best-preserved in Egypt, built by the pharaoh Sneferu (2613–2589 BC).

Description de l'Egypte: A series of publications (1809–1829), compiled by scholars and scientists who accompanied Napoleon on his expedition to Egypt (1798–1801).

Egyptian Antiquities Service: The service was created by the Viceroy of Egypt in 1858 in an effort to curb the illicit trade in Egyptian artefacts. French scholar August Mariette was its first director. The service was responsible for carrying out its own excavations and also for approving and supervising foreign archaeological teams. Mariette created the first national museum in Boulaq.

Fajr Prayer: (Dawn prayer) is the first of the five daily prayers performed by practising Muslims.

Fellâheen: A farmer or agricultural labourer in the Middle East or North Africa.

First Dynasty: Is the period immediately following the unification of Upper and Lower Egypt (c. 3100–2900 BC).

Giza Plateau: The plateau is situated on the outskirts of Cairo and is the location of the Great Pyramids of Khufu, Khafra and Menkaure, and the Great Sphinx.

Hall of Judgement: The Hall of Judgement was the place to which the souls of the dead travelled to have their hearts weighed and their earthly life judged by Osiris and forty-two other judges.

Hieroglyphs: The formal writing system used in ancient Egypt combining logographic, syllabic and alphabetic elements.

Karnak: Is the site of many temples, chapels, pylons and other buildings. It is part of the monumental city of Thebes.

Khafra: An ancient Egyptian pharaoh of the 4th Dynasty during the Old Kingdom. He was the son of pharaoh Khufu.

His tomb is the second largest to be found on the Giza Plateau.

Khedive: The title (equivalent to viceroy) used by the Ottoman Empire rulers of Egypt during the nineteenth century.

Khufu: An Old Kingdom pharaoh and builder of the Great Pyramid of Giza. The dates of his reign still remain a matter of dispute.

Lepsius, Karl Richard (1810–1884): A pioneering Prussian Egyptologist, linguist and modern archaeologist.

Ma'at: An ancient Egyptian concept of truth, balance, order, harmony, law, morality, and justice.

Magic Lantern: An early type of projector using pictures painted, printed or produced photographically on transparent plates (usually made of glass), one or more lenses, and a light source.

Mariette, Auguste (1821–1881): A French scholar, archaeologist and Egyptologist, first director of the Egyptian Department of Antiquities and founder of the first Egyptian Museum at Boulaq.

Mastaba: A type of ancient Egyptian tomb in the form of a flat-roofed, rectangular structure with inward sloping sides, constructed out of mud-bricks.

Memphis: Memphis was located at the entrance to the Nile River Valley near the Giza Plateau, and was one of the oldest and most important cities in ancient Egypt.

Muski: (Sharia al-Muski) Main market thoroughfare of Cairo.

New Kingdom: The period in ancient Egyptian history between the 16th century BC and the 11th century BC, covering the 18th, 19th, and 20th Dynasties of Egypt.

Old Kingdom: The period spanning c. 2686–2181 BC. It is also known as the Age of the Pyramids.

Osiris: One of the most important gods of ancient Egypt. He was Lord of the Underworld, Judge of the Dead and brother–husband to Isis.

Papyrus: Writing paper made from the pith of the papyrus plant, which grows on the banks of the Nile.

Perring, John (1813–1869): A British engineer, anthropologist and Egyptologist, most notable for his work excavating and documenting Egyptian pyramids.

Petrie, Flinders (1853–1942): An English Egyptologist and a pioneer of systematic methodology in archaeology and preservation of artefacts.

Ramesses II (c. 1303–1213 BC): Also known as **Ramesses the Great**. He was the third pharaoh of the 19th Dynasty of Egypt. He is often regarded as the greatest, most celebrated, and most powerful pharaoh of the New Kingdom. He was the builder of the temples at Abu Simbel.

Sakkâra: A vast, ancient burial ground in Egypt, serving as the necropolis for the ancient Egyptian capital of Memphis.

Sarcophagus: A stone coffin, typically decorated with inscriptions and associated with the ancient civilisations of Egypt, Rome, and Greece.

Serapeum (Sakkâra): The burial place of Apis bulls, held sacred by the ancient Egyptians. It was excavated by Auguste Mariette in 1850.

Shabti (Ushabti): A funerary figurine found in many ancient Egyptian tombs. They are commonly made of blue or green glazed Egyptian faience (tin-glazed earthenware), but can also consist of stone, wood, clay, metal, and glass.

Sorbonne: A prestigious university located in Paris, France.

The Great Sphinx, Giza: A limestone statue with the head of a human (the pharaoh) and the body of a lion. It is commonly believed to have been built by Pharaoh Khafra.

Step Pyramid, Sakkâra: The earliest colossal stone building in Egypt, built in the 27th century BC during the 3rd Dynasty for the burial of Pharaoh Djoser by his vizier and architect, Imhotep.

Vyse, Sir Richard (1784–1853): A British soldier and Egyptologist.

ACKNOWLEDGEMENTS

Without the support of family and friends, this book, and indeed my entire writing journey, wouldn't have been possible. My heartfelt thanks to you all, especially my husband, Conor, and my children, Stephen, Hazel and Adam. I'm very grateful to my chief beta readers, Lorna and Terry O'Callaghan, who have read every draft and given me invaluable feedback.

Special gratitude is due to my agent, Thérèse Coen, at Susanna Lea & Associates, London, whose belief in me, along with her sage advice, helped to bring Lucy Lawrence to life.

Producing a novel is a collaborative process, and I have been fortunate to have wonderful editors, copyeditors, proofreaders, and graphic designers working on this series. To Kathryn Taussig, my editor, and all the team at Storm Publishing, thanks for believing in this series and taking it to the next level. A massive thank you to Bernadette Kearns, my original editor – all the books in the Lucy Lawrence series benefited hugely from your input.

I am extremely grateful to have such loyal readers. For those of you who take the time to leave reviews, please know that I appreciate them beyond words. To the amazing book bloggers, book tour hosts and reviewers who have hosted me and my books over the years – thank you.

Last, but certainly not least, I am incredibly lucky to have a network of writer friends who keep me motivated, especially Valerie Keogh, Jenny O'Brien, Fiona Cooke, Brook Allen and Tonya Murphy Mitchell. Special thanks to the members of the

Historical Novel Society, RNA and Society of Authors Irish Chapters, and all the gang at the Coffee Pot Book Club.

Go raibh míle maith agat!

Pam Lecky
July 2024

Printed in Great Britain
by Amazon